## NIGHT STALKER

The hours dragged on. Every drop of snow from a branch sounded like a paw-fall. Every icicle catching the moonlight seemed to be a tiger's eye. She had the sensation that something was following her, but could never confirm it.

Then—eyes again, a pale emerald color.

Her brain envisioned a tiger walking toward her, head weaving to balance the motion of the great forequarters. Hashti froze. So did the eyes. Time suspended itself for a long frosty moment. Then the eyes dipped, wavered, and accelerated directly toward Hashti.

# FOREST OF THE NIGHT

## Marti Steussy

A Del Rey Book

BALLANTINE BOOKS • NEW YORK

To Puck, for dust does not forget the dream which stirs it.

# CHAPTER ONE

❧❧❧❧❧

HASHTI PAUSED MIDWAY THROUGH HER LECTURE ON THE tricks of horse-powered logging. Why were the horses suddenly alert, ears cocked and nostrils flared? Had something frightened them?

Motion flickered thirty feet to her left—a rabbit, darting from its hiding place in a clump of grass. It stationed itself beside a stump, ruffled its neck feathers, and stamped angrily at the young woman. She wondered what emboldened it to face her. Did it have a nest nearby?

Sure enough, the small brown-feathered creature twisted and dove out of sight. The trainer marked the spot, knowing that hidden burrow entrances could mean disaster for her horses. She'd have to look out for other holes beneath the leaves. Rabbit dens always had back doors.

Hashti saw nothing else amiss. She was working in a grove of sweetsap, this planet's equivalent of maple. Snow dusted the ground beneath bushes still trailing a few scarlet shreds of foliage. Sawyers had strewn the hillside with giant tree trunks, sectioned and ready to haul. Between lay the usual debris of logging—horse dung, wood chips, and piles of bare-twigged boughs. The skidway, a makeshift trail for hauling logs to the road, could be picked out only by the initiate. Everything looked perfectly normal, Hashti thought.

Perhaps the rabbit had startled her horses. Or perhaps her lecture had bored them. A little exercise would cure that. She stooped, a heavy steel logging chain in her hand. "Keep the chain as short as you can," she advised as she hitched it to the doubletree. "That lifts the front of the log and keeps it from snagging."

Her pupil, a sturdy handsome blond, glanced from the bay team to the twenty-foot timber. "Lift that thing? It's two and a half feet thick, Miz Hashti!"

She grinned. "Let me show you." Normally, she'd have been working with two men out here, showing Gaylord how to handle the team while his swamper, Sweat, cleared the way for subsequent loads. But Sweat was back in camp, nursing one of the allergic reactions so common in frontier camps. Hashti and Gay were alone with the team and the forest.

Hashti didn't complain. At five foot six, Gay was the shortest man in camp, but his solid build made him a match for any, and he moved with a poise that dwarfed his peers. He learned quickly and worked cheerfully. Hashti liked Gay.

He was one of the few things she did like about New Lebanon. The term "frontier planet" had once filled her with visions of unspoiled wilderness and valiant pioneers, high adventure and unlimited opportunity. The reality, she'd found, was dominated by mosquitoes, mud, and surly, underpaid company slaves.

But like it or not, she had work to do. Gay stood dangerously close to the skidding path. "Stand back," she warned him. He needed to learn some caution, before he got himself or the horses hurt.

His jaw stiffened, but he stepped obediently aside. Hashti straddled the log to give the chain a final tug.

The wind shifted.

Betsy snorted in terror. Her harness creaked. The chain went taut in Hashti's hands. Even as she heard Gay's warning shout, the log shifted between her knees. It was too late to jump for safety. She clung to the chain, riding the log through the brush behind the bolting horses. Branches whipped her face. She spit out a mouthful of leaves and grit. "Whoa! Betsy, Blaze, stand!"

The log caught on a fallen tree and jerked the team to a halt. Hashti pitched forward, somersaulting against the tree's stump. She lay quiet a moment, struggling for breath. By the time she sat up, Gay stood at the horses' heads. He stared apprehensively at his teacher. "You all right, Hashti?"

He should have said "Miz." She let it go as she tried to assess damage. Her face stung, and she'd have a hell of a bruise on her left shoulder, but her body seemed to be in one piece. Her ego? That was a different matter. The barn boss had no business getting knocked over by her own horses. "What happened?" she asked.

Gay, who'd been dubious about horses all along, looked jumpier than the team. "Don't ask me! They just started running. I thought you said they'd stand like rocks!"

"They should." The trainer's reputation rested on the horses' good behavior. What had gotten into this steady, placid pair? Again Hashti scanned the forest, and again saw nothing out of place amid fallen trees and under-brush—not even a feathered rabbit. Embarrassed, she went to the horses, humming softly to calm them, and checked for irritants under the harness straps. Nothing.

"I don't know what got into them, Gay. But you can see why you need a swamper. If you'd held the horses while I hitched, they wouldn't have gotten away. Shall we try it again, more carefully?" She jerked the tongs out of the log. Pain stabbed through her left shoulder.

She didn't want to admit that she'd gotten hurt through her own stupidity, but this was more serious than she'd first realized. She moved the arm gingerly, testing its range of motion. Gay saw her grimace and asked again, "Are you all right?"

"My shoulder's pretty sore," she confessed. "Let's rest a couple minutes." She took the lines from Gay. Betsy tossed her head, jerking against the reins. Hashti sucked in her breath.

Gay's eyes narrowed. "I think Dr. Anna better look at you. Let's go back to camp." He was no taller than Hashti, but he seemed to tower over her as he spoke. Hashti did not protest.

Still singing gently to the horses, she loosened the traces. As Gay finished tossing axes and cant hooks onto the small sled used for transporting tools, Hashti handed him the reins. "You lead them in—they're going to be your team." She hurt too badly to deal with the animals just now.

Gay led the horses along the skidway a hundred yards to the main road. In a few weeks, when the ground was more firmly frozen and a snow base built up, four-horse teams would haul great sleigh-loads of logs down this road to the river. Now, it was merely a muddy five-yard-wide aisle through the trees. The two humans and their team turned south toward camp.

Clear sunshine danced through the trees, a pleasant omen after days of gray. Hashti scarcely saw it. She could have been killed just now, she knew. She'd been careless, even while criticizing Gay for lack of caution. And the camp couldn't afford injuries to her, or to any-one else.

But what had happened? Betsy and Blaze were calm

by nature, well trained, and completely recovered from the trauma of shipping. The matched bays tagged happily behind Gay, snatching at leaves as if nothing had happened. Why the sudden attack of skittishness?

A cool breeze lifted Betsy's black mane. Hashti, warmed by the exertion of logging, had worked with wool sleeves rolled above her elbows. Now the subfreezing wind bit uncomfortably, reminding her that her jacket was still at the skidway. "Gay, I need to go back. I left my coat."

His fingers went to his buttons. "Take mine."

"No, I'll get my own." She didn't tell him that she'd left her beacon in the pocket. The tiny navigational guide would emit a distress signal unless it was periodically reset. Hashti was in enough hot water already without an unattended beacon signaling to those in camp that she was lost or hurt in the woods.

"You sure? You look shaky," Gay protested.

"Just chilly," she told him. "Get the horses on home —it's too cold for them to stand around sweating. I won't be far behind."

"Don't trip on a tiger," Gay yelled after her. It was the standard farewell on New Lebanon.

She smiled and hurried, whistling, toward the spot where she'd left her red and black jacket slung over a blackpine stump. As she eased her left arm into the sleeve, she saw a flash of movement in the yellowed grass. The rabbit? She looked again. A tiger!

He half crouched not more than thirty paces from her, six hundred pounds of carnivore, sniffing like an inquisitive barn cat. He wore not the vivid orange fur of his Terran counterpart, but a luxuriant down mantle some two and a half inches thick, made wind and water-proof by a sleek outer layer of guard feathers. Iridescent burnt-orange and black stripes faded to creamy white on his chest. A black mask across the tiger's face gave extra emphasis to the golden eyes staring at Hashti. Slender white whisker-feathers wiggled as he sampled her scent.

She froze, closed her eyes, then opened them again. The tiger crept two paces forward, making a soft snorting noise.

Hashti took a deep breath, trying to relax her shoulders. She was supposed to know how to handle animals. Never show them that you are afraid. What do you say to a wild tiger? "Uh—hello there. Nice kitty."

He paused, nose twitching. Hashti wet her lips and kept talking, trying for the calm authoritative tones she used on fractious horses. "Easy now. Didn't mean to disturb you. I was just leaving—"

The tiger curled his lips and repeated the snorting noise. His six-inch canines gleamed.

Hashti couldn't run—her muscles were paralyzed by panic. Perhaps that saved her. "Stay. Go home," she told the tiger. Silly, she chided herself! How could he understand her words? Should she throw something? No. Just get out. Slowly. She began to back up. The tiger watched, only the tip of his tail moving. Two steps. Three. Perhaps she would live through this after all. Four steps. Her foot caught in a pile of slash, and she tumbled gracelessly into the tangle of discarded branches. She hid her face and waited to die.

The tiger gathered himself, sprang across the intervening space with low flat bounds, and skidded to a stop half a yard from Hashti. Poised on stiff legs, he reached out and tapped her on the shoulder with a massive forepaw. She cringed. He drew back, watching. Growing bolder, he stuck his nose out to sniff at her face. The tiger had an odd fruity scent and his feathers tickled. A distinctive songlike call rippled from his throat. Then he licked Hashti. His tongue was rough as the file she used on horses' hooves. Squeaking a protest, she drove her fist against his heavy head. "No!"

He pulled back, regarding her with astonishment, then poked his nose forward more cautiously. Panicked beyond reason, she hit him again. He feinted at her with his foreleg. Then, with scornful dignity, he lifted and shook each of his soft-feathered paws. Without a backward glance he sauntered away, leaving Hashti in her pile of pitchy branches talking to herself. "Oh my God. Oh my God, Hashti. What did you just do? Oh my God."

She ran all the way back to camp. Mud sucked at the heavy reinforced toes of her boots. Her legs were burning by the time she stumbled into the long, low, log-walled stable. Gay had hung the harnesses on their pegs and was currying dried sweat from Betsy's shoulders. "Why the hurry?" he asked.

Hashti leaned against the wall, dizzy from exertion. "Tiger. There was a tiger out there. I hit him and he let me go."

She could hardly hear Gay's voice through the buzzing in her ears. "A *what*? Hashti? Hashti, are you all right?"

The pain of his hand on her left shoulder penetrated her daze. "OK. Just tired. Water," she panted. He brought her a cup. She tried not to gulp too fast.

"You all right?" Gay queried yet again. The concern in his voice embarrassed her.

"I'm fine. Not hurt, just scared. Get dizzy when I run too hard. Been like that since I was a kid." Her shoulder ached each time she breathed. She set the cup down. "There was a tiger out there."

"A tiger?" Gay looked skeptical. He knew as well as she that there were large striped carnivores on this planet. But the First-In team, a year ahead of the company crew, had chased the local tigers away. Not one had been seen in the three months Gay and Hashti had been here. The naturalist assured everyone that if a tiger did wander by, it would avoid humans. Hashti had just discovered otherwise.

"A tiger," she repeated. "A huge one. While I was backing away I fell, and he jumped on me. I hit him and he walked away."

"You hit him and he walked away." Gay frowned and brushed his hand across her sweaty forehead.

"Yes, I hit him! What else are you supposed to do with a t-tiger?" Her teeth began to chatter as she cooled off.

Gay wore an odd expression. "Let's go find Dr. Anna. I'm sure she'll want to hear about it."

He didn't believe her. "Gay! Honest to God, that's what happened!"

"I believe you," he said. She was sure he was lying, but her shoulder hurt badly and her fighting energy was gone. She made sure Betsy and Blaze were properly stabled, then let Gay steer her uphill to the main camp.

Swamp City, contrary to its name, sat on a well-drained slope with a southern exposure. The surrounding hillside remained unlogged, thick-needled blackpines giving partial protection from blizzard winds. A hot spring in the center of camp supplied water for bathing and cooking. A quarter mile downhill it drained into a small river, the Merrywater, which would power a sawmill next summer, if all went according to plan. Three miles south lay a freshwater sea. This served as landing place for the tender of the interstellar shuttle that visited twice-yearly. A few miles northwest, a much smaller lake, gone to marsh, supplied ricelike grain and rough hay.

In August, the camp had contained just two cabins. Hashti's horses had hauled the logs for a dozen new

buildings standing helter-skelter amid stumps and sawdust. Swamp City now had housing for everyone, plus
smithy, chemist's lab, camp office, company store, and
warehouse. Its most impressive edifice was City Hall,
built directly over the hot spring. This enormous log
structure could accomodate all hundred and fifty inhabi-
tants of the camp. Hashti had seen it used not only as a
dining hall, but as church, theater, saloon, and court-
house.

The new town's raw wood contrasted sharply with the
weathered walls of the doctor's cabin. This tiny building
had housed the twelve-person First-In team before company employees had ever set foot on New Lebanon. The
team's nonhuman members had left on the ship that
brought Hashti, but Doctor Anna, her husband Ross,
and the boss, Big Red, stayed to guide the newcomers
through their first encounters with New Lebanon.

Gay hammered on the door. His knock was answered
by a thin, hard-muscled man with silver hair—Ross, the
First-In naturalist. Surprise flickered in his gray eyes
when he saw Hashti. "What brings you here, Teamstress? Trouble with the horses?"

"No, I—"

"She needs to see the doctor," Gay answered for her.

Ross motioned them in. Rock and plant samples,
maps, drawings, and reference materials cluttered the
middle room of the three-room cabin. A cookstove stood
against the back wall, and next to it was an exquisitely
grained table of sweetsap wood. This was a sample of
what the colonists hoped to sell to the great interstellar
luxury markets. A rabbit, just like the one who'd scolded
Hashti in the woods, jumped from the armchair and
scooted between Ross's legs. He smiled, picking it up
and smoothing its feathers with one hand as he called
through the door to the right, "For you, Medic."

Hashti caught a brief glimpse of cages and the bright black rodent eyes of testers. Copper poisoning and amino acid imbalances had killed more than a few of those little animals as they sampled native foods for safety and nutritive value, but with their help the First-In physician had learned to compensate for the peculiarities of local biochemistry. The remaining population rustled cheerfully as Dr. Anna stepped through the door, wearing a stained white smock over wool shirt and pants. Like her husband, she had the weathered skin and lean hard body that come from much time under an open sky. Her age was hard to place but Hashti guessed around fifty standard. Anna's short curly hair, once black as Hashti's own, was now liberally flecked with gray, but the First-Inner's dark eyes danced like a girl's. "Hashti! What's the problem?"

"I think I hurt my shoulder," Hashti said, thoroughly embarrassed and still shivering uncontrollably.

"She hit a tiger," Gay said.

"I can speak for myself!" Hashti snapped.

"A tiger?" Ross stared at her. "You got mauled by a tiger?"

"The other way around," Gay told him.

"A stump hit me," Hashti said. "I mean I flew into it. The horses bolted and I fell off the log."

"She told me she punched a tiger," Gay said.

"That's enough," Anna ordered, stripping off the smock and filling a basin to scrub her hands. Her flashing eyes probed the shivering horse trainer. "Ross, open up the stove in the exam room and get Hashti some tea. Hashti, there are blankets on the cot. I'll be with you in a minute."

Ross had been opening his mouth to say something. He shut it, set the rabbit down, and went into the next room to prod the fire. Hashti followed, dropping meekly onto the cot. There would be hell to pay if this injury was serious. Gay was still trying to tell Anna about the tiger. She brushed him aside and entered the exam room.

With its draft wide open, the small stove radiated heat fiercely. "Wait in the other room," Anna said to Ross. "I'll call you if I need a nurse."

"If there's a tiger involved I want to hear about it."

"Out," Anna said, pointing at the door. "You can talk to her later. Hashti, take your shirt off."

Hashti obeyed. She had a fine firm figure, younger and more generously curved than Anna's, but similarly muscled from an active life. Dirt under her fingernails and hay scratches on her hands betrayed her profession, and the tan on her arms showed exactly how she rolled her sleeves. She'd lost some skin from her shoulder despite the thick wool shirt. Anna frowned. "Your skin feels like ice, child."

"So does the rest of me," Hashti reported, trying not to cry out as the doctor pressed and probed.

Anna stuffed a thermometer into Hashti's mouth and continued her examination. "A separated shoulder," she finally concluded. "Not a bad one. Wear a sling for ten days, and take it easy on the arm for a while after that."

"I can't run the stable with one hand!" Hashti protested as Anna pulled out the thermometer.

"We'll get you some help," the First-Inner promised. "Now, there's something else we need to talk about. You're chilled, Hashti. That's dangerous. You can die of exposure faster than the beacon can bring help." She draped a blanket around the younger woman's bare shoulders and handed her another mug of tea. "This is the frontier; we're playing for keeps. This planet will kill you if you don't respect it." Hashti had heard the litany dozens of times. She knew what Anna would say next. "Quiz time. How do you prevent hypothermia?"

"Dress warm, stay dry, keep eating, avoid exhaustion," Hashti answered.

"And the signs of trouble?" Anna prompted.

"Shivering, irrationality, clumsiness, drowsiness," her patient replied, ticking the four-part answer off on her fingers.

"Treatment?"

Obediently Hashti recited, "Get out of the cold, hot liquids, dry clothes, warm bodies."

"Very good. Since you know all that, why is your core temperature down?"

Hashti squirmed silently. Anna finally softened. "OK, I know you were distracted. And you weren't cold enough to be hallucinating. What happened out there?"

"I was standing over a log when the horses bolted with it. I hung on and rode it through the brush. Finally it snagged on a deadfall, and I pitched off against the stump. That's how I messed up my shoulder."

Anna wrinkled her nose. "I'm surprised it doesn't happen more often, with so many untrained people in the woods."

Hashti herself was hardly "untrained." She was a Journeyman Equestrian, nearly a Master, although she'd just goofed like a green apprentice. She avoided Anna's eyes as the doctor continued. "But then nothing in this camp meets the grade. The Company didn't even send medical equipment." Hashti looked again at the bone scanner Anna had used. It bore the starred circle insignia of First-In.

The doctor clamped her lips shut. "Sorry, Miz Hashti. I'm getting off the subject. You say you hurt your shoulder in a logging accident. So why was Gay babbling about tigers?"

"I think it was a tiger that scared the horses, although we didn't know it then. I saw him when I went to get my jacket. While I was backing away I tripped, and he jumped on me and started licking me. I panicked and hit him. After the second time he shook his paws and left."

Anna stared at Hashti, a thoughtful expression on her dark weathered face. Then she draped a second blanket around the trainer's shoulders, and went to the door. "Ross, this is your business."

He hurried in. Gaylord followed, looking anxiously at his friend and teacher. "You OK, Hashti?"

"Just a little bumped up," Anna said. "She'll be fine in three weeks. Ross, I think you'll be interested in her story."

The silver-haired naturalist straddled a chair and started quizzing. Hashti tended to shyness around educated people, but Ross reminded her of her apprentice Master. She repeated the story, realizing how improbable it sounded. Ross listened gravely. When she had finished, he asked for details. "Tell me again what the bunny did?"

"He sat by a stump, ruffled his neck feathers, and stamped at me," Hashti repeated, confused by this interest in a common pest. "Then he dove down his hole. I figured he was scolding us for working too near the burrow."

Ross shook his head. "No. He wouldn't defend it against anything as big as a human. If there were kits— not likely, this time of year—he'd have sat by some other entrance and pretended his leg was broken. Against something his own size, he'd have fluffed out his feathers all over. You say it was just his neck feathers?"

Hashti nodded, frustrated by these tangential questions. "Don't you believe me about the tiger?"

Ross smiled. "I do. Here's why." He rapped on the floor. His pet scampered in from the other room, pausing just inside the doorway with a nervous eye on the visitors. Ross sang a rapid, irregular series of notes.

The animal shrank down, feathers pressed against its sides, its nose quivering. Ross sang again. The rabbit fluffed its neck feathers, shifted its weight, and thrummed urgently against the floor with its hind feet.

"Yes!" Hashti exclaimed. Startled, the rabbit darted into the other room. Hashti lowered her voice. "That's exactly what the one in the woods did. How—?"

Ross smiled. "What I sang was part of a tiger call. When Lady heard it, she sounded the alarm. Yours was trying to tell you there was trouble on the way, but you didn't know the lingo."

Common wisdom said that all First-Inners were a little crazy. Hashti hadn't believed it, until now. Gay's thoughts traveled the same path. "Why should a New Lebanon rabbit care whether *we* knew there was a tiger?" he asked.

Ross shrugged. "I'm sure it was nothing personal. Obviously the main concern is warning other rabbits. But everyone else gets the news too. Almost as if the rabbits enjoy ruining the tigers' hunting." Ross paused, his eyes shifting to Hashti. "The rabbit acted normally. Your tiger didn't. Did he threaten you before he jumped?"

"He made a noise at me. Not a growl, exactly—more like heavy breathing."

"Singing?" Ross asked.

Hashti shuddered. "Just once. After he'd attacked me."

The First-Inner shook his head. "He didn't attack you. If he had, you wouldn't be here."

It had felt like an attack at the time, but Hashti could see Ross's point. She summoned all the objectivity she could muster. "Was he just curious?"

Ross sipped reflectively at his mug of bittertea. "Probably—though I thought the skunk guns had cured that. Tell me again what he looked like, Teamstress."

"He was enormous!" No, the naturalist would want a more specific answer. "Bigger than a small pony. Six hundred pounds, maybe. About up to my waist. Heavy shoulders. Thick, shiny feathers. The stripes blended right into the woods, that's why I didn't see him sooner. A funny pattern on his face—sort of a mask. Gold eyes, white whiskers, big teeth." She shivered again as she remembered his teeth.

Anna and Ross looked at each other. "Sounds like Khan," the man said.

"What?" Hashti asked. "Who?"

"I name them to keep them straight," Ross explained. "This one's been in the area for a couple of weeks, evidently traveling alone. Since he was minding his own business, I didn't say anything. No point in upsetting folks. But now we may have to do something."

"Want me to shoot him?" Gay asked.

Anna scowled. "Guns rarely solve problems, Mr. Hess."

Hashti raised her eyebrows. Gay had a surname? If so, why was he here? She didn't recognize the name, but then only a handful of the Families vacationed at the resorts of her home planet, Carolina.

Meanwhile, Gay scowled back at Anna. "Call me Gaylord. Everyone else does."

The doctor looked amused. "Fine, Gaylord. I still think your approach is primitive."

"Relax, wife," her husband said. "No one's doing anything until we find out which tiger it was." His gaze shifted to Hashti. "Will you show me where you saw him, Tiger Wrestler?"

"She will not," Anna answered. "She's going to finish her tea and take a long nap."

Oh, how tempting that sounded! But the guildswoman had responsibilities to fulfill. "I have to get down to the barn. Teams are due back in an hour."

"Ross can muster them in," Anna volunteered.

Hashti wet her lips. "That's very kind, but I ought to do it myself."

Ross grinned wryly. "I'm no Master Equestrian, but I was a cavalry sergeant on Punjab. I can handle it for an evening. Now, tell me where you had your wrestling match."

"It's, uh, on the new northwest skidway, about half-way up the hill—an old blackpine—" Hashti found it surprisingly hard to pinpoint that otherwise unremarkable spot in the woods.

"Where we had lunch?" Gay interrupted. "I'll show him."

"Done," the naturalist agreed. He disappeared into the cabin's third room and returned wearing a worn but warm-looking sweater, with an odd device strapped across his chest. "I thought I was finished with this damn thing."

"If you spill any you're not coming back in this house," Anna warned. "Skunk gun," she explained to Hashti.

"Why not a real one?" Gay asked.

"Let's not meddle more than we have to," Ross answered. "A tiger that's been skunked doesn't come back, and he tells his friends not to come back either. This one just didn't get the word."

# CHAPTER TWO

✿✿✿✿

ANNA KISSED HER HUSBAND GOODBYE, THEN TURNED back to Hashti. "As long as you're here, let me update your chelator."

Hashti looked unhappily at the injector in the doctor's hand. "Again, already?"

Anna nodded firmly. "Once a week—unless you want brown rings around your eyes. Not to mention your brain and liver rotting away."

Hashti held out her arm. Anna made a deft pricking motion, squeezed slowly, then smiled and wiped a single drop of blood from the puncture. "Better than dying of copper poisoning, no? I assume you're taking your iron?"

Hashti nodded. "And lacing it into the grain. You'll check the horses this week?"

"I'll test, but I doubt they need shots. Grain doesn't have all that much copper. Meat's the big offender." Anna disassembled and put away the injector. Then she handed Hashti a yellow pill, an ice bag, and a thick flannel nightgown. "Stay here the rest of the afternoon," she suggested. "It's warm, and nobody will bother you."

Hashti hesitated. "I really ought to check the horses myself, doctor."

The First-Inner laughed. "Don't be silly. Ross needs some honest work to do. He spends too much time watching birds and trees. I've cages to clean; I'll be with the testers if you need me." She tightened the stove's draft and left.

Hashti hated to have Ross do her work, but she'd been short on sleep since the day she landed on New Lebanon. Exhaustion neutralized guilt. She pulled off her boots, slipped into Anna's gown, and went to bed without even setting her boot liners to dry.

She fell into a restless, flickering sleep, drifting between dream and daydream. Big, placid old Betsy grew stripes and fangs and used her for a catnip mouse. Ross chewed her out for not feeding the horses, only it wasn't Ross, it was her old teacher Master Will. Gaylord kept popping up at odd places and sliding his arm around her—

She started awake. Darkness told her she must have slept several hours. Coals settled in the stove with a quiet murmur. Ross and Anna were talking in the next room. "The Teamstress still asleep?" the naturalist asked.

"She sure is. Keep your voice down."

"Bet she needed it. Company works the kids too hard. Bedding down those teams was a job even for me."

"You're getting old, dear."

"Come here, woman, and I'll show you how old I am!"

Anna laughed. "You're incorrigible. What did you find in the woods?"

"It was Khan, all right. The claw that won't retract is a dead giveaway."

"What did he want with Hashti?" Anna asked.

"No clue," Ross answered, sounding troubled. "Just nosy, so far as I can tell. We don't need nosy tigers."

"What next?"

"Skunk him, I guess. That's stopped every other tiger."

"Give skunk guns to the jacks?" the doctor asked.

"Hate to. They're so jumpy, they'll skunk anything that moves, including themselves. But they'll likely meet Khan before I do." Hashti heard the thud of boots being pulled off and tossed aside. "Soon as I get dry socks on," Ross announced to his wife, "I'm headed to City Hall for dinner. You coming?"

"I'll stay here in case the young lady wakes up. Tell Big Red she needs help in the barn for a couple weeks."

"Already talked to him." Ross stamped his feet back into the boots. "Want me to bring you something?"

This had gone far enough, Hashti thought. The couple shouldn't miss dinner together on her account. She climbed out of bed, straightened her sling, and knocked on the door. "I'm up, Dr. Anna."

"Are you decent?" At Hashti's affirmative answer, Anna pushed open the door. "How's the shoulder? It's dinnertime, if you feel up to it."

Hashti pulled on her heavy woolen work clothes, wincing at the reek of horse sweat, and stepped with Ross and Anna into frosty darkness. Low-hanging woodsmoke stung her eyes, and frozen mud crunched underfoot as she walked toward City Hall. High above the smoke sparkled a distinctive, ring-shaped constellation, and two moons which sent double shadows crisscrossing the packed-dirt paths between buildings. From the looming hulk of the dining hall, smells of steaming venison and odd local vegetables lured loggers from every direction. These big rough men had come to the frontier because there was nothing for them at home. They stared curiously at Hashti—news of her accident had spread throughout the camp—but the First-Inners' presence shielded her from questions.

An enclosed porch, the length of the building, buffered City Hall against blasts of cold air pouring through the outer doors. Loggers shucked their boots when they entered. Hashti and her companions added their own boots to the jumble and hung their wraps from pegs on the wall. Then they moved on into the single cavernous room which occupied most of City Hall. Its sixty-degree air felt steamy warm on wind-chapped faces. By the flaring, uneven, yellow light of pitch torches, the forty-five-by-sixty foot room looked even bigger than it was. Thick posts, dotted around the room at fifteen-foot intervals, supported the rafters. Empty space at the far end of the room testified to the camp's hope that the next shuttle would bring new hands.

At the room's front by the kitchen entrance stood the Company table, with cushioned chairs reserved, by tradition, for the university-trained. Oldearth's chemist, lawyer, and bookkeeper held three of these seats. The other three went to the First-Inners, making "Company Table" something of a misnomer.

Close by stood the guild table. Although still a journeyman, Hashti held a courtesy seat here with the masters. Tonight they treated her as a celebrity. No one seemed to realize that she'd gotten into trouble through carelessness. She finally gave up explaining that she'd been hurt by a tree rather than the tiger. Everyone praised her coolheadedness and courage—they'd have thought differently if they'd been there, she was sure—and pestered her for descriptions of the tiger. Her adventure completely eclipsed normal conversational complaints about off-colored meat and tryptophan gravy.

Hashti had trouble evading questions long enough to eat, and eating presented its own problems as she tried to cut her venison with one hand. She heard Ross and Anna at the Company table, and Gay on his bench at one of the broad common tables, giving their own versions of the story.

Finally, as dinner bowls were stacked and sweetsap pudding served, the camp boss rose from his chair and called the unruly crowd to attention. Big Red stood half a head taller than most of the men, with shoulders to match, and by torchlight his hair glistened bright as the stripes of his red plaid flannel shirt. Like Ross and Anna, he wore the gem-flecked earring of First-In. He was foreman because the Company hadn't provided one. Hashti had been in the shuttle tender's cargo bay, trying to coax a sedated but still-dubious Blaze from the gently bobbing tender onto an even less stable raft, when the company's lawyer, Lael, informed Big Red of his new status. The First-Inner's outrage had been something to behold. "The hell you say I'm running this camp! I'm no stooge for Oldearth Company! You're well-enough educated. You run it!"

Lael, a fashionably plump blonde who made Hashti feel like a skinny backwoodser, shook her head. "I know nothing about lumbering. My specialty is frontier law, and I've got a store to run. Besides, your Circle did contract to supply adjustment consultants."

"Adjustment consulting doesn't mean running the damn camp! And you know the men don't want to take orders from a First-Inner."

Lael shrugged. "Want it or not, they need somebody to give orders. Recruiters must have been on a tight budget."

Big Red glowered as he accepted the sealed packet of personnel records. "I'll do what I have to, but so help me, Oldearth will pay!"

However reluctant he had been to assume authority, he had done a good job. Those who didn't respect him for his competence respected him for his six-and-a-half foot frame and solid fists. Now his booming voice quelled the chatter of a hundred and fifty people with scarcely an effort. "Listen up, crew. You all know the barn boss met a tiger this afternoon." Eyes moved again toward Hashti. She ducked her head. Big Red let curiosity build for a moment before he went on. "Contrary to rumors, she'll be fine in a couple of weeks. In the meantime, teamsters get to the barn early and help look after your horses. Lance, as of now you're a stablehand."

Hashti had noticed how the gawky sixteen-year-old lingered when "gofer" errands brought him to the barn; he had no business with horses but was fascinated by them. A wide grin spread across his face. Big Red had chosen well.

The huge redhead was still talking. "Mr. Ross has identified the tiger and says one good whiff of skunk will prevent further incidents. Each team send somebody to the Company table after dinner and we'll give you a gun. They aren't hard to use."

A worker rose from his place at a common table. "You're gonna send us against tigers with nothin' but perfume?"

Big Red looked him in the eye. "You ever seen a tiger that's been skunked?"

"No, sir."

"I have. It works. A face shot temporarily blinds the tiger. Even a miss will make it want to hunt elsewhere. You can blind yourself, too, but wait half an hour and you'll be able to find your way home. Just remember you've got a short range—thirty to sixty feet. Shoot and dodge, or you'll be knocked down by a blind, smelly tiger. Any other questions? Good. Have some dessert."

Pudding was easy to eat with one hand; Hashti did it justice. As she scraped the last remains from her cup, she saw Lael rise from the Company table and mince provocatively toward guild territory. Hashti sighed.

Lael assumed a tone of great friendliness. "Are you OK, Hashti? That's awful about the tiger! You must have been scared silly!"

"I've been in more comfortable situations," Hashti admitted.

"It's a good thing you had Gaylord with you," Lael gushed, unaware or unconcerned that Gaylord had not, in fact, been there. "Now there's a man with looks, no? Too bad he's not taller. Has he told you where he's from?" Her eyes were tight.

"Didn't ask," answered Hashti, dropping her spoon into the empty pudding cup and shoving it toward the center of the table.

Lael raised her hands in a gesture of dismay which, not incidentally, emphasized her feminine endowments. "You spent the whole day in the woods with him and never asked where he's from? You're hopeless!"

Master Tam, the carpenter, was seated at Hashti's elbow and had watched the encounter with amusement. Now, unexpectedly, he interrupted. "Miz Hashti works for her living, Lael. She's got more important things to do than chat up every man she meets."

His distribution of courtesy titles was not lost on the lawyer. She glared, opened her mouth, and shut it again. Other guildsmen around the table grinned. Lael opted for a strategic retreat. "Nice seeing you and Tam, Miz Hashti."

Tam tore his eyes from the rearward portion of Lael's anatomy to shake his head at Hashti. "Who taught you to be so polite? You don't have to put up with her crap."

"I grew up on a resort planet," Hashti explained. "The nastier they are the nicer you have to be."

Tam smiled. "You'll get over it. You want the rest of my pudding, Journeyman? I saw how you packed yours away."

Hashti, cheeks bright, nodded assent. As she retrieved her spoon and plunged it into the second dessert, her new stableboy approached. "When do you want me at the barn, Miz Hashti?"

"Quarter after four will be fine," she told him.

His eyes widened. "In the morning?"

"In the morning." She smiled. "You can sack out in the mow after the teams leave."

"Yes, ma'am. Guess I better get to bed."

As Lance wove his way out through a throng of jacks receiving skunk guns, Hashti heard a hiss. Loud protest erupted. "Curse you, Sweat, haven't you got any brains at all?" An acrid stink washed across the room. Sweat, a heavy ungainly man whose face bore the marks of more than one brawl, bellowed and pawed at his eyes as the crowd bore him away.

"Put him in the sauna!"

"Hell, no! Tie him in the barn."

"Not fair to the horses. Dump him in the lake!"

Anna made her way toward Hashti, wincing. "I knew there'd be trouble. At least it'll teach everyone to be careful. Here's an ice bag—keep it on your shoulder tonight. I suggest you get out of here, before they draft you for cleanup."

Sleep with an ice bag? In this weather? Hashti shivered, but such were the rewards of carelessness. She paused briefly in the mud room to don her boots and mittens, then trudged downhill toward the barn. Her hand was on the stable door when a weird, terrifying song pierced the darkness.

She froze.

The melody was artful, but alien. Ross's few notes,

earlier today, proved only a pale imitation of the haunting cry now echoing from the hills. It wandered across three octaves, now fast, now slow. A roar cut through the chilly darkness, and a second tiger voice rose, interweaving with the first.

Hashti hurried into the barn. The horses stamped and snorted. They knew predators prowled the forest. Hashti stroked shoulders and murmured lullabies, trying to reassure her charges. The tigers were still calling when she collapsed on her pallet two hours later.

Gay burst into the feedroom the next day, smelling terrible. "Hashti, I got him! I skunked your tiger!"

She'd been showing Lance how to mix a bran mash. The boy looked from Hashti to Gay. "I'll finish mucking stalls, Miz Hashti. Call me when you're done." He fled with an alacrity that embarrassed her. Was she so transparent?

Victory flushed Gay's face. "I was out on the northeast skidway when the tiger came right down the middle of the road. What a brute, Hashti! No wonder you were scared when he knocked you down. I almost panicked myself. But I put the fear of God in him. Too bad—what a pelt! My mother would kill for a wrap like that. I hated to put skunk all over it. I wish Ross would let us shoot the beasts."

The smell in the small feedroom was getting overpowering. Perhaps Lance's precipitous departure had had nothing to do with courtesy. Gay saw Hashti edging away, and frowned. "Aren't you glad I got the tiger? I thought you'd be happy to know I skunked him."

"I'm glad, Gay. I never want to see him again. But—" How could she put this? "You smell. Like you've been using a skunk gun."

"Oh." He looked properly abashed. "I forgot. My

nose is already numb. Anyplace around here I can clean up?"

"The basin in my room probably hasn't frozen yet," Hashti said, glad she had straightened her domain this morning.

Gay returned a few minutes later, still reeking. "Something wrong?" Hashti asked.

"Too damn cold to wash down here. Besides, your soap smells."

"It smells better than you do," Hashti pointed out.

"It smells like you, is what it smells like! You want me to walk into the bunkhouse with that stuff on me? You'd have a lively time explaining, Miz Hashti."

She hadn't thought about that. Rumors flew fast enough unassisted. Gay sniffed at his sleeve. "I guess I am pretty rank. I'll go on up to camp and get rid of this shirt. I need to tell Ross I got the tiger."

"Mister Ross," Hashti prompted, softening the reminder with a grin. Gay had a terrible time with honorifics.

"Oh, yeah. Mister Ross. I'll be by later for my victory kiss." Gay vanished into the corridor, his words lingering behind.

Hashti had little time to ponder them. Lance chattered endlessly as he helped with the chores. Politeness kept Hashti from asking why the boy had come to this planet, but his conversation revealed an intimate knowledge of pickpocketing techniques. She drew her own conclusions.

Her guesses about Lance fit with her generally unpleasant impression of Oldearth's recruitment policy. They'd offered her, as barn boss, a standard profit-sharing contract. The other guildfolk, honest, competent men, had been hired on similar terms. Together, the guild crew had the skills needed for lumbering on

New Lebanon, though they'd been given no foreman to coordinate those skills.

But Lance, underage, the law on his heels, had certainly gotten a substandard deal. Hashti suspected that most of the laborers' contracts were as meager. Why had the company wasted topnotch guild talent on a camp with such inexperienced, demoralized workers? And why had a man like Gay been desperate enough to accept Oldearth's terms?

It didn't matter. Hashti was here, now, and must do her part in training and motivating the crew. Profit meant a nest egg for her, and a Guild Master's cap, as well. If the camp failed, she'd be in debt to Oldearth Company for her passage home. Until the debt was paid, she'd have to accept any assignment the company gave her. That began a spiral few could escape. She'd gambled her career on the sweetsap wood of New Lebanon.

As if to illustrate her thoughts on the quality of recruitment, a scar-faced swamper walked in. It was Sweat, Gay's malingering partner, the man who'd inadvertently fired his skunk gun. Strands of greasy brown hair had escaped from his ponytail to trail across his cheeks. Hashti looked up from the foot of the lame horse she'd been examining. "Can I help you?" she asked.

Sweat ignored her and looked to Lance, who was fetching a bucket of ice water.

"You want something?" Hashti asked again, standing up in the stall.

Sweat brushed the hair off his face with a large, clumsy hand. His eyes swept Hashti up and down. "What're you offerin'?"

Fed up with advances from men she hardly knew, she answered curtly. "Nothing. Why are you here?"

Sweat looked back at Lance. "Big Red was wonderin'

if you could put together an extra sleigh haul team, for when snow comes."

Lance shrugged and pointed his thumb toward Hashti. "She's the boss."

"Thought you was workin' here now," Sweat said to Lance.

"Miz Hashti runs the place," the boy answered. "I just shovel shit."

"What do you need?" Hashti asked a fourth time, coming out of the stall.

Sweat frowned. "I was askin' Lance."

"Lance doesn't have the answer!" Hashti snapped. "I run this barn. Now give me the question!"

Sullenly Sweat asked, "Can you scratch a couple o' skidders and put together an extra sleigh haul team?"

She ran through the possibilities in her mind. "I can. Now scram."

Sweat departed, muttering under his breath about stuck-up bitches. Lance stared after him. "What's his problem?" the boy asked. "Doesn't he know who's boss around here?"

Hashti grimaced. "I'm ten years younger, six inches shorter, and a hundred pounds lighter than he is. Not to mention I'm female. He can't believe I'm really the boss."

"But you're a Guilder!" Lance protested. His street wisdom had some odd gaps, Hashti reflected, if he thought guild status cured all problems. "The teamsters don't treat you like that, do they?" Lance asked.

"They're better," Hashti admitted, remembering a few pointed confrontations at the beginning of her career on New Lebanon. "They know me now. Have you got the bucket?" She bent down to look at Liza's hoof again.

As she expected, the hoof was hot to the touch. Somewhat clumsily, since she had to work one-handed,

Hashti planted the mare's leg in ice water. Liza snorted reproachfully. By the time Hashti finished her ministrations, tended to other stable chores, settled in the returning teams, and soaked Liza's foot once more, the horsewoman had, as usual, missed dinner.

Even the dishwashers were gone, although the wooden washbasins were still damp and a soapy smell lingered in the air. Hashti set her lamp on a counter in the kitchen wing of the dark City Hall and began to scrounge. The gentle burble of the spring covered the rustle of tiny feathered pests scurrying for cover, but from the corner of her eye Hashti saw them flee. Until Ross could find some small native wildcat or owl amenable to domestication, mice would continue to share the camp's larder.

A covered kettle contained the remains of tonight's stew, a bluish-gray mixture of swamp pilaf and rabbit meat. Hashti ladled a generous helping into her wooden bowl. Then, her nose wrinkling, she filled a cup with tryp gravy. Cold, it tasted like the bacterial culture from whence it came. Hashti set the cup in hot spring water to warm.

However distasteful it might be, she knew the barely tolerable gravy provided a crucial complement to New Lebanon's proteins, not to mention that a jolt of tryptophan at supper helped everyone to sleep well. As Hashti poured the stuff over the remaining half of her dinner, Gay walked in. "Saw a light here and thought it might be you," he said casually. "Everything all right in the stable?"

"Stable's fine. What are you doing up so late?"

Gay kicked at the side of a vat that held hot water from the spring. "Thought I might see you when you came up for dinner. I talked to Ross. He says I skunked the wrong damn tiger!"

"What?" She should have warmed the gravy longer, or skipped it entirely. She forced herself to swallow anyhow. "What do you mean, the wrong tiger?"

"There's a new tigress in the area," Gay explained. "That's what all the noise was last night. Ross says it was the new one that I zapped. I told him any tiger that walks up to me in broad daylight needs to sniff skunk, whether she's new or not." The stocky blond lumberjack hesitated, watching Hashti scrape and rinse her wooden bowl. "Getting colder tonight. I thought you might want help with your stove."

"That'd be nice," she replied as she put the dish away and reached for her coat. "It's hard to build a fire with one hand. I hate undressing in a cold room."

Gay's hair shone copper in the light of the oil lamp he carried. Neither of them said much, but Hashti was acutely conscious of her companion's well-muscled shoulders and the blond stubble along his jaw. Their footsteps crackled loudly over the soft sigh of wind in treetops. Then the barn roof rose comfortingly over them, blotting out the stars of an alien sky. Betsy whickered as she recognized the footsteps of her driver.

Gay paused to scratch the bay mare's jaw, then hurried ahead to the woodpile by the far door. Hashti walked more slowly down the aisle, greeting each horse and checking for problems. She watched the mares with special care. In their bellies were the foals who would serve Swamp City as it grew. In a season or two, when Hashti was done training drivers, she'd start educating a new generation of teams. In five years, when these unborn foals were working at full strength, she'd have proven her right to a Master Equestrian's cap.

Her present inspection showed nothing amiss. Gay, holding a double armload of wood, waited outside Hashti's little room at the end of the corridor. She pushed the door open for him. He dumped the wood by her little feed-barrel stove, and knelt beside it to lay the fire. Hashti sat on the bed, watching well-seasoned kindling burst into flame. "Thank you," she said. "This room gets bitter at night."

"My pleasure," Gay answered, closing the door on the blaze. He sat on the foot of Hashti's bed, closer to her than the small room required, and looked around.

Not much to see. Seven by ten feet was a lot, compared to shipboard quarters or a slot in the bunkhouse, but stove and bed pretty well filled the space. Plank walls abutted the tackroom and corridor; the outer walls were log. Hashti had chinked them herself. She had also caulked the window shut, but only lightly—she wanted an escape route should the building ever catch fire. With the window covered, the only light came from Gay's lantern. Hashti's straw-stuffed mattress rested on a wooden shelf across the width of the room; underneath was her trunk of clothes. Spare mittens, boot liners, and underwear hung on a rack by the stove. On a board nailed to the wall sat washbasin, oil lamp, tea mug, and the few personal treasures she had tucked into her baggage allowance. Gay's gaze lingered on a picture of Hashti with a horse and an older man. "Your father?" he asked.

"Master Will. I 'prenticed with him back home on Carolina. I bred and trained the horse myself—my Master's Demonstration. We sold her to a vice-president of Oldearth, and that's how I got this job."

Gay took Hashti's hand, turning it so that he could see the horsehead signet on her guild ring. "Must be nice to have a trade," he commented.

She wondered why Gay didn't have one, but such questions were taboo on New Lebanon—few folk came to the frontier for reasons as innocent as Hashti's. Gay's callused hand was warm, as she had known it would be, and he had a nice grip—firm but gentle. No wonder the horses responded well to his touch! She liked his voice, too, not least because she could understand what he said. Most of the men here spoke such thick dialects that she had difficulty following them. Gay spoke with pure, almost upper-class diction. "I suppose the sore arm will keep us from skidding together, Hashti. I'm sorry."

A separated shoulder would keep them from more than that. "I'm sorry, too," she replied, her hand tightening to underline the point. She was glad Gay understood her constraints. "Dr. Anna said I'd be feeling better in a few weeks."

"I intend to spend more time with you then," Gay said.

Hashti liked men who spoke before they grabbed. Gay had class, she thought, along with his ready wit and well-knit body. Of all the propositions she'd had here, his was the first to tempt her.

But, as the encounter with Sweat this morning had shown, Hashti was not a free agent, and fairness demanded that she put her cards on the table. "I'd love to spend more time with you, Gay." Her blush lent authenticity to the statement. "But consider me off limits, as long as you're on the skidding crew."

He cocked an eyebrow. "Why such a hard line?"

"As Master Will used to say, 'You can't drive stallions if you smell like a mare.' You know there's no privacy in this camp. If I took up with you, every teamster and his brother would accuse me of favoritism or pester for similar favors. I work with men or romance them. Not both."

Gay smiled. "And if I should happen to be transferred off the skidding crew?"

Hashti flushed again. "I'd be glad to celebrate with you."

"Then I'll talk to Big Red in the morning," Gay promised. He leaned forward with half-closed eyes. "Shall we seal the deal?"

Hashti, ignoring her fluttering pulse, met his gaze squarely. "I just told you I don't fool with men who work for me. Wait 'til you're off the skidding crew. Plus a couple weeks for this shoulder to heal," she added, as an unwary twitch sent pain stabbing through her back. "I'm black and blue all over."

"You'll need a better excuse than that to get rid of me, Miz Hashti!" Gay chided. "I'm after more than a roll in the hay."

Maybe. His flushed face and involuntary squeeze said he'd not turn one down.

Gay did not report for work the next morning. His bunkmates told Hashti he was in Big Red's office. They guessed she was somehow involved. "Why'd you send him home so early, Miz Hashti? He's so stung he don't wanna work for you no more. A dame like you should have pity on us poor laborin' men. You want a better offer, I got one for you—"

She accepted no offers and gave no explanations, but she was eager to hear how the interview had gone. She waited. And waited. And waited.

Ross stopped by late in the afternoon, as she was taking her frustration out on a dirty harness. "That'll be the cleanest harness on New Lebanon," he remarked. "I thought you weren't supposed to use that arm."

Hashti looked guiltily at the hame strap in her left hand. "I'm just steadying this thing. Not straining my shoulder at all."

"Mmmmm. I won't tell the wife, but don't let me catch you at it again." He seemed in no hurry to leave. "She asked me to check on you earlier, but I was busy with your handsome friend."

"Doing what?" Hashti's attempt to sound casual was

spoiled by a cake of saddle soap spurting from clenched fingers.

Chuckling, Ross retrieved the soap for her. "Showing him where the game hide out. Wish he'd spoken up when he got here! I could've spared myself three months of hunting if the young pup had told anyone he could shoot."

"He can?" Hashti asked, surprised even though she'd heard Gay mention it in Anna's office. On civilized planets, marksmanship was a skill of the sporting elite. Only on the frontier did ordinary folk handle guns. Gay did not look or act like a native frontiersman.

"He can. And well. He also gave me a message for you. Something about taking you into the woods for breakfast—tomorrow, if possible. Shall I convey an affirmative answer?"

Hashti's face fell. "Tomorrow's Middleday." There are many ways to fit a planet's calendar to the familiar twelve-month pattern. Here, it had been done by adding an extra day to the week. Swamp City's citizens had Sundays off, worked Monday through Wednesday, got a half holiday on Middleday, and worked again Thursday through Saturday.

"What's wrong with Middleday?" Ross asked. "You're supposed to have time off."

"Time off," Hashti reminded him, "means the horses stay in the barn and the teamsters don't help feed them. Sundays and Middledays are the busiest, down here."

"You've got an assistant now," Ross said. "Let Lance work the morning and you take the afternoon. I'll tell Gay you're coming."

Hashti considered several responses, and settled on, "Yes. Please."

The First-Inner smiled at her expression. "Put that

harness together and call it a day, Tiger Wrestler. I'll help Lance check in the teams."

"What? I can do it!"

"But why, if somebody else will? I rather enjoy being with horses again. Or don't you trust me?"

"I trust you, but—"

"Fine. Finish that harness and get out. You've a date to get ready for."

# CHAPTER THREE

❧❧❧❧

SWAMP CITY'S MEN BATHED IN A LEAN-TO ON THE WEST side of City Hall. Lael and Georgia, the Company book-keeper, hearing plans for that rough and exposed facility, had offered three bottles of offworld liquor to whoever would build them a private sauna. Naturally enough, the two other women in camp, Anna and Hashti, were granted use of the steam bath. Tonight, Hashti discovered to her frustration, her shoulder injury made it nearly impossible to wash her own hair, and for once she was glad to have the sauna's owners join her on its steamy benches. Georgia dashed two heavy buckets of cold rinse water over Hashti, then toweled and combed the horsewoman's dark unruly locks. As Hashti dried her hair beside the woodstove, Lael brought a cup of bitter-tea and sat to chat. Only when the lawyer began to inquire about Gaylord did Hashti's distrust return. "I've got to leave now, Lael. I really need to get some sleep."

Well-scrubbed and well-rested, she greeted Gay an hour before sunrise the next morning. His eyes widened slightly. "You look nice this morning! Not that you don't usually, but, uh—"

"But I usually have hay in my hair?" Hashti asked, amused by his reaction.

"Let's say I can usually tell what guild you're in," Gay hedged. "Anyway, you look nice. Shall we go?"

They headed away from camp, leaving dark slushy bootprints as they skirted the roots and puddles of a cedar bog. Stars, thick and bright in this part of the galaxy, reflected generously on new-fallen snow. By the time Gay and Hashti climbed the ridge to the south, stars were fading in the paleness of dawn. Two miles further south across the forest lay the immense lake in which the shuttle tender had landed. Steam shrouded the lake like a great calm cauldron. Hashti squeezed Gay's mittened hand. "It's beautiful."

Nearby, dark gray bedrock thrust up through the trees to form a bald. "Let's eat here," Gay suggested.

"Looks good," Hashti agreed. They settled in the lee of a six-foot rock outcropping, pushed snow aside, and built a small fire.

"I've had it with grass seeds and tryp gravy," announced Gay, unloading his pack. "Today we eat right. Bread. Tea. Berries. And—sausage!" Hashti didn't mind the usual porridge of native grain, but Gay's treat looked even better. A lover on cook's crew would have its advantages. He strung half a dozen of the blue-tinged venison sausages on a stick and propped them over the fire alongside the teapot. Finally he sat back beside Hashti. "How does it feel, being Guild here where the only other men your age are common laborers?" he asked.

A bold question, thought Hashti. She replied honestly but diplomatically. "At least they aren't Family."

Gay's eyebrows rose. "What's wrong with Family men?"

Hashti shrugged. "They're great for a fling, but they don't stick around. Getting mixed up with one is begging for trouble." Everyone on Carolina's resorts knew how much heartbreak came from whirlwind affairs with gentry. Not that Family didn't marry—but they married only their own kind.

Gay frowned. Too late, odd facts about him snapped together in Hashti's mind. She looked from the hunting gun he carried—a rich man's toy, on her world—to Gay himself. "Where'd you learn to shoot?"

He looked away. "Does it matter?"

She knew he was Family. He knew she knew. Why press? Only because she hated evasiveness. "Tell me, Gay. I don't tumble into bed with strangers."

"Will you tumble if I tell?" he asked teasingly.

"I won't if you don't."

Gay leaned over to kiss her. "You're marvelous, Hashti. Have you ever been told you have beautiful eyes?"

"Several times. Always by men who had very little interest in my eyes. Tell me who you are."

He sobered, inclining his head in a formal gesture of introduction. "Gaylord Hess." Seeing no response, he added, "My aunt is governor of Vandalia. My dad's area manager of Interstar."

Hashti whistled. No wonder Gay stood out among the rough-edged recruits! His eyes searched hers anxiously. "Not all Family men are trouble, Hashti. Some of us do stick around, for someone worth sticking around for."

She tried to match this new identity with the lumberjack she'd known. "Why are you doing common labor on the frontier?"

Gay tightened his jaw. "I'm sick of being sneered at. I need to prove I can make it without my Family's help. Here, it's the strength of your back that counts."

Hashti blinked. "Who sneers at you?"

"Everyone. Little things, like what you just said about Family lovers. After university I went to—"

"University?" But of course. Family got the best education money could buy. "What did you study?"

His lip curled. "Business. What else? How to make

the most money from somebody else's work. Then they gave me a lumber division on New Rio—a damn sight better equipped and planned than this mess, I might add!" He paused, clamping his jaw in frustration. "The men were polite to my face, but behind my back they cracked jokes about silver spoons. Of the women, half wanted a Family wedding and the rest wanted to play kiss and tell."

Wouldn't any red-blooded woman try for Gay's pillow—without regard to his Family standing? He continued before Hashti could voice her opinion.

"I got sick of hearing I didn't know what real work was. So I signed with a fly-by-night recruiter who'd been hiring away our men. I'm going to learn this business from the bottom up."

Silly, thought the guildswoman. He was lucky to have connections. Why not play them for what they were worth? But Gay's eccentricity added to his charm, setting him apart from rich young men who thought they got rights to the trainer when they hired her horses. "How many people here know who you are?" she asked Gay.

"Not many. I gave the recruiter a fairy tale, which he couldn't question since he was handing out illegal bonuses. Lael read the papers twice before she signed them. She knew I'd lied, but she assumed I was ducking the law. And since she thinks I'm down on my luck, she's not chasing me." He smiled.

Hashti smiled too. Nice to know at least one man wasn't wrapped around Lael's finger.

"Then there's the First-In doctor," Gay continued. "She ferreted everything out during my touchdown physical, and asked me to be Red's aide. I told her that wasn't what I came for. And now, you know. Guess I have trouble keeping my secret from women." He groped for Hashti's hand. "I'm sorry. You understand why I didn't want to tell you. It doesn't matter, does it?"

It did matter. Gay fell too neatly into the pattern—a courteous, extravagant lover who'd be gone in the spring. A winter on New Lebanon would cure him of his egalitarian ideals, and Hashti knew better than to expect that he'd take her along when he left. But in the meantime, why be lonely? "Since it got you onto cook's crew, I came out ahead. Will you find us something new to eat? I'm tired of wild geese and venison."

"Don't complain. You should see our backup stores." Reproof gave way to disgust on Gay's face.

Like any other frontier camp, Swamp City ate off the land. Law required only that the company supply a half-year's emergency rations—enough to last until the next shuttle. "What did Oldearth give us?" Hashti asked.

Gay wrinkled his nose. "Lard, cornstarch, and vitamin pills."

Running a stable had taught the trainer at least a little about nutrition. "That's revolting. It's also inadequate. We need protein."

Her companion looked away. "They provided that, too. After a fashion."

"Well?"

"You don't want to hear this."

"Quit telling me what I do and don't want to hear. What about protein?"

Gay examined a mud spot on his boot. "They said if things get that bad, we won't need the horses anyhow."

Hashti clenched her teeth. "You were right. I didn't want to hear."

Gay poked angrily at the fire. "Are you surprised? It's of a piece with everything else the Company's done and not done. This place is more primitive than a prison camp."

"I thought this was standard procedure!" Hashti objected. She'd heard the reasons a thousand times. Machines were expensive and required special tools, fuel, and spare parts. Labor was cheap. So frontier colonies were equipped with bodies, brains, and "appropriate technology." The Company put workers on a planet. The workers got pay if and when they produced export revenue. If they wanted to leave, they bought their own tickets—or signed debt contracts.

Gay laughed harshly. "I know transport up and down gravity wells is expensive. But Hashti, they expected the chemist to blow his own glassware! That's crazy. They could have quadrupled their profit by outfitting us properly."

"Then why didn't they?"

"Don't ask me." His voice held an edge.

"You said you studied business," Hashti pressed. "Why didn't they equip us?"

Gay poked at the fire. "I think it's a snare venture. I've heard about them, but I never saw one before. Ugly business."

"But I've got an ordinary profit-sharing contract . . ." Hashti's protest trailed away as Gay's words soaked in.

He mistook her silence for lack of understanding. "You do. But what if there's no profit to share? Normally, a company tries to optimize its investment/profit ratio. Company makes money, the crew all get a piece, morale is high and everybody comes out ahead. In a snare venture, the company doesn't try for a profit. They want just enough income to cover costs. That way, without losing any money, they get a stranglehold on prime guildfolk like you. The only way for you to get off the planet is to sign a debt contract for your ticket. Once you're under a debt contract, they can send you places no Master in her right mind would sign for. And even if the next place makes a profit, it'll take you a damn long time to buy free."

"They can't do that!" Hashti protested. "They'll be blacklisted by the guilds!"

"You're right," Gay agreed. "They will—if they make a habit of it. But Oldearth's too smart for that. In a given instance, who can tell a snare from an honest failure? Your contract looks like any other horse trainer's. Can you prove they've trapped you?"

"No," she answered dully, still absorbing the implications. "So that's why this whole camp seems so half-baked. It's supposed to fail."

"That's how I read it," Gay said grimly. "Want to know what happened to our foreman? He backed out when he read the transport's bill of lading. He knew we weren't well enough equipped to succeed."

Hashti's head drooped as she remembered the hopes that had brought her here. What if Gay's suspicions were correct?

He pulled his mitten off and stroked her black hair. "Don't give up yet. If the camp fails, I can buy both of us out. But Oldearth missed a few guesses. Who'd have known we could set the camp on a sweet hot spring? Who'd have known we could get the buildings up so fast? And who'd ever have guessed the First-In consultants would take such an active interest in us?"

"Isn't that what they're paid for?" Hashti asked.

"Technically speaking," Gay answered, "they need only advise us on things like what's safe to eat and what winter weather will be like. They ordinarily stay clear of organizational and production-related decisions. But Big Red's running this camp for us—without him we'd have a rabble, not a work force. The doctor could have tended her testers, given us our copper shots, and called the job done. But she went through all our building and equip-

ment designs, and made a lot of good suggestions. She
has more ideas than some engineers I've known. Ross
lets you think he just ambles around watching animals,
but he laid out the camp practically single-handed, has
done two-thirds of the hunting, and all of the pest control." Gay leaned forward to turn the sausage skewer.
"Whatever you think of First-Inners, they do know how
to survive on the frontier. And ours have gone out of
their way to help us."

"They have," Hashti agreed. Until now she had paid
little attention to the politics of interplanetary com-
merce. "But why, if they don't have to?"

Her informant shrugged. "Who knows why First-
Inners do anything? Maybe for their reputation. Circles
don't like being associated with failures. Maybe for the
challenge. Maybe from the goodness of their hearts. I'm
just glad they're helping."

The sausage skewer slipped sideways. Gay propped it
back, then hitched himself closer to Hashti. "Breakfast
in five minutes. Shall we enjoy ourselves in the meantime?" She snuggled against his shoulder and ignored the
sun rising over the lake's mist.

It takes a lot of snow to produce two mugs of tea, and
a lot of wood to melt the snow. All too soon Gay left to
replenish the fuel supply. He politely refused Hashti's
offer of assistance. "It's a two-handed job. Sit back and
relax; I won't be gone long." His broad back, disappear-
ing down the hill, brought to mind an old ballad. Hashti
sang it as she waited, making sure to change the song's
beloved from brunette to blond and his eyes from blue to
brown. She was experimenting with other variations
when she heard an odd whuffing sound, like the noise
she made trying to blow stray hair out of her eyes, or the
greeting of two horses sniffing at each other. It came
from her right. She looked up. There stood a tiger.

It was the same one she had encountered before—she recognized the black mask. She broke her song off mid-measure. Gay was out of sight. The tiger whuffed again from his position about ten yards away, then stepped stiffly, cautiously forward.

Gay's gun lay a few feet from Hashti. But she had only a vague notion how to use it, and in any case it required two hands. She remember Ross's comment on her previous encounter. "If he'd meant to kill you, you wouldn't be here." The tiger did not appear malicious, although she had his full attention. Eyes locked on hers, muscles braced, he crept forward.

Hashti wet her lips. "No, boy. Back. Stay back."

He froze, one paw in the air, and whuffed yet a third time. Encouraged, she kept talking. "Good boy. Go home now. Go away." To her dismay, he resumed his advance.

It took him perhaps two minutes to reach her at that stilted, attentive pace. He circled wide around the fire, then stuck his head out to sniff at Hashti's face and her left arm in its cotton sling. At this distance she could see the individual barbs of his feathers, and the faint bluish tinge which copper-tinted blood gave his lips. He nosed at the mug in her right hand. She dropped it, splashing hot tea across her boots. The tiger started, then resumed sniffing. Nose twitching, he hummed five notes. The melody seemed oddly familiar, like the last part of the first line of an old nursery song. "Twinkle, little star." Thoroughly confused and very frightened, Hashti gave no answer.

The tiger's inspection complete, he dropped back on his haunches and sat watching her. Since he had offered no threat, she relaxed a little. "What do you want?" she asked the magnificent animal—as if he could answer! "What are you looking for?"

He responded with an odd string of notes, and looked expectantly at the woman. She had no idea how to respond. Then the tiger noticed the fallen mug. With a forearm thicker than Hashti's thigh he batted at the cup and gave chase, dribbling it halfway across the clearing. Finally he pounced on the object, lifting it between his paws and flinging it high into the air. It thudded into the snow by Hashti's feet.

The tiger acted for all the world as if he wanted to play, but the horsewoman had seen stable cats excite themselves into frenzy with games like this. She wanted nothing to do with a frenzied tiger. Neither did she want to cross him. Nervously, she reached out and rolled the cup back to him.

Like a hockey player intercepting a pass and driving it into the net, he scooped up the mug and returned it to her. It stopped just beyond her reach. As she lifted her hand, the tiger knocked the cup a few inches further away, inviting her to contend for possession. She sat back on her heels against the rock. "Oh, no. I'm not going to argue, sir. You're a lot bigger than me." He understood the gesture, if not the words. Snatching up the cup himself, he rolled over on his back, bit playfully at his prize, and tossed it into Hashti's lap.

She heard a smothered gasp. Gay stood, white-faced, thirty feet away at the edge of the clearing. His skunk gun drooped dispiritedly towards the ground—he could not fire at the tiger without soaking the woman as well. "Hashti!" he croaked. "Get away from that beast!"

She found his terror oddly irritating. It was a touchy situation, but the tiger had offered no threat, and the interaction challenged every trainer's instinct in her. "I'm OK," she assured her would-be protector. "Just don't startle him."

The tiger turned when he heard the man. The animal's

lips drew back in a spitting growl. Hashti knew a snarl when she heard one. "Back off, Gay," she warned.

Instead, Gay raised the skunk gun. If she'd stopped to think, Hashti would have seen his point. Tigers mustn't get used to approaching humans so boldly. But Hashti didn't think. Acting from a gut conviction that you don't punish an animal that hasn't misbehaved, she threw herself between Gay and the tiger.

The gun's foul-smelling charge sprayed wildly across the rocks, a ten-foot blackpine sapling, and Hashti. Meanwhile the tiger charged, arching over the woman in a flash of power. He toppled Gay with a shoulder blow. As the logger fell, Khan's jaws brushed at his neck, but the animal did not bite. Instead he sat back, bristling, forepaw poised to strike if Gay moved.

Through the watery blur the spray brought to her eyes, Hashti saw Gay lying motionless. Feeling desperately responsible, she scrambled to her feet and ran toward the tiger, shouting and waving her good arm. "Get out! Get away from here! Let him go!"

Khan jumped back with a hiss, watching her warily. "Go on!" she shouted. "Git!" He retreated a few steps further. She kicked snow in his face. At that the tiger wheeled and ran. Hashti turned anxiously to Gaylord.

He was already climbing to his feet, intact and fighting mad. "What the hell were you doing, Hashti?"

She could barely see through her skunk-induced tears, and the stench of the spray made her stomach lurch. She stumbled to the edge of the clearing and vomited, each spasm wrenching her abused shoulder. Still queasy, she rinsed her mouth with snow and looked back at Gay. "I was trying to keep you from starting a fight. If you hadn't been so trigger-happy we'd have been fine."

His hands twitched as if he wanted to shake her. "That was a full-grown tiger, not a pussycat!"

"He didn't try to hurt me," she answered, rubbing her eyes on her sleeve.

"If he had, you'd be dead," Gay growled. "You god-damn silly bitch."

She spun to face him. "I don't care who your aunt is, you can quit talking to me like that."

His fists clenched. "I didn't say a word about my Family!"

"No," she shot back, "but you're acting like a spoiled rich brat."

Her jibe hit below the belt; she could see Gay flinch. He gritted his teeth. "Fine, Madame Make-It-On-Your-Own Horse Trainer. I hope your guild ring helps you next time a tiger jumps you, because I'll be damned if I will."

In angry silence they dismantled their breakfast camp and stamped out the fire. Two hours ago, Hashti thought, she had been clean and happy. Now she smelled like a skunk and was fighting with Gay. Hollow with misery, she picked up the mug the tiger had played with and handed it to her companion. "Truce?"

He stuffed the mug into the pack on his knees, tied the pockets shut, and finally looked up at her. "Truce. I'm sorry I missed the tiger. I didn't mean to skunk you, Hashti."

That wasn't the apology she wanted. He shouldn't have fired the gun at all. But truce is truce. She watched silently as Gay stood and belted the pack around his waist. He snugged the strap and checked for slippage before he spoke again. "I was scared half to death when I saw him standing over you. Ross is wrong about the tigers. They're not at all standoffish. Let's get back to camp before we meet any more."

But they seemed fated to meet tigers today. They had pushed their way back through a mile of virgin under-

brush and were stepping with relief onto a cleared logging road when Gay halted, blocking the path with an
outstretched elbow. Hashti bit off her protest in mid-
breath as she saw the sleek buff and black figure of a
tiger sauntering down the road toward the humans. The
animal was smaller than Khan, and her stripes ran in a
curly question mark pattern. She perked her ears inquisitively and emitted that odd whuffing noise, from a distance of about forty feet.

Gay replied with a barrage from the skunk gun. The
tigress hissed in outrage and circled, shaking her head
and pawing at her eyes. Gay backed away, pulling Hashti
with him. The tigress stumbled against a tree and slashed
at it in frustration. Then she stopped and seemed to recover her bearings. Still pawing occasionally at her face,
she trotted away through the trees.

"Right between the eyes!" Gay exulted, sliding the
gun back into its sheath. Yet worry crept into his expression as he stared after the animal. "She looks awfully
familiar." His face darkened even further when he knelt
to examine her tracks. "Yes, it was Sabra!"

"Who?" Hashti asked. She looked at the pug marks,
bigger than her hand could span, pressed into the fresh
snow. They were obviously tiger tracks, but beyond that
Hashti could read little. "How do you know?"

"Ross showed me. The tiger with the mask—Khan—
has a rear claw that won't retract. This one, Sabra, with
the funny stripes, has unusually long middle toes. I
skunked her day before yesterday."

Hashti looked dubiously at the marks. "Are you sure
she's the same one? Mister Ross said a tiger that's been
skunked never comes back."

Gay frowned a moment longer at the imprints in the
snow. "I'm losing faith in his opinions."

Ross himself seemed taken back by their report. He

hurried off to investigate the sites of the encounters, and returned with troubled eyes. "You're right, Gaylord. It was Sabra." The troubled look lined itself even deeper when Sabra, two days later, confronted a pair of sawyers and received yet a third dose of skunk. Then the next day, Saturday, the real excitement began.

Big Red had summoned Hashti for a conference in the camp office. The small room doubled as the boss's quarters. A rumpled quilt covered a cot along one side wall, and a teapot sang on the stove. The First-Inner motioned Hashti to a chair at his sweetsap table, twin to the table in Anna's cabin, above which hung pictures of planets that Big Red had explored with his Circlemates. Hashti stared, fascinated by the alien figures surrounding Big Red, Ross, and Anna.

The tall redhead seated himself across from her, propping his feet on the bed. "Have we got enough horses, Miz Hashti?"

She jerked her attention back to everyday matters. "Enough for now," she answered. "But too many are geldings. It'll take a long time to build up the herd."

"There are native ponies on this planet," Big Red told her. "Want to try your hand with them?"

Hashti considered. Wild horses, anywhere, of any kind, tended to be tough and strong. But, unlike domestic species selected over millennia for trainability, wild horses were usually unreliable and recalcitrant. Furthermore, the feathered pelts of New Lebanon ponies would probably chafe intolerably under collar. "I guess not," Hashti answered slowly. "I'll leave them for the exotic animal collectors."

"Ross said you'd say that," the boss responded, sounding relieved. "I'm glad you did. They live on the plains, and that's five hundred miles from here. But you're the expert, and I thought I ought to ask."

"I've enough on my hands as it is," Hashti assured him. "By the way, I need a driver for Betsy and Blaze. Gaylord's old team."

Big Red smiled. "Ah, yes. His transfer to cook's crew has worked out beautifully." Hashti blushed, but Big Red's thoughts were on a different track from hers. "Gay's not only set up a new scheme for sharing scut work, but he's teaching one of the other fellows to shoot. Born leader—if I don't watch out he'll take over the camp. Maybe I should encourage him—"

Shouting erupted outside. Someone pounded furiously on the plank door of the office. Big Red glanced apologetically at Hashti. "I can't put together two sentences without somebody having a crisis. Excuse me, Journeyman." He raised his voice. "Come in, come in, don't break the door!"

It was Sweat, crimson-faced, panting, and stinking to high heaven. "I quit. Done. Not goin' back 'til you shoot the damn tigers." He tore off his cap and hurled it to the floor.

Big Red raised his eyebrows. "Pick up your hat and we'll talk about it."

"Ain't nothin' to talk about," Sweat growled, retrieving the cap. "I'm not workin' with tigers aroun', that's all."

"Why not?" Big Red asked, still sprawled calmly in his chair.

"Just got tumbled by one, dammit! Jumped me while I was limbin' a blackpine! I damn near landed on my own axe! Coulda' been killed!"

"You skunked him, I take it," Big Red said.

The disheveled lumberjack shook his head and fists in helpless frustration. "No! No way! Never saw him comin'! Took me from behin'! Didn' get the gun out 'til I was down, then it went off all over *me*."

"I can tell," Big Red answered dryly. "OK. A tiger caught you from behind while you were limbing, knocked you over. What did he do then?"

"Yodeled! He stood over me and yodeled! Then went marchin' away like he was king of the world." Sweat hit his palm with his fist, shouting again. "He coulda' killed me!"

"He didn't, though," Big Red said. "Calm down."

Hashti had been sitting unnoticed off to the side. The vision of Sweat in a pitchy pile of slash, spraying himself with skunk while a tiger in lederhosen stood over him singing, presented itself with irresistible humor. The guildswoman began giggling, holding her nose to stifle outright laughter, her ears popping with suppressed mirth.

Sweat whirled toward her, a flush of embarrassment on his face. "You just try gettin' hugged by a tiger, and see how you like it!"

"She has and she didn't," Big Red interjected as Hashti plunged her face into a bandanna. The boss assumed his most commanding tone. "Go get the skunk off yourself, Sweat, and come back here in an hour. I want Mister Ross to hear this."

"I'm not goin' in the woods 'til that tiger's dead," Sweat reiterated.

"Fine. You can split wood for the kitchen. Now go, and be back in an hour."

Big Red sighed with relief as the door closed. "Thank God he's gone. This place will smell for a week. Miz Hashti, be careful who you laugh at. Sweat's put people through the window for less. You got someone in mind to replace Gay?"

As teamster, he meant. She shook her head. "Just someone with good sense and a level temper."

"I'll see who I can find," Big Red assured her, rising

from his chair and opening the door. "In the meantime, I better talk to Ross. These tigers are getting out of hand."

They got further out of hand the following week. Monday, Sabra toppled a sawyer into the snow. That night tigers sang long and loud. Tuesday, a new tiger made his debut by butting a swamper into a thorny tangle of berry bushes. The same tiger was well skunked when he accosted Ross later in the afternoon. The animal took revenge the next day, pouncing on Stan while the hapless old man gathered wood for the dorm's stoves. Then Sabra dumped another worker in the drifts.

No one was hurt. The tigers merely pounced and left, but men were frightened. The attacks were interrupted by two heavy snowfalls, allowing workers to pack and ice the roads for sleigh hauling. Logging should have accelerated rapidly now. Instead, production slowed almost to a standstill as people tried to work while watching over their shoulders for tigers.

The real hazard had not yet emerged. If not as barn boss, then as victim of Betsy and Blaze's abortive runaway, Hashti should have seen it. But she was preoccupied with a sore shoulder, Gaylord, and the details of daily work, until a red-shirted lumberjack puffed into the barn calling for her. "Miz Hashti!" he panted. "They need you at the landin' right away. A bad accident."

She snatched her cap and ran, slowing to a lung-burning jog after a mile and a half. The footing was bad —iced ruts too slippery to run on, and choppy snow between that churned like sand underfoot. Finally Hashti reached the hill that sloped down to the river. The road forked here; the grade, although short, was steep. Sleighs, loaded twenty to twenty-five feet high with logs, descended on a path liberally strewn with hay, which kept the runners from sliding onto the heels of the horses. The other road boasted cleanly iced ruts for pulling empty sleighs up the hill.

From her vantage point at the top, Hashti saw logs scattered like straw across the foot of the return road. A sleigh lay half-buried in deep snow on the river ice. Anna bent over the driver. The lead team from the wrecked sleigh stood shivering to one side. The pole team remained in their traces, one horse standing, one lying awkwardly in the snow. Clearly, a loaded sleigh had taken the wrong branch and plunged out of control down the icy comeback road. When it stuck in the snow at the bottom, logs had cascaded forward onto driver and horses. Hashti ran down the hill.

One of the men who unloaded logs caught her as she slid to the bottom. "Hero and Herc are hurt, Miz Hashti."

"How's Sam?" she asked, glancing at the driver. Anna was helping him onto the light sleigh that normally performed the happy task of bringing hot lunch to the woods.

"A log bounced off his head. He was pretty confused, and we were scared to let him move. But Dr. Anna says he'll be fine. Lead team's fine too." Hashti's informant nodded at the massive grays standing by a stack of logs.

"Get some blankets on them," she ordered. "And get them walking, if you can spare anybody. They shouldn't stand when they're sweaty. How did it happen?"

Behind the man's ice-rimed beard, his face was scared. "Sam lost control before the horses ever started down the hill. He keeps askin' where the tiger is. One of them must've spooked the team."

Hashti shelved the information and turned her attention to the injured team. Hercules limped badly as she led him forward, but it was only muscle soreness. Time would heal him.

Then Hashti urged Hero to stand. The big gray struggled fruitlessly. His spine was injured; he had no control over his hindquarters. His brown eyes followed his trainer with the dull patient trust of a wounded animal. She wiped her own eyes on the back of her mitten, and probed further. No response.

Anna watched. "Is it as bad as I think it is, Miz Hashti?" she asked quietly. "I couldn't see anything to do for him."

Hashti nodded. If Hero had been a valuable racehorse on a civilized planet, he might have been rehabilitated. But he was only a draft beast in a frontier lumber camp. Swamp City had no sophisticated surgery facilities and no equine therapists. "He's had it, Dr. Anna. Do you have anything I can give him?"

The First-Inner bit her lip. "Back in the cabin. Not here. But I could get him pretty drowsy with what I've got in the kit."

Hero shivered in the biting wind. "It would be a kindness," Hashti replied.

Anna rummaged in her bag for a red-marked vial, which she warmed between her hands. Hashti couldn't get Hero's harness off, but she removed his bridle. Kneeling in the snow, she held Hero's head on her lap while Anna gave him the injection. Hashti scratched the itchy spot under the big gray's chin, meanwhile crooning his favorite lullaby, until he no longer responded to voice or touch. She kissed his crooked white blaze. Then she pulled her knife and slit his throat.

# CHAPTER FOUR

HASHTI SLUMPED SOBBING ON HERO'S WARM BODY. Anna's thin strong arms embraced her. "Cry it out," the First-Inner muttered. But the frontier grants little time for mourning. Hero's lame teammate waited in the snow. Hashti looped Herc's reins, hung them on his collar, and began the long, limping walk home with him.

Back at the barn, she stripped off her blood-drenched coveralls, wanting to burn them, but knowing she couldn't pay the price Lael would charge for new ones. Instead Hashti set the red-blotched clothing to soak, bundled herself in layers of dry wool, and returned to Hercules. The adjacent stall yawned achingly empty. Did Herc wonder where his partner had gone? Sam had left a sour wild apple in Hero's feedbox. Herc sniffed inquisitively. Hashti handed him the treat—Hero would never claim it now. She looked up at the nameplate she had carved for the gray gelding, and remembered the awful plunge of her knife into his jugular. Hercules watched curiously as she scaled the partition between stalls to pull down the nameplate. It was useless now, but Hashti couldn't burn it any more than she could leave it hanging. She set it facing the wall behind the molasses barrel in the feedroom.

She picked up Herc's grooming bucket and went to work on his dappled gray coat. He nickered and rubbed

his head lightly against her, as if he knew her need of
comfort. She brushed her agitation away and had settled
into quiet grief when Lance brought a summons from Big
Red. "He sends regrets over Hero and wants you in
headquarters at six bells."

Hashti did a quick calculation. "I ought to be back
before the teams come in. If not, be sure to check
Cherry's shoulder and see if the new collar pad stopped
the chafing." She broke the ice in her washbasin, dashed
the tear stains off her cheeks, and headed up to camp.

Lael, Georgia, and Big Red were seated around the
table in the crowded little office. Anna and Ross sat on
the cot. Of all the Company table, only the chemist was
missing. His absence was no surprise, for important as
Mr. Jack was to the camp, synthesizing lubricants, medi-
cines, and any other needed substances from local ingre-
dients, he always avoided politics. Placing herself on a
trunk at the foot of the bed, Hashti realized that she
herself was the only representative of guild or commons.
Big Red greeted her matter-of-factly and came straight to
the point. "We've got a tiger problem and we need some
decisions."

"You're damn right you have a problem," Lael said,
looking bored and sulky as usual. "You're going to have
a rebellion on your hands if you don't get rid of the
beasts. Sweat threatened last night to steal a gun."

So Lael not only preyed on the men's loneliness and
poverty, but told tales on them as well? Hashti lowered
her opinion of the storekeeper another notch. Meanwhile
Lael urged, "Kill the tigers, and be done with it."

"We can't," Ross said.

"Why the hell not?" Lael asked.

"We can't afford to up the ante," the naturalist answered.

"What ante?" Georgia asked.

Ross sighed. "Look. An animal attacks for one of two reasons—because it wants to eat you, or because it wants to defend itself against you. First-In took care of the first before you ever got here. After sampling the bait we left, no tiger would think of dining on a human."

"What about a tiger that wasn't here then?" Hashti asked. Khan, Ross had said, had been here "a couple weeks."

The naturalist smiled at her. "I drop another bait now and then, just as a reminder. And the tigers pass the news."

"They what?" Hashti said.

"Tell each other about it." Ross saw her eyebrows rise. "Look, how do you teach a green horse to pull?"

"Team him with an old steady horse. Why?"

"You see, animals do teach one another. These tigers aren't loners—the complexity of their singing tells you that. When one gets sick on something, she warns away the others. It didn't take much to get them to leave us alone."

"But they aren't," Lael said.

Ross hesitated, then answered a shade too defensively. "They aren't trying to hurt anyone."

"That isn't how the laborers tell it."

"They're scared and so they exaggerate," Ross said. "Ask the Teamstress about her encounters—notice that she's alive to tell."

Eyes swung towards Hashti. "Well?" Big Red asked. "Your tiger experience is second only to Ross's—that's one reason you're here. Were the cats trying to hurt you? If not, what did they want?"

Hashti licked her lips. "No," she answered, remembering herself cringing in the slash pile, Khan's sleek-feathered form looming above; Sabra's gentle whuff; Khan, chasing her tea mug around the snowy clearing. "I was scared silly, but neither tiger tried to hurt me. They seemed—curious. Even a little playful."

"Trouble is," Anna said, "tigers can hurt us without trying—witness this afternoon. Sam could easily be dead. We were lucky to lose only the horse." She glanced quickly, apologetically, at Hashti. "Sorry, Miz Hashti. I know it hurt."

"Better a horse than a human," the trainer murmured politely. She'd known Hero a lot better than she'd known Sam. Liked him better, too. But some things one doesn't say.

"Anna's right," Lael said, latching onto her unexpected ally. "We can't have curious tigers wandering around. Let the tigers spread word that we *kill*."

"Dead tigers tell no tales," Ross objected with a flash of his customary humor.

"Then kill them in front of witnesses!" Lael retorted.

"Hold on," Ross said, serious again. "I told you, hunger isn't the only reason animals attack. Threat triggers fighting, too. Put a tiger in danger, you endanger yourself."

"Are you saying you're *afraid* to shoot tigers?" Lael asked.

"I am," the First-Inner admitted. "So should you be. You know what happened on Jelna-Five."

"Those were fish!" Georgia objected. "What do they have to do with feathered tigers?"

"Behavioral convergence," Ross answered.

"Behavioral what?"

"Convergence," Ross said. "Similar selective pressures producing similar answers. For instance, green trees. New Lebanon's plants have copper rather than magnesium in their photosynthetic pigments, but in the end they've evolved colors like those on other planets of this atmosphere and solar spectrum. Or warm bodies—a common response to climates like this."

"Jelna-Five fish and feathered tigers?" Lael prompted.

"I'm getting there!" Ross said. "Behavior converges just as anatomy and physiology do. Similar problems evoke similar behavior. Dogs and humans both hunt prey too large for an individual to catch. So both hunt in packs. That leads to progressive mutual excitation responses, which humans call mob psychology, and protection of weak packmates, such as injured peers and pups. Very large, successful, top-of-the-chain carnivores such as tigers or Jelnan fighting fish don't waste energy on inedible, nonthreatening species. But the Jelna-Five colonists surrendered their neutrality by spearing fighters. The fish soon learned to attack back—as I think the tigers will do, if we initiate aggression."

"A rifle makes short work of aggressive tigers."

"Only if you see them in time," Ross countered. "This is the tigers' forest, not ours. They move silently, nearly invisibly, in it."

"With those stripes?" Georgia asked.

"Adaptive coloring," Ross responded. "Black stripes on a bright background, perpendicular to the silhouette, are hard to see. That's why so many animals have them —convergence again. Ask someone who's been jumped whether they saw the tiger coming." He toyed with his teacup. Hashti saw brown age spots on his hands. "I'm scared to shoot the tigers," he said.

"Keep talking," Anna said, fingering her earring.

Ross set his cup aside. "We've been here a while. The tigers know we aren't tasty or threatening. They should ignore us. Instead they're streaming into the area. And pouncing. When they've pounced and gotten away with it, they leave. I agree with the Teamstress, they seem curious and playful. That's normal for cubs. Not adults. Why waste such energy on us? And why do lone hunters indulge in social serenades? Do they hold territory in common? Do they rear cubs communally? I don't have the answers and I don't want to mess with something we don't understand—for the tigers' sake, and ours. What if we provoke some sort of group defense? It's hard enough to deal with tigers individually."

There was silence. Big Red cleared his throat. "Shooting poses problems from our side, too. We have only twelve guns, and fewer folk than that to handle them." Big Red ticked the names off on his fingers. "Myself, Mister Ross, Doctor Anna, the cook, and Gaylord. All of us have other things to do than stand tiger watch."

"More men can learn to shoot," Lael argued. "Gaylord's teaching Kevin."

"Kevin's got coordination, a level head, and a lot of experience outdoors," Big Red answered. "He's the exception, not the rule. Think of Sweat. Even Gaylord couldn't make him safe with a gun." Hashti shuddered in private agreement. Lael frowned.

"This camp's tense as a bowstring," Red continued. "Hand out guns and men will shoot each other—accidentally and otherwise. Bullets don't wash off."

"So what do you want to do?" Georgia asked.

"Stall," the First-Inner answered. "Until we learn how to discourage the tigers without provoking them. Or until they work through their curiosity."

"I thought we agreed we had a problem!" Lael snorted.

"We do," Big Red said. "But let's define it accurately. The problem is not tigers per se, but interference with our work."

"Getting knocked over by a tiger qualifies as interference," Lael interrupted.

"It does," Red agreed. "The pouncing has to stop, and it will, if we make it unpleasant enough for the tigers and do so consistently. Mr. Jack is working on some new, more potent, skunk formulas." Hashti tried to imagine a more potent skunk formula. Her head spun. "We'll cut back on the number of work teams and assign each one a guard. That should make it nearly impossible for tigers to pounce and get away."

Hashti nodded. The tigers would learn fast, if punishment came consistently.

"Your job," Big Red told Lael and Georgia, "is to boost morale. The men are not going to be eaten. Convince them of that. Make heroes of the ones who meet tigers."

"*What*?" asked Lael. "I'm a lawyer, not a cheerleader!"

"But the men care what you think," Big Red answered dryly. "Remember—if everyone's cringing in the bunkhouse, this camp won't run a profit, and if it doesn't, your franchise won't be worth much."

He looked appraisingly at Hashti. "What about the horses' morale? Circus horses work around tigers. Will ours, Journeyman?"

A risky business, thought Hashti. She remembered stodgy old Betsy snorting and blowing, and Hero's blood on the snow. Could the camp avoid accidents like the ones Hashti and Sam had had? What would Master Will have done? "Provided the tigers don't actually attack the horses," she answered slowly, "the horses just need to get used to them. You start by sacking—wave a tiger skin around, rub it on the horses, get them used to the smell and look of it. Or you put a tiger cage next to the barn." She bit her lip, knowing these suggestions flew in the face of all Ross had said about not threatening the tigers. "I'm afraid it takes a tiger to get horses used to tigers."

Big Red did not question her judgment. He asked only, "Will one be enough?" Hashti nodded. The boss leaned back in his chair. "Well, Ross? Will the planet blow if we take one tiger skin?"

Ross smiled. "We could probably get one, Boss Man. Just one. For a good cause."

Into the chemist's cabin went wood ash, ginger beer, fish livers, and rabbit grease. An even more noxious mixture came out, to be loaded in skunk guns and given to the guards who now patrolled wherever men and horses worked. This reduced the labor force, but better a few men on guard than more injuries.

The tigers found the new system a challenge. They ran in distress when a skunk charge found its mark, but returned the next day or the day after to topple their assailants. Volunteers for guard duty became ever scarcer.

Gaylord and his friend Kevin left early each morning to range the woods with rifles, seeking game for the camp larder and a tiger for Hashti's equine desensitization project. Gay would stop by the barn on his way back. "No tiger today." He'd stay to help sweep the aisles, or drink a cup of bittertea. The barn always seemed brighter while he was there. Then he'd be gone again, off to butcher deer and boil porridge for twelve dozen ravenous lumberjacks. Hashti sighed and wished her shoulder would not take so long to knit.

Homesickness, fear, and discouragement gnawed at the camp. At this rate, the loggers would have little to show when the shuttle returned in May—and without something to show then, they'd receive no more personnel or equipment.

Amidst the anxiety, the weather grew colder. Gay gave up dawn hunting in favor of dusk. Inexperienced jacks suffered frostbitten noses and toes. Leaden-gray snowclouds replaced the crystal blue of early autumn. Every day the sun came up later and set earlier, leaving a scant eight and a half standard hours of daylight. With the solstice only a few weeks off, Swamp City's citizens tried to plan their New Year celebration. Enthusiasm was hard to muster.

On Tuesday, the tenth of December, three weeks and a day from Hashti's first meeting with Khan, Gay stormed into the barn with good news. "Got a tiger for you, Hashti! But we can't budge her. That sucker is heavy! We need a team to drag her in."

"How heavy?" Hashti asked. "And where'd you shoot her?"

"I didn't shoot her," Gay replied. "Kevin did. Out by where you first saw Khan. Kevin's waiting there for us."

Gay had no idea how heavy the animal was, but Hashti guessed that a female tiger would weigh four hundred pounds. A single horse could do the job, especially with a well-packed road to travel. She harnessed Hercules, who was ready for some exercise, and they set out in the gray of late afternoon.

They had barely turned onto the road when a rifle report snapped through the woods. Gay raised his hands in frustration. "There's dinner. That guy has all the luck. He not only gets my tiger, but deer come to him as well!"

"He had a good teacher," Hashti said soothingly.

But Kevin had not shot a deer. They found him pacing back and forth, anxiously watching the road to camp. Amid the stumps and dead branches lay not one, but two dead tigers. Gay's jealousy broke out in self-righteous indignation. "Why the hell did you shoot again? Ross said just one!"

Kevin, whose thick burr marked him as a native of the island world Atlantis, looked pale and frightened. "I had to shoot him, Gay. He was spitting and growling at me. When he charged, I knew he meant business."

Gay frowned. "Good luck convincing Ross of that. Can we take them both at once, Hashti?"

She glanced at her horse. No point stressing him so soon after his injury. "Let's do it one at a time." The men trussed the first tigress while Hashti backed Hercules into position. He sidled and snorted like a hotblooded racer. "Don't be a wimp," the trainer chided. "You're a lot bigger than she is. And besides, she's dead."

The big gray continued to move on stiff legs, nostrils flaring and ears pointed like tracers at the body. Hashti let him sniff and consider for half a minute, then gathered up the reins. "All right, handsome. Time to earn your keep."

He danced sideways. She spoke more sharply. "Get over, Herc!"

The bit jingled as he tossed his head. But Hashti had spent seven years with Master Will learning to outsmart brawn. She leaned on the point of Herc's hip, realizing as she did so that her left shoulder didn't hurt anymore. Thrown off balance, the horse moved over. "Thank you," Hashti said. "A little further, please." This time he shifted obediently. Gay hooked the carcass to the single-tree. Mindful of the last time she and Gay had skidded together, Hashti kept a firm hand on the reins and a close eye on her horse. He gave no further trouble.

"You want to wait here?" Gaylord asked his friend.

Kevin glanced at the second dead tiger and shook his head. "I've had enough of sitting in the woods with tigers, thank you." They headed briskly for the stable.

Ross exploded, as predicted, over news of the second tiger. "How'd you monkeys get so trigger-happy? We need one tiger skin, not two! If you shoot any more, I'll skin you along with the beasts!"

Gay, standing behind Ross, set his jaw and rolled his eyes. Kevin, target of the blast, was more contrite. "Honest to God, Mister Ross, I was scared. He was after me. I wouldn't have used the rifle otherwise. I won't again. But I needed it."

Ross stared hard at him, then sighed. "OK. But no more." He appraised the tigress they had dragged in. "You're getting a valuable horse blanket here, Tiger Wrestler."

Hashti too looked at the carcass, lying in the center corridor of the stable. Dead animals had always saddened her, and she found this one particularly disturbing. Live tigers moved with massive power and fluid grace, confident and capable. This one lay awkwardly twisted, the thick muscles reduced to so much stiff meat. The tigress's golden eyes stared unseeing at crude wooden walls. How dull those eyes were, contrasted with the alert and interested gaze of a live animal! Even the thick down pelt was bedraggled and disarrayed from the two mile trek through the woods.

I killed her, Hashti thought, thinking of her plan to desensitize the horses. Irrationally, she muttered an apology and explanation to the animal's body. It eased her conscience only slightly.

She still had Herc's reins in her hands. "If we're going to stand around, Herc needs a blanket," she reminded the men. "Or if you're ready, we can go fetch the other tiger."

Ross shook his head. "It's nearly dusk. The mighty hunters can bring their other trophy home with First-In's motorsled—if they leave their rifles here. They've shot enough tigers for one day." Gay and Kevin greeted this suggestion with enthusiasm. Hashti shrugged and began to unbuckle Herc's harness.

Herc, and later his friends, disapproved heartily of the feathered body in their barn. By the time Hashti had them settled in their places, she heard the motorsled pulling up outside. Ross must have heard it too, for he came in the north door as Gay and Kevin entered from the south. "Where's your tiger?" the naturalist asked.

Gay spit out an oath. Kevin, looking more shaken than before, answered. "Gone. Tiger tracks all over, and nothing but a few feathers and bones left. Looks like the other tigers ate the body. We didn't spend a lot of time looking—we were afraid they were still around, and we didn't want to discuss it with them in the dark."

Ross's eyes narrowed, but he said only, "That showed sense. Come on, let's skin the one we've got. When we've got the pelt off you can help me drag the rest to my cabin. I'd like to get a closer look at the beast's anatomy."

They gathered their implements and set to work, to the horses' consternation. Kevin wrinkled his nose as he watched Ross make the opening cut along the tigress's belly. "I'll never get used to blue meat," he said. "How can it possibly be edible?"

"Not hard," Ross answered. "Planets of similar composition, size, and orbital parameters end up with similar biochemical block sets. This planet's a lot like the one we evolved on, so life here uses the same simple amino acids and sugars we do. On a flip of the coin, even stereochemistry matches, so we can eat here. In the grand scheme of things, copper blood's a negligible variation."

"What about tryptophan?" Gay asked. "That's an amino acid, isn't it? How come that's missing?"

Ross shrugged. "Yeah, it's an amino acid, but a relatively complicated one. And it's here. Just not enough of it for us. Pretty minor glitch."

Kevin shook his head. "That depends what the cook does with the gravy. I still think blue meat is weird."

"It does look odd," Ross agreed. "Yet see how familiarly things are arranged inside this tigress. She has a liver, and bladder, and womb, just like a red-blooded tiger would. Funny how those same organs turn up from planet to planet. Seems to be a successful arrangement."

"How come she's got no tits?" Kevin asked. He glanced quickly at Hashti, then away, his fair skin reddening.

Ross took the question in stride. "Don't use them. Milk hasn't been invented on this planet."

This was news to Hashti. She paused, halfway through filling Cherry's feedbox. "How do they feed their babies?"

"Regurgitation," Ross said. "As on most planets." He resumed his cutting.

Cherry nudged impatiently at Hashti, who shook herself and dumped the rest of the grain into Cherry's box. She wondered if the tigress had cubs, and felt worse than before about the whole enterprise. But tears wouldn't help either the mother or her cubs, if she'd had any. Hashti put away her grain scoop, and went to check the stove that warmed the watering trough.

Ross's unhappiness did not infect the camp at large. Big Red declared an evening of celebration, complete with two casks of ginger beer. Hashti took time first for her own ritual of celebration, namely, a sauna. Permeated as her life was by manure, sweat, and horse dander, it took only clean hair and the lingering rose scent of her soap to make her feel like a lady.

Returning from the bath, she donned the one nice outfit she'd brought to New Lebanon. Fawn jodhpurs

and a finely knit black lambswool sweater made a far
sleeker combination than her usual shapeless work pants
and horsehair-covered plaid shirt. A tiger's-eye neck-
lace, echoing the gold and black of her guild ring and
clothing, seemed singularly appropriate for this occasion. Her cheeks were flushed from the ice water that
had concluded her steam bath, and hazel eyes flashed
beneath her carefully brushed black hair. Hashti looked
good tonight, and she knew it.

City Hall was awash in people and laughter when she
finally arrived. Gay had been watching for her, and hurried over as she struggled with icy bootlaces. He was
resplendent in a shirt of pale blue satin with yellow em-
broidery. "Take your wraps?" he offered.

She stripped off her wind jacket and heavy wool shirt.
Gay stared at her gleaming tiger's-eye pendant, or perhaps at the curve of her sweater beneath. Hashti held her
shoulders a little straighter than usual. When he looked
back at her face she winked. "My sling's gone."

Gay grinned and elbowed her lightly. "So I see. Come
on. Kevin and I saved a seat for you."

About half the tables had been stacked against the
back wall, clearing the center of the room for dancing. A
dozen amateur instrumentalists and two fine singers
were warming up. The tiger pelt, its sticky bluish blood-
stains somehow removed, adorned the company table.
The stripes shimmered blue-black and fire-orange in the
lamplight. To either side stood casks of beer. On the
guild table, lumps of sweet dough sizzled in a cauldron of
hot fat. Hashti snagged three of them and rolled them in
sugar. Missing dinner had its compensations—she had
more room left for dessert. Being small had its advantages too, she thought as she wriggled through the forest
of lumberjacks and seized a foaming mug of ginger beer.
Thus provisioned, she joined Gay and his partner.

They had reserved her seat with some effort, for people crowded around to congratulate Kevin. Gay responded to the fuss with his usual suave humor. Kevin himself seemed nonplussed, but he smiled when the musicians struck up a rolling chanty. "Hey, Kevin," they called. "Here's a song from home for you!"

Grinning, he let himself be placed at the head of a line of dancers. The crowd dissolved at his departure, and Hashti sat back with Gay to watch the dance. Kevin was as blond as Gay, but taller and more slender. He swayed through an ocean-wave pattern with easy grace. "You didn't tell me Kevin was a dancer," Hashti commented. "Bet he'd be good with horses. Dancers usually are."

"Can't he do anything wrong?" Gay snapped, his irritation finally surfacing. "First he got my tiger, now my woman is bubbling over him."

"Gay! Calm down!" Hashti nudged him with her hip. "You'll get yours later. In the meantime, shall we dance?"

He nudged back, smiling. "No, thanks. I prefer other forms of exercise."

Kevin returned with a bittersweet expression on his face. Hashti knew how music from home affected one. "Missing Atlantis, Kevin?"

The corners of his lips twisted. "At home I got seasick. Now here, I get homesick!"

"I know a cure for that," she told him, extending her hand. *"Sharrawun lu?"*

His eyes widened. "You speak Skitch? Where'd you learn?"

"Carolina. We had a lot of patrons from Atlantis. Now, how many times will I have to ask you—*Sharrawun lu?"*

"Uh—yes! I'd love to!" he stammered, grasping the proffered hand. "If Gay doesn't mind . . ."

Gay drained his mug. "Go ahead. I've got some talking to do tonight."

Hashti hadn't danced since her Journeyman's party,
and she'd forgotten how much she loved it. Guildfolk
and common mixed freely on the floor. Even the First-
Inners joined in to demonstrate an exotic Khathan jig.
Gay stayed on the sidelines, in lively conversation.
Hashti even saw him talking to Lael, as the latter fin-
gered the downy thickness of the tiger pelt. Lael's usual
expression of boredom and contempt was gone. Hashti,
pausing to shove up the sleeves of her sweater, caught
Gay's glance and extended a hand in invitation. He
shook his head and waved her back into the line that
snaked its way among the benches.

Her presence among the dancers did not go unremarked. Did anything she did here go unremarked, she
wondered. Late in the evening, when the casks were dry
and the crowd beginning to thin, the fiddler called, "This
one's for Miz Hashti. Ready for a horse dance?" The
dance he referred to was a strenuous one in which each
group of dancers played a three-horse racing chariot.
Kevin appeared from nowhere, seized Hashti's hand,
and pointed mischievously at Gay. They tugged him onto
the floor to complete their trio.

Gay was a fair dancer, steady, although he concentrated too hard to enjoy himself fully. Fortunately he had
stamina. The dance began fast and got faster, full of running, kicking, and spinning. Kevin and Hashti hurled
themselves into it, counting on Gay for ballast. The musicians challenged them, picking up the tempo until
groups dropped out in exhaustion. Hashti was glad dancing had kept her away from the beer. Hands grew slippery with sweat, and her partners gripped more firmly. A
break at this speed would send all three flying. The room
was a blur of tables, interrupted by the thick wood pillars

the dancers needed to dodge. Finally Gay's foot caught on an uneven plank in the floor, and the trio spilled amidst general laughter. Hashti stumbled to her feet, and found the room still spinning. Only Gay's arm kept her from hitting the floor a second time. She sagged against him with a kiss. "Who cares who shot the tiger?"

The troika marked the end of the dancing. Kevin picked himself up and mopped the sweat from his eyes. "Let's get out of this steambath," he suggested.

The three friends donned boots and wraps and stepped outside. As clouds dispersed the temperature dropped; it was well below zero already. A light north-easterly wind crystallized the moisture of Hashti's breath and peppered it back against her face. She suffered her own pang of homesickness as she saw the ring constella-tion directly overhead. Carolina's sun glowed with icy brightness in that circle.

Far in the distance tigers cried, an unsettling sound, like a chorus of the damned singing comic operetta. Kevin shivered. "I wish they'd shut up. It gives me nightmares."

"They're just animals," Gay said. "They die when you shoot them."

It was too cold to stand and argue. Hashti, though not at all tired, yawned elaborately. Kevin caught the cue. "Time for me to hit the sack," he announced.

Hashti, despite her yawn, was sorry to say good-bye. "I'm glad to have met you," she told him. "The dancing was fun."

Kevin squeezed her hand. "Thanks, Miz Hashti. I see why Gay likes you." Blushing, he crunched away toward the bunkhouse.

Hashti and Gay stood for a moment under the frosty stars, watching Kevin depart, listening to the eerie howls of the tigers. Then Hashti took Gay's mittened hand in hers and led him to the stable.

# CHAPTER FIVE

HASHTI WOKE THE NEXT MORNING TO A SHY KNOCK ON
her door. The timer on her beacon said that she should
have been up half an hour ago. "Miz Hashti?" came
Lance's inquiring voice.

"I'll be right with you," she called. Reluctantly she
rolled over. Gay was gone. The fire was dead. Light
spilling through the cracks of the door showed hoarfrost
on the hinges. Hashti's socks and underwear jeered at
her from the far side of the room; she had forgotten to
bring them to bed. How cold was it out there? Probably
best not to know. She climbed out of bed, dragging her
blankets with her, and dressed as rapidly as possible.

By midmorning, when she and Lance finished their
chores, the temperature had risen from twenty-five degrees below zero to ten below. The bracing cold and yesterday's excitement left the horsewoman too keyed up to
stay indoors. Lance, yawning, borrowed her room for a
midday nap. She herself belted on a pack and went to
inspect her teams.

The first person she met was Sam. After the accident
at the river, he had refused to return to sleigh driving.
Four horses were more than he cared to handle, he said,
and he wanted to keep his feet on firm ground. So Hashti
had put Sam and his uninjured lead team to skidding.
Today she found the matched pair of grays lunching on

succulent twigs, while Sam and his swamper strained
with cant hooks to position a giant log. Hashti asked
Sam why he was doing the horses' work.

He started violently at her voice, then leaned on his
cant hook while he mopped the sweat from his face.
"They're too jumpy for fine stuff, Miz Hashti. Nervous
about tigers, seems like. So we're only usin' them for
long hauls."

The horses stood, calmly stripping bark from whipbranch shoots. Remembering Sam's fateful plunge down
the comeback road, and her own pounding heart when
Betsy and Blaze had bolted, Hashti kept her face
straight. But this behavior couldn't be allowed to continue. "They're pulling a fast one on you, Sam. See their
ears waggling? If they're suspicious, they prick their
ears. If they're really scared, they lay them flat back.
Right now they just want lunch."

He looked dubiously at his team. "I'm sure we had a
tiger watchin' us a few minutes ago. Gay was tellin' last
night how the tigers scout you out before they jump. An'
he told us how Kevin got attacked. It isn' really safe to
be workin' with horses here, is it?"

So that's what Gay had been telling people while
Hashti danced? She filed the information away for later
consideration. In the meantime, she had a lazy team to
contend with. They didn't smell any tigers—they
smelled their handler's timidity. "Let's see how they act
now," Hashti suggested, collecting the reins and backing
the horses into position for hitching. They looked reproachfully at her, but obeyed without further discussion. The swamper hooked the chains. Clucking to the
team, Hashti pivoted the log a few feet to clear it from
the stump, then took it on out to the pile waiting by the
sleigh road.

An embarrassed Sam followed her and unhooked the

chain, muttering, "Tiger must be gone now." She handed
Sam the reins. The off horse balked. Hashti glared at the
animal. He fell into line with a soft snort of disgust.

Hashti spent fifteen minutes helping Sam reassert his
authority. She did not want the team resuming their
tricks the minute she walked away. "Remember—*they*
move the logs," she cautioned as she left. "Their backs
are a lot stronger than yours."

Sam grinned sheepishly. "OK, Miz Hashti. Don't trip
on a tiger!"

He was not the only nervous logger she met that day,
and not the only one who'd heard stories from her boyfriend. Gay hadn't even seen the threat display which
had frightened Kevin into shooting a second tiger, but
Gay had told everyone about it, and it got more serious
each time. What was her blond beau up to, Hashti wondered? He must know that this panic jeopardized the
camp! Her irritation increased when she met Sweat on
her way back to the barn. Since he refused to go into the
woods, he'd been put to clearing manure from the ruts of
the ice road. He held Hashti personally responsible for
every pile. Now he greeted her with nasty glee. "Hear
you had yourself a good time last night, Miz Hashti. Not
good enough for Gay, though. He and his buddy been up
there with Lael all mornin'."

Hashti knew better than to get upset over malicious
gossip from an unreliable source. Sweat was probably
lying. Even if he wasn't, there were dozens of reasons
for Kevin and Gay to visit the store. But she was still
fretting when Ross walked in half an hour later. "Can I
talk to you for a few minutes, Tiger Wrestler?" he asked.
"Someplace we won't be disturbed?"

"Sure. Let me finish this hoof." She pared a bit
deeper, surveyed the result, and decided she had done a
good job. "Lance, we'll be in my room if you need any-

thing." She led Ross to her quarters at the far end of the corridor. The stove still held the coals of the fire Lance had built; water bubbled in the teakettle. Hashti, apprehensive about this interview, offered Ross a cup of bittertea. What was on his mind?

He sat back with the steaming mug, propping his feet on Hashti's mitten rack. "The wife and I cut into Kevin's tigress this morning."

"Find anything interesting?" Hashti asked politely.

"A few things," Ross replied just as casually. "Its brain is too big."

Hashti knew anatomy only from a horse trainer's perspective, but everyone knew what brains were for. "Does that mean it's smart?"

"That's the easiest explanation. When we finish the dissection we'll know more." Ross watched the tea swirling in his cup, then looked up at Hashti and made a right-angle change of subject. "How brave are you, Tiger Wrestler?"

What? "I'm—it depends what you have in mind, sir."

"I'm going tiger-trailing tomorrow. I'd like you to come along."

"What for?"

"There's a place I want you to see—the place where the tigers sing. I found it last winter, during their mating season. They put on a real show, strutting and jumping, twirling and bouncing, singing like demons the whole time. Eventually, of course, they went skittering away in pairs to mate. So I wrote the whole thing off as an elaborate courtship ritual. The trouble is, they keep it up even when they're not breeding. We could hear it from here last night. Louder and stronger than ever. What are they doing? I'd like a second opinion. From you."

"Why me?"

Ross twisted the mug in his hands. "You're a trainer.

You know how animals act. You have an open mind and good intuition. And, crazy as it may sound, there's something happening between you and the tigers. Twice now you've had unusual encounters. Did you know Khan's watching you?"

"Me?" This conversation was throwing Hashti off balance.

"Khan's left us alone except for the two times you saw him, but I find his tracks. He hangs around the stable, with a few trips along the edges of the main camp. This morning he followed you along the sleigh road."

Hashti thought guiltily of Sam, who'd been so certain a tiger lurked in the bushes. Perhaps he hadn't imagined it after all. She did not like the thought of a tiger tailing her. "What does he want?"

"I don't know. I have a hunch we might see him on this trip." Hashti blanched. The First-Inner half smiled at her. "I'm not sure I should ask you to go. But so far your encounters with Khan have been harmless. And we need to learn about the tigers. Fast."

"What's the hurry?" Hashti asked, although she suspected the answers.

Ross stared again into his swirling tea. "We're now skunking virtually every tiger who pounces. With ninety-five percent negative reinforcement, the tigers ought to stop. Instead, attacks are accelerating, as if the tigers find it a game! What sort of animal risks skunking for the sake of play?"

Hashti sat silently. Ross's expression darkened. "Then there's the tiger that threatened Kevin. That was no game. And it happened just after he'd shot a tigress. If the tigers catch on that fast, what happens now that Kevin's shot two?"

Gay hunted with Kevin, had gone with him to collect the second carcass. What about him?

"All the signals say to freeze, stop everything," Ross concluded. "But just when we need to stop and take stock, Gay's rabble rousing, trying to force a showdown. He wants to junk the skunk guns and do some real shooting. He's got too much invested to listen to reason." The First-Inner set his cup aside and looked straight at Hashti. "This is not proceeding according to the rules. I have to find out what's going on, before we get into something we can't get out of."

She looked back at Ross, a cold lump in her stomach. Deliberately seek out a tiger who'd been shadowing her? Who might be smart? Not her idea of fun. But if Ross was right, if she were in a unique position relative to the tigers, then she had a responsibility to the camp. "I'll go. When do you want to leave?"

Ross grinned hugely. "You've got pluck, Tiger Wrestler! Master Tam's shaving down a pair of skis for you. Tomorrow's Middleday. Show up at six, and we'll eat breakfast before we go."

Gay stopped by in midafternoon, an hour after Ross's visit. The pulley system which normally transported hay had broken down, and Hashti was filling mangers the old-fashioned way. Neither she nor Gay had had more than three hours of sleep, and she had reason to think her friend was hungover. Still, he greeted her on a positive note. "Hi, beautiful. You sure impressed Kevin. Every other sentence he's talking about you."

Cold, hungry, tired, and worried as she was about Betsy's cough, Hashti smiled at Gay's words. "Tell him it was mutual," she said. "I haven't met a dancer like that in a while."

"He must dance as well as he hunts," Gay answered. "I'm glad you two hit it off together. Just don't forget which one of us you go with when the dancing's finished."

"I remembered last night," she reminded him.

He grinned warmly. "Yes, you did. Which reminds me, I heard you're going skiing with Ross tomorrow. You canceling our lunch date?"

"Guess so," Hashti admitted. "I'm not sure exactly what he wants, but I think it'll take most of the day. He has some place he wants to show me."

Gay frowned. "Where's that?"

"It's a place where tigers sing," Hashti said.

"What the hell?" Gay bellowed. "What kind of bee has he got in his bonnet?"

"He dissected Kevin's tiger this morning," Hashti started to explain.

Gay cut her off with a wave of his hand. "I know, I know. Some crazy thing about their brains. He tried to tell me about it. Damn First-Inner's gotten daft as an alien. You, I expect sense from."

Gay's disrespect for the naturalist angered Hashti. She jammed her pitchfork into a bale of hay. "At least Mister Ross doesn't spread scare stories. I already told him I'm going. Let's drop the subject." She turned away to fetch her wheelbarrow.

Gay caught her by the shoulders and turned her back. "Wait. Are you serious about this? What will you do when you find the tigers?"

She lacked an answer for herself, let alone Gay. She shook his hands off. "See what color their eyes are. Let's talk about something else."

"I'm interested in this," Gay answered. He cocked his head. "Is there something you're not telling me?"

Hashti sighed. "I tried to tell you, and you wouldn't listen."

Gay's eyes narrowed. "That? That was too crazy to

be true. What's really on his mind? Are you sure he's told you everything? You know what they say about First-Inners. Don't go with him, Hashti."

She stalked away towards the feedroom. "Don't be silly, Gay. He's twice as old as I am, and he's married."

"Lael says he's not too old to notice a pretty girl," Gay called after her.

Hashti spun around. "Lael will say anything about anyone if she can get something out of it. And while we're on the subject, where were you this morning?"

Gay set his jaw. "A business discussion. Which I was going to tell you about, before I heard this feather-brained notion of an expedition with Ross."

"I'm listening."

"Forget it. If you stay in camp where you belong, I'll be glad to tell you. In the meantime, take good care of that tiger pelt. Kevin and I have Finder's Claim on it."

O-ho! So that was where the wind lay—Gay smelled a profit from the tigers if he could get permission to shoot them. But before Hashti could quiz Gay further, Lance returned from the smithy with a batch of new double-trees. By the time they were put away, Gay was gone.

The argument left an ache in Hashti's chest, but, ex-hausted, she slept soundly anyhow. At six the next morning she rapped gently on the door of Ross and Anna's cabin. Anna, wearing a thick wool robe over her flannel nightgown, opened the door. A heavy logging boot peeked ludicrously from under the hem of her gown. The other foot was thickly bandaged. "Dr. Anna! What happened to you?"

The First-Inner shook her head in disgust. "Stupid ac-cident. We worked late over Kevin's tiger, and I twisted my ankle dragging the carcass out afterward. So things are a little slow this morning. But come in, breakfast's almost ready. I want to check your shoulder before you hit the trail."

Anna guided Hashti into the clinic room and administered a rapid-fire series of strength and range-of-motion tests. "You're fine," the doctor declared a scant five minutes later. "Just don't push yourself too hard. Skiing's tough on muscles that've been favored." Opening the door, she waved Hashti ahead of her back into the center room.

Ross stood by the small stove, whistling as he poured batter onto a griddle. "Mornin', Tiger Wrestler. You look bright-eyed and bushy-tailed. Can I have an energy transfusion?"

"Now don't tease her," Anna chided, limping across the room to set out a pan of syrup. "Not her fault you're a worn-out old man."

"Less worn out than you'll be, if you don't get off that ankle," he scolded back, chasing her to a chair with his spatula. Turning to the stove, he flipped two cakes high into the air; they tumbled neatly onto the griddle. The next one plopped, soft side down, on the floor by the stove. Anna clucked. "Serves you right for showing off. Our guest will think we have no couth."

Ross grinned at her as he scraped the pancake off the floor. "I have lots of couth. I just didn't get enough sleep. That dissection was a bear."

He must have worked on it all day and into the night, Hashti thought. "Does it always take so long?" she asked.

Anna shook her head. "Heavens, no. But this was really delicate work—and it paid. I knew a bit about local neuroanatomy from other animals here. Based on that, the tiger's associative centers seemed way too big. So we pulled the brain, set up a reactivator, and did a channel trace starting with auditory input. The impulse spread to a cortical tangle that looked a hell of a lot like advanced parietal development, and tied a dozen Bateman's knots before it triggered an outgoing vocal pattern. The beta nucleoli stained as heavily as yours. Look how convoluted the lobe is!" She waved at a jar full of glistening, rumpled, white tissue.

Hashti smiled weakly. She'd learned nothing from the explanation, and was just as glad. It wasn't her notion of breakfast conversation.

Ross saw her expression as he brought his platter of hotcakes to the table. "Who has no couth, wife? Don't let her bother you, Teamstress. The bottom line is that the tigers' brains appear to be wired for thinking and talking—not just 'I'm hungry' and 'you're cute,' but real twenty-four karat speech."

"They talk?" the trainer asked in amazement. For all Ross's brooding remarks about big brains, Hashti had never expected anything like this.

Anna frowned. "They can't. Verbal intelligence follows manipulative ability. The tigers lack fingers, tentacles, or even prehensile noses; they have no tools or technology. So they shouldn't be smart. But for dumb animals, they sure have funny nervous systems."

"Maybe Khan will tell us," Ross suggested.

Anna bit her lip. "Do be careful, you two."

Ross made a disparaging face. "We'll be fine. I'm more likely to be hurt by the idiots in this camp than by a tiger. And don't forget, I'll be escorted by the planet's champion Tiger Wrestler."

"You be careful just the same," Anna answered. "Now sit down and pass the syrup. I'm starving."

Hashti was hungry, too—she'd worked for two hours before she came up here. But the conversation was diffi-

cult to push out of her mind. Tigers talking? All animals
have modes of expression, but Ross seemed to be refer-
ring to real speech. Could Khan be an intelligent alien?
Hashti shook her head to clear it and attacked the pancakes.

All too soon Ross pushed back his chair and patted
his stomach. "The best thing about this work is the food.
You eat like a horse, work it all off, and then eat some
more. Come on, Tiger Wrestler. We've got a long day
ahead of us."

Stepping outside, they found darkness giving way to
the shadowless gray of predawn. Since the previous
morning the temperature had climbed into the high
teens. The air seemed muggy and humid. Ross handed
Hashti a pair of arched boards with metal and leather
contraptions fastened to the centers. "You skied before?" he asked.

She looked dubiously at the boards. "Not on anything
like that."

"You'll catch on fast." He showed her how the bind-
ings worked; they attached directly to her wool-lined
logging boots. "You have spare boot liners along?"

She patted her bulging pockets. "Right here."

"Good. I'm afraid I've got another load for you," he
said, hefting a backpack. "You'll need to tighten it up a
little. Anna's taller than you are."

"What's in it?"

"Just basics—food, tinderbox, cup, first aid, sleeping
bag. Got your beacon?"

"Inside pocket." It hadn't left her since the day she
met Khan. "Why a sleeping bag?"

She wished she hadn't asked, as Ross solemnly intoned, "This is the frontier..."

". . . We're playing for keeps, this planet will kill me if I don't respect it," she finished for him.

"And don't you forget it," Anna warned, materializing from nowhere. "Keep the beacon with you, and don't stray without an emergency kit. Signs of hypothermia?"

"Shivering, irrationality, clumsiness, drowsiness," Hashti answered, trying not to sound impatient. "Avoid by dressing right, staying dry, eating well, and avoiding exhaustion. Treat by getting out of the cold, hot liquids, dry clothes, warm bodies."

"Just checking your memory," Anna said with a grin as Ross held up the pack for Hashti.

Obediently the trainer slid her arms through the straps. The pack was surprisingly light and superbly balanced. She realized why when she saw the starred circlet embroidered on the belt. This was First-In equipment—probably Anna's own pack. Ross winked at his wife as he checked the shoulder straps. "What say, love? Fits the Tiger Wrestler pretty well, doesn't it?"

"Leave her alone," Anna said.

"But wife, she's a natural! Clever, outdoorsy, good intuition . . ."

"Right—she's a rising star. Don't deflect her trajectory."

"You're a fine one to talk!" Ross answered, as Hashti listened to the exchange in open-mouthed confusion. "Who was it that recruited me," he continued, "when I was forty-three standard and headed for medals?"

"You were sitting in the army being bored and getting shot at," his wife retorted. "Whereas Hashti's got a handsome beau and good guild prospects." She paused, then resumed in a softer voice. "Let's wait and see."

Wait and see about what? Hashti got no answer from

Ross. He sighed good-naturedly. "Oh, all right. When we get around to it, can I say I told you so?"

Anna laughed and limped over to kiss him. "I'm sure you'll say more than that. Now good luck, and be careful. If you don't hustle, sunrise will catch you in camp."

"Yes, ma'am!" Ross saluted her with military precision, and set off with Hashti down the ice road.

# CHAPTER SIX

❧❧❧❧

THIS WAS NOT HASHTI'S FIRST TIME ON CROSS-COUNTRY skis. She'd dated a ski instructor on Carolina, and they'd spent many a morning grooming woodland trails while the patrons were still abed. But then she'd worn slender blades of skis clipped to slipper-light shoes; the whole kit had weighed less than one of the felt-lined, armor-toed boots she wore now. Hashti's present skis could support a man with a heavy pack on soft, untracked snow. Master Tam had shaved and shortened them for her, but still they seemed broad and clumsy, dragging at her feet as she shuffled down the road. When the path turned uphill, Hashti attempted a proper springing trot. In minutes her heart was racing.

"Hey, take it easy on an old man!" Ross called, twenty yards behind her. "We have a long way to go. These skis aren't made for speed."

"I noticed," Hashti replied, pulling off her mittens and tucking them under her belt. She slipped her bare hands back through the loops on the ski poles. "Where are we going?"

Ross caught up with her. "We'll follow the Merrywater south to the big lake, then go east up the shore to the Rock."

"The Rock?" she asked.

"The place I told you about. It's a big granite

outthrust by the lake, with a stone shelf protected from
the wind on three sides by even higher rock. We'll watch
from the outcropping above and to the north."

"Do tigers live at the Rock?"

Ross gave her a troubled look. "To tell the truth, Tiger
Wrestler, I don't know where they live. But that's another story. Let's save our breath for skiing."

The firm road made for fast travel, or would have if
they'd had skinny skis and no backpacks. But the slick
surface sent Hashti's feet splaying in odd directions
every time she hit a bump or dip. Conditions improved
when they reached the Merrywater. Ross had been this
way recently, leaving a neatly packed trail. Now refro-
zen, the snow supported the travelers easily, even with
their packs. Their skis slid obediently along the the prepared ruts.

The sun was well over the horizon when they reached
the lake. They treated themselves to honeybread,
washed it down with sugared tea, and turned east. The
lake's level ice was coated with snow just thick and wet
enough to track well. Ross broke trail, and Hashti shuffled behind him in a rhythmic reverie, her pulse an even
hundred fifty.

At ten in the morning Ross pointed ahead. The hills to
the left met the lake in a rock bluff, peaking two hundred
fifty feet above the water line.

"The Rock," Ross announced. "Ready for some
climbing?" Turning inland, they traversed the hill at a
broad angle. A firm planting of skis usually secured purchase. Only occasionally did Hashti need to step sideways up the slope to keep from backsliding.

Ross pointed out the tracks of deer and rabbits, and
showed Hashti how to tell fresh prints from old by the
condition of the snow. Soon they found tiger tracks,
most stale and iced over, but still displaying peculiarities

that identified individual tigers. Hashti saw where a tiger had stalked a deer, the cat's rear paws landing directly in the prints of the front ones. He had missed the deer. Tigers left nonspoor evidence as well: bark ripped by claw sharpening, yellow spots in the snow, a scraggly clump of down where a tiger had rubbed its back against a rough old stump.

The two humans traveled about a mile during their climb, taking an hour and two rest breaks. Hashti had thought herself well conditioned by stable work, but uphill poling exhausted her arms; particularly, as Anna had warned, the out-of-condition left shoulder. Ross, for all his jokes about being an old man, set a trying pace. Hashti pressed herself to the limit keeping up.

An hour before noon they scrambled onto a rocky knoll overlooking the diamond-iced water of the lake. Dropping her pack, Hashti stretched her arms toward the sky, which had paled from yesterday morning's crackling blue to an indistinct near-white. Then she flopped forward, fingers brushing her toes, trying to relax away the ache of the climb. The deep gray, quartz-veined rock of the bluff glistened dark and wet where snow from her boots touched its sun-warmed surface. Finally Hashti sat on a dry open spot and pulled out her beacon. It reported that the morning's struggles had brought her only five miles. As the crow flew the distance to camp was even less, about three miles. It seemed ridiculously short—on Carolina, twenty miles made a pleasant morning's ski. But there, Hashti had worn neither logging boots nor a pack. There, she'd not had to push her way through virgin snow and underbrush. Here, three overland miles might take hours to traverse.

Hashti looked around again. Behind her a wall of blackpines, abused by wind and lightning, followed the hill to its crest. To either side, east and west, the rock sloped downward, scrub bushes fighting for purchase on it. In front of her the granite fell away in a steep precipice, giving an uninterrupted view of the lake. "Where are the tigers?" Hashti asked.

Ross pointed west and downward. "See that big old blackpine? Look in the rocks just beyond it." Hashti peered in the direction he'd indicated. The tree grew from a cleft in the rocks, forty feet below the knoll and two hundred yards away. Beneath it—yes! A big thick-feathered cat sunned in a sheltered nook. His coat bore bold black rosettes in lieu of stripes. "Is that a tiger?" Hashti asked softly.

"Yes," Ross whispered back. "Most of them are striped, but other designs turn up from time to time. I haven't seen this fellow before. He must be new in the area."

"How many tigers live around here?"

"I don't know," the naturalist answered. "My records show seventeen different tigers visiting this rock during the past year—heaven knows how many have come that I never knew about. The number's risen sharply during the past month. But of the tigers I've recorded, not one has hung around. They stay for a day or a week, and move on. Your friend Khan has stayed a month. That's a record."

"Where do they come from?"

Ross's eyes searched the distance for an answer. "I don't know. I've never heard of so many cats sharing a spot. There are so many and they return so seldom, they must come from awfully far away."

"Mating?" Hashti suggested. "Like trout?"

"If they all came at once that might be it," Ross said. "But although they mate only in midwinter, they visit in all seasons."

Hashti frowned. "If they mate in midwinter, don't the cubs come at a clumsy time of year?"

"No, they're born in April. The gestation period's much shorter than a horse's. A tigress can't afford to get too pregnant to hunt, so the cubs are born small, but they develop fast. I think they start hunting before the end of their first year, though they stay with their mothers a long time beyond that."

"Oh. Is there anything you don't know?"

Ross grinned. "Lots. For instance, how does their territorial system work?"

"Maybe they don't have territories," Hashti suggested, then knew that was silly. Not all animals defend strict boundaries, but all have home ranges.

Ross's thoughts agreed with hers. "They've got to have territories. Every creature smarter than an alga does. It's just a question of how they're organized. Tiger ranges must be enormous, and obviously they overlap. Do they hold territory as groups? And what special significance does the Rock have?"

A breeze shook the bushes, showering them with dislodged snow. Ross brushed his shoulders, frowning. "I don't like the way the wind is picking up, and there's not much to see with just one tiger here. Let's eat lunch. If another tiger doesn't come by the time we're done, we'll leave."

It seemed foolish to turn back so quickly, but if the First-Inner was worried about the weather, Hashti would take him at his word. It had been hard enough to get here under good conditions. "You want to skip lunch and head back now?" she asked.

Ross shook his finger at her in good-natured admonition. "Rules two and three for avoiding hypothermia: Don't get exhausted, and keep eating. We've worked damn hard and I for one need a break."

Lunch was pleasant, with a magnificent view and hot tea to compensate for frozen sandwiches. As they sipped hot chocolate afterwards, Ross sucked in his breath. "Look down there, Tiger Wrestler."

She stared down past the big blackpine. Two young tigresses strolled into the clearing. The waiting tiger lifted his head. Ignoring him, the newcomers sniffed at the cliff face. One turned her tail to it. Hashti could not be sure, from this distance, but the tigress's posture suggested that she was urinating on the rock. A minute later, her companion followed suit. "Calling cards," Ross whispered.

"What?"

"They have special scent glands under their tails, and each animal's smell is unique. By smelling the rock, a tiger can presumably tell who else has visited recently."

As Ross explained this, the big spotted tiger sauntered toward the newcomers, giving a short musical call. They responded with their own strings of notes, then stretched their noses out to sniff at him. "Whuffing," Hashti told Ross.

"What?"

"They're whuffing. Snorting in each other's faces. Khan did it to me, and even Sabra tried. I think that's how they say hello."

The whuffing was followed by general head rubbing and body sniffing. "Looks friendly," Ross observed. "It'll get even friendlier in a few weeks when mating season starts. This, I think, is just social."

Hashti had never seen tigers in heat, but she agreed that this was not foreplay. It looked a lot like her breakfast encounter with Khan.

Greetings completed, the females settled themselves in the sun, lying head to tail and licking contentedly at each other. Hashti had often seen horses standing head to tail, swishing flies off each other on hot summer afternoons, but here there were no flies. She looked questioningly at Ross.

"Preening," he answered. "Smoothing the feathers and spreading them with oil from a special gland of the tongue. It waterproofs the outer layer of feathers, keeps the down dry. It's also New Lebanon's standard way of exchanging pleasantries."

The tigresses' companion rose and swayed lazily toward them, joining in the mutual grooming. The three exchanged short sequences of notes. Then the big male roared and tossed his head. The females looked expectantly at him. "Watch this," Ross whispered.

The jaguar-spotted male strutted into the center of the clearing. Raising his voice, he launched into a turning, twisting melody full of trills and grace notes. Although he never simply repeated himself, subtle echoes made themselves felt. Then the song broke in an ear-shattering snarl. The tiger flattened himself against the rock, only his tail twitching. He sprang, twisting in midair to bring down some invisible prey, then stood proudly, resuming his song.

"Heap big hunter," Ross muttered under his breath.

Hashti nodded briefly in agreement. "Looks like he's bragging, doesn't it?"

The song went on, a gripping display of art and sheer carnivorous power. Hashti wished desperately that she could translate it. Certainly the tiger must be boasting of his fights and kills.

Then shadow swept the theater as the sun ducked behind a cloud. A freshening breeze cut through Hashti's sweater. Ross tugged at her sleeve. "When he finishes the ladies will take their turn. They can keep it up for hours. But I don't like the looks of this sky. I think we'd better go."

With tigersong still ringing, in their ears, the two re-shouldered their packs and slid from their vantage point down to the trail they had made coming up. Ross froze, hushing Hashti's inquiry with a lift of his hand, then squatted on his heels to examine fresh pug marks in the snow. His voice had a nervous edge to it. "Guess who wandered by while we were eating?"

Heart pounding, Hashti scanned for a flash of orange and black. "Khan?"

"Come here and I'll show you. Look at the left hind paw—that's right, the rear paws leave smaller prints. Now look at his middle toe. See the point slanting off? Evidently he can't retract that claw. That's his trade-mark."

Hashti thought she saw what Ross was talking about, although even on a print as fresh and clear as this it was a subtle sign. Biting her lip, she looked up at the gray-haired naturalist. "What do we do now?"

He shrugged. "The print is about an hour old, so Khan may have left already. Let's go home. I'd just as soon not chat with him now, anyway."

Hashti felt the same way. Heavy gray clouds scudded across the sky and the wind grew ever sharper. "Fine," she said. "Give me a minute to get my windbreaker on."

Ross smiled and cocked an eyebrow. "Good idea, Tiger Wrestler. Myself, I'm going to slip behind that blackpine. The tea ran right through me."

Waving him on, Hashti shucked her pack, dug her windbreaker from its corner pocket, pulled the tightly woven jacket over her head, and drew the hood close about her face. She had strapped on her skis and was reaching for the pack to put it back on when she heard, above the lashing of the trees in the wind, a familiar whuffing snort. She turned her head. Khan sat thirty feet behind her. He whuffed again.

She tried to keep her voice calm and quiet. "Mister Ross? We have company." Khan's attack on Gaylord replayed itself in her mind. She felt horribly exposed with her back to the tiger, but pivoting on cross-country skis is easier said than done. Spreading her poles wide for support, she lifted her right foot, swung the ski around on its tail, and lowered it into its original track pointing the opposite direction. Her feet were now splayed at a hundred and eighty degree angle from each other. She lifted the left ski around and placed it by its partner. Khan found the procedure fascinating. When she was finally facing him, Hashti took a deep breath and whuffed as loudly as she could.

Khan's lips drew back from his teeth in a peculiar grimace, more a yawn or smile than snarl. Then he stood and sauntered toward her. Balls of ice dragged from the tips of his belly feathers, and a bur had matted itself onto one ear, but other than that, Khan could have come straight from a grooming. A magnificent animal!

Ross whistled, long and low, behind Hashti. "Oh, Lord. You call the shots," he said. "I'll skunk him if you want." Glancing over her shoulder, Hashti saw Ross reach for the leather holder strapped across his chest.

Khan saw, too. He bared his teeth again, and this time he was indubitably threatening.

"Don't touch it," Hashti ordered Ross. "He knows what it is."

Ross lifted his hands, as if to prove their emptiness. "Whatever you say." Hashti wasn't sure whether he was addressing her or the tiger.

Khan, who had frozen during the discussion, advanced again, his heavy forequarters swaying like a woman's hips. Shutting fear from her mind through sheer will, Hashti forced herself to think of this as an animal training problem. Be calm, authoritative, and don't startle or threaten him, she told herself. Never mind that you've violated a trainer's first rule by putting yourself in a vulnerable position. You can't change it now. She pulled off her mitten, squatted down, and extended her hand.

Khan paused three feet from her and whuffed again.

She whuffed back.

He sniffed delicately at her outstretched hand, her face, her hand again, and sang. "Twinkle, little star." It was a civilized hum, not a forest-shattering wail such as the spotted tiger still emitted.

Ross's report of the dissection flashed through Hashti's mind. "They're wired for real speech," he'd told her. What was Khan trying to say? "You smell funny"? "Take me to your leader?" "What happened to your feathers?"

Not knowing how else to react, Hashti repeated the five-note phrase.

Khan rubbed his body along a nearby sapling, sharpened his claws a few strokes, then came over and bumped Hashti with his great glistening head. With her feet strapped to the clumsy skis, she was knocked off balance. She caught herself with a bare hand, wincing as it was scraped by the snow's icy crust. Thank heavens she hadn't gotten the pack back on, she thought! Otherwise she'd have toppled completely over. Khan gave her a startled look and rubbed again, more gently this time.

"It's OK, fella," she told him. "You just have to take it easy. You're a lot bigger than I am."

As she wondered how to further their conversation, Khan strode to a spot fifteen feet away, where the slender stem of a dead thistle rose from the snow. It was capped by a spherical pod two inches across. The tiger sent the round brown seed-case rattling against Hashti's boot, as he hummed a tune three notes long.

"He's talking to you," Ross muttered under his breath. "I swear to God, he just said 'catch.'"

Testing the guess, Hashti repeated this new phrase and tossed the thistle seed back.

The tiger purred broadly, caught the seed between his forepaws, snapped playfully at it, and returned it to Hashti.

From the corner of her eye she saw a snowflake sail by, but this was no time to quit. Letting the seed lie, she packed a snowball and tossed it at the tiger, again singing the three notes.

Her missile shattered when the tiger slashed at it. He jerked away as the snowy fragments sprayed across his nose. As if conscious that he'd been "had," Khan turned his tail to Hashti. A kick of his rear paw showered her with snow.

Ross chuckled. "Guess that fixed you, Tiger Wrestler."

The woman and the tiger played for nearly an hour, at the end of which she could sing "catch," "blackpine," "icicle," "tiger" (or was that Khan's own name?), "paperbark," and "sweetsap." "Twinkle little star," she concluded, must be her own name. She also learned the notes for "gotcha"—Khan had a rowdy sense of humor. Hashti had no sooner gotten used to Khan's rubbing than he took to pouncing. He never hurt her, merely seemed to find it fun. He was more wary of Ross, sniffing noses with the naturalist in a dignified manner, but swiveling his ears outward warningly when Ross tried to enter the game. The First-Inner resigned himself to watching from the sidelines, alternately frowning in silent concern and laughing.

As Hashti sparred with the tiger, snow began in earnest. The flakes were small, but fell in such profusion that soon they reduced vision to forty or fifty feet. Khan tumbled Hashti into a snowbank, whuffed in her face, sang something new, and left. She waited five minutes, then ten. No tiger. Ross looked at the snow swirling about them. "Let's get out before this gets any worse."

Their tracks had not yet been obliterated. The clumsy wooden skis seemed almost efficient as Ross and Hashti descended to the lake. But there they discovered that the entire ice pack had been blown away by the storm wind, leaving an expanse of slate-gray water whipped into towering whitecaps. Foam spumed twenty feet into the air as waves crashed against the rocks.

Their trail had blown to sea with the ice, and they dared not expose themselves to the wind-driven spray along the beach. They retreated from the lake and began struggling through brush parallel to the shore.

Snow had drifted deeply here, and underbrush grew more thickly than in deep forest. Fallen limbs and bramble bushes wrapped themselves around Hashti's skis. The more she fell, the more tired she got. The more tired she got, the more likely she was to fall again. Thunder boomed across the snow-veiled sky. Hashti had never heard thunder in a snowstorm before. Her head down to escape the wind, she skied straight into a cedar branch. It dumped its coating of snow in her face.

Exhausted, she stopped to brush herself off. Her mouth felt like cotton. She forced herself not to lick the snow from her lips. Eating it would sap her strength still further. Instead, she fumbled for her insulated canteen, and gratefully gulped the lukewarm bittertea.

Ross circled back, squinting at Hashti through the driving snow. "Tired, Tiger Wrestler?"

She shrugged away her pride. "I need a rest, Mister Ross." Gay was right, she thought. She belonged in her nice warm stable, not this bleak winter wilderness.

Ross's expression was serious but calm. "I'm tired too. Let's dig in for the night."

He searched briefly and chose a large cedar tree, somewhat protected from the wind by its fellows. Underneath the tree's wide, sloping branches, the snow was packed and trampled. Ross nodded at the depression. "Deer been sleeping here." He pulled a lightweight, waterproof sheet from his pack. It whipped madly in the wind, but, they soon had it clipped to the cedar's branches, forming a snug little tent eight feet across, four feet high at the highest point, with the tree trunk near the center. They spread the floor with small branches and a second tarpaulin. Finally they brushed the snow from themselves and crawled in. Ross sat against the tree's massive trunk and patted the floor next to him. "Have a seat and snuggle up, Teamstress."

She sat, careful to lean against the tree rather than Ross. He handed her a hotbottle. "Here. Your blond boyfriend will call challenge on me if I let you go hypothermic."

She guzzled the warm liquid. Ross watched critically. "You're soaked," he said. "I'm going out to pile snow. You get that wet stuff off and yourself into a sleeping bag."

After romping with Khan and fighting through the underbrush, Hashti was indeed snowy from the outside in and sweaty from the inside out. Hitherto exertion had warmed her, but post-exercise chill would soon set in. Flinching from the biting air, she stripped, pulled on a dry undersuit, and wriggled into the sleeping bag from her pack.

Outside, Ross used a ski to scrape more snow against their makeshift tent, transforming it into an igloo. The tarpaulin ceased its frantic snapping. The low doorway faced west, away from the wind, sheltered by the flat lacy needles of the tree's hospitably drooping branches. "If it were colder," Ross told her as he returned, "we'd dig an entrance below floor level so cold air wouldn't roll in. But the temperature's so close to freezing right now, I'd just as soon maintain ventilation. We don't want the drift melting around our ears."

It was hard to imagine ventilation being a problem, the way the wind howled outside. Hashti could feel the cedar's trunk shake as its crown was whipped by the storm. "How hard is it blowing, anyway?" she asked.

"Hard enough," Ross answered. "Forty miles an hour in the open? Gusting to eighty or ninety, maybe. Too hard to ski against."

She shivered, remembering how she'd had to lean into the blasts to keep her balance. "I'm happy to sit it out. The sleeping bag feels good."

Ross glanced sideways at her as he took his mittens off and slapped them against his boots, knocking the snow loose. "I thought it might. You warmed up enough, or do I need to crawl in with you?"

The fourth strategy for hypothermia treatment—skin-to-skin contact. Ross, silver-haired or no, radiated a virility that made the prospect attractive. "I'm fine," Hashti answered, blushing.

Ross grinned and winked. "I need to change socks. Promise not to peek at my naked toes!"

"I promise," Hashti laughed, ashamed of her wandering desires.

Ross pulled on dry socks, removed the wet liners from his boots, and slid waist-deep into his own sleeping bag. Then he began rummaging in his pockets. "Aha!" He broke a fudge bar and handed half to Hashti. "This should do something for that tired feeling in your legs."

She didn't need to be begged. The candy's savor was heightened by the wind raging outside. Ross studied her.

Hashti raised her eyebrows as she met his gaze. "Well?" she asked.

"I was wondering what Khan saw in you. If he were human I could guess. Why a tiger finds you fascinating is another question entirely."

She'd been too distracted by the storm to think about anything else. Now the other events of the day tumbled through her mind. "Do you really think they can talk?" she asked.

"You tell me," the First-Inner answered.

Hashti started a reply, then bit it off.

"Go with your hunches," Ross counseled. "Sometimes your mind gives answers before it can give reasons."

Hashti nibbled thoughtfully at the fudge. "It sure felt like he was teaching me words."

"I thought so, too," Ross said. "Although it's theoretically impossible."

Hashti paused mid-bite to look inquiringly at him.

"The hand-brain theory," he reminded her. "We talked about it at breakfast. There's a vast gap between the continuum of 'animal' thinking and communication, and the grossly enhanced symbolic and abstract reasoning capabilities that we call 'intelligence.' Animals have little use for our sort of intelligence. Instinct, conditioned reflex, and such mental abilities as they already have serve them much better. Only in combination with manipulative ability and primitive tool-using does rational thinking come into its own. At that point, when intelligence, social development, and technology become mutually reinforcing, you get a quantitative, qualitative jump to what we call civilization. Simply put, tigers are too successful on the pounce-and-bite level to bother with smarts. But if your conversation with Khan wasn't a conversation, what was it?"

Having no answer, Hashti kept silent.

Ross swallowed the last of his fudge and dusted his fingers. "At least the tigers communicate in a mode we can sense and duplicate. If Khan had accosted you with infrared modulation, you'd have had a tough time replying."

Hashti considered that. "I'd never have known he was talking, would I?"

"We might have guessed, after the autopsy."

"I still couldn't have answered."

"We'd have had to rig a cross-modal synthesizer—a little box that converts one kind of information, like infrared, into something the user's biologically equipped to handle, like sound. But they're a real pain to use." A howling gust nearly drowned his words. He winced, then smiled reassuringly at Hashti. "We have plenty of time to ponder our good fortune. This storm's not slowing down any."

Despite the blizzard, their snow-buried shelter was cozy. "I feel like a little animal in its burrow," Hashti reported.

Ross squirmed into a more comfortable position and squinted at the silvery-white tarp which formed their roof. "Myself, I like burrows equipped with furnaces, fireplaces, and featherbeds. Not to mention hot showers and brandy. And my wife. We old married types get spoiled. Speaking of which—" He poked at his beacon. It squeaked back at him, not the usual alarm beep but a shorter, shriller sound. Ross sighed. "Too bad. Nobody home." Then, as the beacon's noise subsided, he spoke directly into it. "Hi, Gimpy. This is your feeble old man. I haven't strength to make it home through wind, snow, and etc., so I'm camping under a cedar tree with the nubile young thing. See you tomorrow, weather permitting."

Hashti stared at the beacon as Ross returned it to his belt. "That thing carries voices?"

"Sure. A receiver in our bedroom takes messages if no one's around, and transmits a general alert if an emergency signal comes in." He pulled the beacon back out and handed it to her. Smaller and lighter than her own, it sparkled with complex controls and an intricately worked circle insignia. "Made it myself," Ross explained with pride. "Old First-In custom. A beacon's too important to trust somebody else's work, and having made one, you've a better idea how to repair it."

"What does it do?" Hashti asked.

Ross showed her the controls. "It's got a dead-man alarm, navigational recording, and clock, just like your beacon. But it also has a remote trigger, and two-way voice communication over a range of about forty miles, with the antenna we have rigged in camp." He turned the beacon over. "These clips on back lock the beacon to a data condenser, which records spoken reports in compact form. You can recover input through the condenser itself, or transmit to the central console's decoder. Makes note taking a lot easier."

"Pretty expensive equipment," Hashti said.

Ross spread his hands in a what-can-we-do gesture. "Yes. People bitch about First-In fees, but it all goes back into equipment, travel, and research. We don't have any technological monopoly. We design and produce the best because we know exactly what we need, and our lives depend on it."

On Carolina they said First-In fees went to alien voodoo and spaceport dives. Hard to reconcile with Ross's plaid-flannel practicality! Hashti eyed the gaudy, gem-dusted gold hoop which peeked from beneath his cap. Like any child, she'd stolen earrings from her mother and played at exploring the frontier with her stuffed donkey and rabbit for alien Circlemates. Like any mother, hers had shaken her head and asked if Hashti couldn't find a more respectable game. Later, like any teenager, Hashti had sighed over the silk-clad heroes of frontier romances. But by then she was plaiting manes and polishing buckles under Master Will's demanding eye, safe from the lure of the gypsy Circles.

Neither Hashti nor her mother had ever dreamed that such a safe, conventional guild career would leave Hashti blizzard-bound on a tiger-infested frontier planet, huddled in a snowdrift with a bona fide First-Inner. Ross seemed like an old friend, neither hero nor renegade. Hashti's thoughts returned to his strange conversation with Anna just before leaving camp. "How'd you get into First-In?" she asked.

He grinned. "I used to be career army. Then my unit escorted the First-In team who negotiated the Punjab settlement. The Circle's doc was cute, but absolute hell to escort. Every time I turned my head she'd be off to look at something. You'd think a woman of forty would know better. Finally I used primitive tactics to distract her." His eyes twinkled. "Willful woman, that one. Since First-Inners can't marry out, she brought me in."

Anna and Ross acted like they'd been married forever. Had they really met so late in life? Hashti considered the new information, then returned to her original line of questioning. "She brought you in? Just like that? Wasn't there a lot of training and stuff?"

He shrugged, but the way he watched Hashti was not at all nonchalant. "First-In adopts trainees by personal recommendation. You have to be endorsed by at least three Circle members, one of whom is of another race. The medic made a point of introducing me to her teammates. By the time we left Punjab she had the recommendations lined up."

"What happened then?" Hashti asked.

"I spent a probationary year learning languages and

getting acquainted with the Circle. Living with aliens is tough. Crazy little things, like the way they eat their food or honor their dead, can bother you more than you'd ever imagine. That's why most planets are settled by only one intelligent species. And it's why folk are so nervous around First-Inners. They can't understand our tolerance for alien customs, let alone our participation. They're terrified to admit there's more than one way to bed a mate or bathe a baby. By making superheroes or witch doctors of us, they excuse themselves from opening their own minds. Anyway, by the end of the year I knew I wanted in, and the Circle knew it wanted me. So here I am."

"Who decided you were going to be a naturalist?"

"Oh, I did. It had been my hobby for years. There's room in a Circle for almost any specialty, so long as you don't suffer from professional tunnel vision."

"You didn't go to university?" Hashti asked, confused. Ross did sit at the Company table.

"I did First-In's standard general studies track and a bit of specializing. But most things I learned on my own. The Circle gave me a library and told me to use it, along with keeping my own two eyes open. I planned to spend this winter classifying the voluntary and involuntary behavioral components of thermoregulatory adaptation in a boreal climate."

"The what?" Hashti asked. "Why?"

"Thermoregulation means temperature control. Some of it, like having a down coat, is structural. Some of it is behavioral—you keep warm or cool by how you act. Behavioral adaptation further divides into things like shivering, which you do automatically, and things like getting out of the wind and huddling up, or building a fire and making tea, which are voluntary. The study gives me a stockpile of ideas to draw on when I get stuck. Like this afternoon."

And a good thing he'd known, too, Hashti thought. "Where I come from," she confessed, "a naturalist is someone who brags about how many species of birds she's photographed."

A merry expression danced in Ross's eyes. "I've seen the type, too, Tiger Wrestler." He hunched down, his hands raised as if guiding the framer on a holocamera. His voice rose to a ridiculous falsetto. "Oh, George, look at that! A pink-toed, double-breasted, half-feathered willy-hoot! What a darling fellow. Isn't he just the cutest? Get ready. Get ready. Here he comes. Got him! Oh, the guys at the club will be just green with envy. Let's go have a drink!"

Hashti laughed. Ross straightened, saying remorsefully, "I shouldn't make fun. At least they're showing an interest in the world. I take an occasional bird picture, myself, although the wife's the one whose work really benefits from visual documentation."

"Doctoring?" Hashti asked, wondering whether pictures of her own bruised shoulder lay in Anna's files.

"More the anatomical engineering stuff," Ross answered. "The doc's certified in Frontier Medicine and she's saved more than a few lives, but what really fascinates her is anatomical adaptation—the ways bodies solve problems. How a shoulder joint is built, how an eye adapts to changing light conditions, how sweat glands coordinate cooling and waste disposal. Once she understands those things, she suggests equipment designs to duplicate them." Ross chuckled. "That pack you wore balances the way a pregnant Sherpa lizard does. The stoves in City Hall imitate a dolphin's bloodstream. Cuts firewood consumption by a third. Not that we're short on wood, but we have better things to do than spend time cutting it."

Hashti had pigeonholed Anna with Carolina's physicians and veterinarians, who disdained any change from their grandparents' ways. She struggled to realign her image of the gray-haired doctor. "You mean she uses the stuff she knows to plan packs and heating systems?"

"Exactly," Ross said.

"No wonder everyone's confused about First-In," Hashti concluded.

"It's not so confusing," Ross assured her. "A company pays First-In to scout and advise incoming comany employees. How we scout a planet is our business. On a job like this, with only a dozen members on the team, there's no way we can include specialists in all the relevant disciplines. Instead, each of us cultivates a broad range of interests, and we stretch the knowledge we have to cover what we don't know. Face it: no matter how acute your expertise, you interpret the unknown by analogy. The analogy's source is less important than its usefulness. So we give each team as much racial and professional diversity as we can to widen the pool of possible analogies. That's why you find an economic sociologist, for instance, on New Lebanon."

"Who's an economic sociologist?"

"The Boss. He studies the economic links between various aspects of society—politics, religion, sex, music, you name it. You might think he should be on diplomatic assignment. But," Ross said, tapping the tree trunk he leaned against, "the Boss can explain this cedar tree nearly as well by social economy as I can by behavioral climactic adaptation. Put us together and we're dynamite."

"It does seem like he should be doing diplomatic work," Hashti objected.

Ross sighed. "I suppose someday he will. A First-

Inner's career tends to parallel the organization's, just as an animal's development reflects its species' evolutionary history." He paused, eyeing Hashti. "See? There's an analogy right there."

Hashti nodded, and Ross went on. "First-In began as an explorer's guild. Someone realized that if interracial teams opened new planets, there'd be fewer charges of treaty violation. Soon after, people saw that Circlemates, who live together and work together and understand each other as well as people of different species possibly can, make ideal translators and mediators. So now Circles handle interracial diplomacy as well as exploration.

"Most individual First-Inners likewise begin on the frontier. When we grow old and wise and want soft beds, we switch to diplomacy." He smiled mischievously. "The wife and I may never graduate. And Freckles won't, without us. The three of us work too well together."

How could anyone, even Ross, call Big Red "Freckles"? "Are you always teamed together, then?" Hashti asked.

"Usually," Ross answered. "Our Circle has about two hundred members, embracing all four hominid races and the seven other land-going species from Earth-type planets. Working teams have twelve to sixty members. For diplomatic reasons each team includes at least three races, and for psychological reasons we'll have at least three members of each race. Also there has to be a good mix of specialties. Beyond that, it depends who likes to work together. Teams shift a lot since usually folks of the appropriate species stay behind a while as transition consultants."

"Which is what you and Doctor Anna and Big Red are doing," Hashti said, fitting the pieces together in her mind. "Where will you go when you leave New Lebanon?"

"Back to the Core," Ross answered. "That's what's left of the Circle when the smaller teams are in the field. It includes administrators, trainees, very old folk, and children who aren't traveling with their parents. It's what we come home to between assignments."

"Where is it?"

"Varies. Core handles the Circle's largest, longest-term projects, but eventually it finishes even the big ones and moves on. The lack of a fixed base protects our reputation for neutrality."

"Where is your Core now?"

"The interplanetary trade conference on Sharon, which ends soon. We're looking for a new base. I hope it's on the frontier. I hate being stared at. I got my fill of that on the grand tour."

"The grand tour?"

"Visiting the home planets of my Circlemates. I understood them a lot better after I'd done it. But what an experience!" Ross told Hashti, in hilarious detail, about the visits. Carolina was not the only place suspicious of First-Inners.

Most people's eyes focus on something neutral when they reminisce. Ross's locked on Hashti. When she began to fidget under his gaze, he broke off and asked, smiling, "How about you? How'd somebody as little as you get mixed up with anything as big as those horses?"

"I always liked them." Briefly she sketched her upbringing on Carolina's sports resorts and the long years of apprenticeship. "And so," she concluded, "just after I made Journeyman, Oldearth offered me this job. Master Will said he'd back me for a Cap if I did well."

"I should hope so," Ross said. "Oldearth got a real deal. You're good. They got you for Journeyman's wage.

And they can saddle you with crap a Master wouldn't
need to tolerate."

His observation fed Hashti's smoldering resentment
against the Company, but resentment wouldn't do any
good now. She was here and had to do what she could
with what she had. She changed the subject. "Where do
the tigers go on nights like this?"

"Oh, niches in the rocks, undercut banks of stream
beds, low-hanging trees like this..." Ross paused. "I
told you I haven't figured out their territorial system."

A particularly vicious gust sent a curl of snow swirling
through the doorway. It emphasized the general snug-
ness of their hideaway compared to the deadly whiteness
beyond. "Wherever the tigers are, I hope it's as cozy as
this," Hashti said.

Ross yawned. "Maybe someday we'll find out. In the
meantime, let's catch some sleep."

# CHAPTER SEVEN

❧❧❧

THE STRANDED TRAVELERS MADE PILLOWS OF THEIR packs and settled in for the night. Let me hear no romantic stories, Hashti thought, about the wonders of a night spent in the woods in a snowstorm. As a teenager on Carolina, eager to prove her hardiness, she'd done mountain camping. This was every bit as bad. No matter how she adjusted her position there was always at least one rock, root, or iceball digging into some vulnerable part of her anatomy. Whenever she was about to doze off, a cold gust would find its way down her neck. Worst of all was the aftermath of the tea. Three times Hashti wakened to stagger out of the shelter and expose herself to the elements. Each time she wondered whether Khan would pounce on her out of the blackness. Afterward she had to warm up her bag and try to go to sleep all over again. Finally, blessedly, she awakened and could see the roof above her. Morning!

In an instinctive search for warmth, she had wriggled backward during the night. She now found herself firmly pressed against Ross. Gingerly she rolled over to look at him.

He grinned. "Anyone ever tell you you have a warm back? Although I bet you steal covers, when you have the chance. Sleep OK?"

"Brrrrrrrr."

109

"Me, too. Next time I camp in a storm, I'll bring a snowproof, windproof tent. Forget this improvised stuff! But the storm's over and we're still alive. Breakfast?" He held out another fudge bar.

Hashti accepted. "Where I come from, this is not considered proper breakfast. But then a cedar tree isn't considered proper lodging."

"It was warmer than outside! Chow down and we'll head home."

"Do you want to try to find Khan again?"

Ross hesitated, then shook his head. "He obviously knows where to find us. And unless Khan has an urgent desire to see you, we'd best get back and talk to the Boss. This changes a lot of things about the way we have to deal with this planet."

Outside the sky was brilliant blue. Snow plastered the windward side of every twig and trunk. Damp bark glistened darkly on the sheltered sides of the trees. Evergreen branches trailed to the ground under the weight of their white frosting. Every so often a snow clump slid loose with a wet plop, and the unloaded bough tossed gratefully in the light breeze. A beautiful day, without question. But the lake was still open, forcing the skiers to continue their struggle through the woods. Even the trail along the Merrywater had vanished in the oblivion of new snow. As the sun climbed higher, wet snow began to stick to the skis. Every few yards Ross and Hashti stopped to shake or scrape caked slush away. By the time they reached Swamp City, Hashti was as tired as she'd been during the storm, and twice as bruised. She knew exactly what she wanted—a hot meal, a long leisurely sauna, another hot meal, and a warm, soft bed for the night. She knew better than to count on it.

Smells of pine pitch and roasting venison greeted the pair as they came up the last long slope into camp. In the open yard in front of City Hall, Master Tam supervised construction of the traditional Phoenix Nest, a structure of dry brittle wood a bit higher than an enormous table. The folk of the camp would place their grievances of the present year upon it, and when the flames had done their work, the settlers would roast New Year's dinner on the coals. Hashti wondered why the Nest was being built so early—the solstice was still two and a half weeks away. Perhaps Big Red thought the workers needed a sign of hope.

Tam waved. "There they are! We were worried about you. You still have all your fingers and toes?"

Ross swung his pack onto the ground. "Barely. Colder than a witch's tits out there, Wood Butcher."

Sweat, fetching boards for the construction, leered. "Not with Hashti Hot Shit along. Bet you had yourself a good time, Mister Ross."

Hashti fidgeted uncomfortably under Sweat's gaze. Did this man hate her, desire her, or both? Ross remained unruffled. "No such luck, Sweat. It seems the lady is spoken for. I'll take my wife next time. She cooperates."

Everyone laughed, and the group dispersed. Ross and Hashti dumped their packs in the silvered First-In cabin and then sought lunch in City Hall. Hashti looked hopefully for Gay or Kevin in the kitchen, but both were out hunting. The cook, winking, promised to let them know she was back. Hashti ate until her stomach could not expand an inch farther. Then she returned to the barn.

Lance greeted her with a puffy face and red eyes. Guiltily, she remembered that plow teams had been out around the clock during the storm. Lance had probably had less sleep than she. She pulled a wisp of hay from his disheveled dark curls and shook her head in mock disapproval. "You look a mess, young man. Get yourself up to the bunkhouse and catch about twelve hours sleep before you show your face here again."

He looked anxiously at her. "I did the best I could, Miz Hashti. I'm almost caught up now."

"You did fine," she reassured him. "Now go get some sleep." She smiled as she watched him go. Lance showed promise. If Hashti made Master, Lance would be her first apprentice.

Her room was in disarray. It'd been a warming house for plow drivers returning from the storm. Her washbasin, two-thirds full of water, sat on the floor. Someone must have been thawing frostbitten feet. Sighing, Hashti began to straighten up.

She was nearly finished when she heard voices outside. "I don't see her, Gay." That rolling "r" could only be Kevin's.

"Here I am!" she called, stepping into the corridor to greet the two young men.

Gay hugged her, then stood back, shaking his head. "Where the hell were you last night?" he asked. "I told you this gadding about with First-Inners would lead to trouble."

"You were right," Hashti answered. "I've seen enough snow to last me the rest of the winter. A drift is not the warmest place to sleep."

Beneath the teasing, Gay was genuinely relieved to see her. "I hope you learned your lesson. New Lebanon is bad enough behind log walls with a fire in the stove. Going out to look for tigers is just plain stupid."

"You haven't asked me if we found any."

"You're back in one piece. That's enough."

Kevin nodded in agreement. "Begging your pardon, Miz Hashti, but you were lookin' for trouble. Tigers are pretty, but they've no love for us." A shiver of apprehension rippled across his body as he remembered the tiger that had charged him.

Gay had a triumphant look on his face. "Well, we won't have to worry about them much longer. I've been talking to Lael, Hashti. It seems Oldearth Company bought only timber export rights for New Lebanon. Anything else we can exploit for ourselves, free and clear."

Ashamed, Hashti remembered her agitation when Sweat told her that Gay had spent the morning with Lael. Of course Gay was up to something constructive. "That's great! I'm glad to know the Company finally out-cheaped itself. But what, besides trees, do you plan on exploiting?"

Gay gestured toward the tackroom, where the glistening orange and black striped tiger pelt soaked in a stinking barrel of brine. "Tigers! That feathered skin's valuable, Hashti. Thick, soft, exotic. All we have to do is get it to the right market. We should be hunting tigers, not whittling at the forest while they snap at our necks."

Hashti's heart sank with disappointment and foreboding. "You can't shoot the tigers, Gaylord. They're intelligent."

"What? Are you still worried about this nonsense of Ross's?"

"It's not nonsense," Hashti said. "I talked to Khan yesterday."

Kevin's eyes were wide; Gay's narrowed critically. "Go on," he told her.

She described her romp with Khan. Kevin winced as she told of the tiger's predilection for pouncing. Gay shook his head slightly. When she finished, he gave her a worried half-smile. "You are something else, Hashti. Your parents must have been gray by the time you were three."

"Does this mean I shot two intelligent aliens?" Kevin asked.

Gay shook his head. "I sincerely doubt it. But since Hashti thinks so, and there are nasty penalties for warring on intelligent races, I'll tell Lael the plan's on hold. We won't say anything to the camp until this gets sorted out." His arm slid around Hashti once more. "Listen, friend. Please don't run off into any more snowstorms. There's got to be a safer way to talk to tigers, if you insist on doing it."

"If there is, I'll be glad to take it," she assured him, relieved to find him reacting so reasonably. She hadn't realized how much she missed Gay. His body was warm and solid against hers.

Kevin, as if reading her thoughts, blushed. Clearing his throat, he glanced around the empty barn. "Where's Lance?"

"Bunkhouse. I told him to take the rest of the day off."

The slender Atlantan picked up his rifle. "Gay, I want to scout out that hill to the north. I'll meet you down by the cedar bog in an hour."

Gay's hand tightened on Hashti's waist, but he hesitated as he looked at his hunting companion. "Sure you don't mind going out alone?"

Kevin paused just a moment before answering. "I'll be fine."

The three walked together to the big double door. Hashti smiled shyly at the young hunter as she pushed the door open. "Thanks, Kevin."

He grinned and ducked his head. "My pleasure, Miz Hashti. I hope someone does the same for me sometime."

She flushed and thanked him once more. What else was there to say?

"Don't trip on a tiger!" Gaylord called. He watched after Kevin for a moment, then pulled the door shut and dropped the bar. "This is no trivial favor, Hashti. He's refused to go out alone ever since that tiger jumped him."

"We had better do justice to his generosity, then." She held out her arms.

All too soon, Gay glanced at his beacon and rolled away. "Your teamsters will be in soon. Wouldn't they love to find me here! I better catch up with Kevin."

Reluctantly Hashti dressed and followed Gay into the corridor, tying a bandanna over her hair as she walked. Inflooding sunlight dazzled her as she unbarred the door. An odd dark lump lay across the ice road twenty yards from the stable. Even when Hashti's eyes adjusted to the light, they refused to comprehend what they saw. Finally the scene came into focus, and she screamed. "Kevin! Gay, get out here! It's Kevin!"

She ran to the limp body and probed desperately for a pulse, but she knew already that she'd find none. Kevin's head lay twisted at an odd angle, surprise and fear glazed into his eyes. Beneath his white turtleneck Hashti found a set of clean, deep incisions, almost as if he'd been knifed. But this murder was no human work. Tiger spoor showed sharp and clean in the snow between the road's iced ruts. Hashti sat back on her heels, caught between misery and disbelief. "Oh, my God."

Gay, ashen-faced, rocked the body in his arms. His voice was bitter with grief. "The tigers like to play, do they?"

The camp gathered before dawn the next morning, in the square in front of City Hall. The Phoenix Nest, intended as the center of their solstice merrymaking, had become a bier, draped in the scalloped blue and white of Atlantis. Kevin's slender body lay pale and still atop it.

Ross stood across from Hashti, his face grim in the starlight. He'd not announced the discoveries of their journey—not while everyone was still in shock. Who would believe Hashti's tale of tumbling in the snow with Khan, when Kevin had just died in the jaws of another tiger? Yet his death made the matter more urgent. Tonight at dinner, Ross said.

The naturalist wore his usual baggy pants, black turtleneck, and thick wool shirt. But Anna and Big Red had donned dress uniform, for the first time since they'd met the company workers' shuttle. They looked like First-Inners from a frontier drama. White silk shimmered in the half light as they stepped forward.

"Damn monster lovers shouldn't be leadin' this," someone hissed. "If they ran this camp right, Kevin wouldn't be dead."

The disturbing whisper went unanswered. Anna and Big Red faced each other across the bier, their breath hanging in clouds of pale mist as they began the ancient Litany of Dust.

"From dust are born the suns, the seas, and life," Anna proclaimed.

"Dust we are, to dust we shall return," Big Red answered.

"It swirls in hope and song, and then swirls on," Anna chanted in a clear strong voice.

"But dust does not forget the dream that stirs it," Big Red promised. He turned, arms outspread, to face the assembled camp. "Tell of this dream that stirred the dust!"

There was a moment of shuffling hesitation, until Master Tam stepped forward. "My first week here, I made a chair that fell apart when Kevin sat on it. It seemed like an omen for my whole stay on this planet; I was ready to hand back my guild ring. Kevin only laughed and said I'd never known humiliation unless I'd been seasick on Atlantis. He made me feel a lot better."

Lance moved up and took Tam's hand. "On the ship, I tried to take Kevin's coral box. He caught me, but he never told anyone else. He said if I was clever enough to pick pockets, I was clever enough to make my way in a guild, and he suggested me for the job in the stable."

One by one people stepped forward with their small remembrances. "Kevin danced with me," Hashti choked out when her turn came. She took her place in the chain, with a spurt of panic. Had she said "Kevin died for me?" No, that was only her guilty conscience.

Kevin's family was far away on another world, oblivious to his fate. In their place, Gay had sat the vigil. Now he came forward to accept a small packet of Kevin's private treasures. Joining hands with mourners on either side, Gay closed the circle.

Approaching dawn whitened the eastern horizon. "From dust are born the suns, the seas, and life," Big Red declared.

"Dust we are, to dust we shall return," Anna answered.

"It swirls in hope and song, and then swirls on," Big Red intoned.

"But dust does not forget the dream that stirs it," Anna promised. She faced east and raised her arms, catching the first rays of the rising sun. Then in one deft motion she lowered her hands and lit the pyre. Fire roared through the tinder-dry wood. Kevin's body vanished in flames.

Choking with grief, Hashti could barely swallow a token bite of the funeral breakfast. She told Lance to take his time. Then she headed for the barn, eyes cast down, willing that no one would speak to her. As soon as she was out of earshot of the crowd, she began to sob. Why Kevin? What had he done to anyone? And what part had Hashti played in his death?

Ross walked into the stable half an hour later. "Tiger Wrestler?" he called.

"Over here," she replied from her nest in Betsy's manger, where she sat twisting and untwisting the short fringes of her scarf.

Ross leaned against the stall partition, all the twinkle gone from his gray eyes. Diffidently he offered her a packet. "You didn't eat much. Here's a muffin."

"No thank you," Hashti answered. "I'm not hungry."

"Why not?" Ross asked.

She stared at her scarf fringes. Ross lifted her chin with a gnarled finger, forcing her to meet his eyes. "I know you liked him," Ross said. "There's nothing wrong with that."

"I killed him," Hashti muttered. "It was for me he went out alone."

Ross didn't ask for an explanation. There are no secrets in a camp, they say. He let go of Hashti's chin, shaking his head. "Don't be silly, Tiger Wrestler. At least you saved Gay. Kevin was a marked man."

"I sent him out to die," Hashti persisted, too depressed for logic.

"No," Ross said with haunted eyes and an odd catch in his voice. "You didn't send him out to die, Teamstress. I did. I had all the clues in front of me, but still I let Kevin shoot a tiger, and then I let him keep hunting. I should have shot a tiger myself, when I first suspected a problem. As soon as the wife and I looked at it, we'd have known. Instead Kevin killed the tiger—and Kevin paid the price."

Ross's obvious pain jolted Hashti from her own sorrow. "That's stupid," she told the First-Inner. "How could you know? You told me yourself there was no precedent for the tigers being intelligent."

Ross's face remained dark. "It's First-In's job to see beyond precedent. But we blew it. We were blind as a bunch of company bureaucrats. It was so obvious that this planet fit the classic pattern. The big cats belonged here. We never looked twice at them, just skunked them away." His rough, strong hand, resting on the edge of the manger, clenched in impotent frustration.

Awkwardly, Hashti reached for it. "Don't second-guess yourself. You put the pieces together before anyone else did."

Silence stretched between them. Hashti felt Ross's pulse and her own where their hands touched. She wanted to let go, but Ross gripped as if drawing support from her. Finally his gaze dropped to meet hers. "All right," he granted, his lips curved in a sad smile. "Guilt gets us nowhere. I'll quit blaming myself if you will, Hashti."

It was the first time he'd ever called her by name. They looked away from each other, unsure how to break the tension. Then Ross let go of her hand and held out the muffin again. "Hungry now? You'd better fortify yourself. You've got some challenging work ahead."

She paused with the muffin half into her mouth. "What now?"

"I'll talk to the camp tonight. Everyone's frightened and angry, understandably, but shooting must be banned. At the expense of logging, if necessary. The rest is up to you."

"What 'rest'?" she asked, with an uneasy feeling in her stomach.

Ross's gray eyes locked on Hashti's gold ones. "For whatever reason, Khan favors you. So you're the one who has to learn who tigers are and how we should deal with them. I'll help all I can. But you're on the line."

"I'm no First-Inner!" Only a Circle member could communicate with aliens. Or so she had always been told.

"Hashti. Forget the First-In mystique. Aliens are only as different as your fear makes them. You have more in common with the tigers than you do with your horses. Even without technology, the tigers hunt, mate, teach their children to speak, just as your own ancestors did. You can bridge the gap."

Hashti opened her mouth to reply. She was interrupted by a shout outside. "Tiger!" It was Sweat's voice.

Hashti could not see Sweat from her position in the manger. But Ross, looking out the wide stable doors, went pale. "Oh Lord! Who gave him that thing?" He sprinted down the corridor, shouting, "Put it away, Sweat! Don't shoot! That's Khan! He won't hurt you!"

Hashti scrambled out of the manger and ran after Ross. Sweat was standing on the path down from camp, ninety feet from the barn. Khan stood frozen by a couple of blackpine saplings, a stone's throw from Sweat. The man had a rifle leveled at Khan's black-masked face. Ignoring Ross's shouts, Sweat fired. Snow spattered a few feet to Khan's left.

Ross closed in on the frightened logger. "Drop the gun!" he repeated, reaching for it. Startled, Sweat swung toward Ross, his grip tightening in surprise. Hashti screamed even before she heard the shot.

The impact threw Ross backward into the snow. He doubled up, rolled over, and tried to rise as Hashti knelt by him. He pulled himself up by her shoulders, then collapsed with a groan in her arms. Horrified, she felt blood soak her sweater.

Sweat stared at them, panicked. "I didn' mean to! It

was an accident!" he blubbered, gesticulating with the gun still in his hands.

"Point that thing somewhere else!" Hashti hissed.

Even as she spoke, Khan shot across the snow and tackled Sweat from the rear. Embracing the man's neck and shoulders with his forepaws, the cat pulled him down in a deadly embrace. As the two hit the ground, Khan kicked viciously with his rear claws. Fabric tore, bone shattered, the gun went spinning across the road. Sweat howled in pain and terror. Hashti yelled too. "No, Khan! Let him go!"

With a final kick that knocked the breath out of Sweat, Khan pushed him away. Twisting expertly onto his feet, he snarled at the man in the snow and trotted toward Hashti. Men ran down the road from the camp, shouting. Among them was Gay, gun in hand. "Get out of here!" Hashti yelled at Khan, reaching for an iceball with her free hand and pelting it at the cat. "Go!"

He pulled up short as the icy missile landed, and shook his head at Hashti with a confused snort. Then, glancing over his shoulder at the approaching mob, he ran.

The whole thing had taken perhaps fifteen seconds. Ross still slumped against Hashti, gasping for breath. She laid him down in the snow and fumbled with the buttons of his plaid shirt. "Try to stop the bleeding," he mumbled, his words slurring.

"I'm trying," she answered through clenched teeth. She had her hand under his sweater now, her fingers slipping in slick blood. The hole was easy to find. A pressure point to staunch the bleeding was less apparent. The blood welled from deep within his chest.

He tried to speak again but the words were lost in coughing. Crimson spray spattered across the snow. The wind bit coldly at tears on Hashti's cheeks. Ross's chest rose and fell with a horrible gurgling sound.

Then Anna came stumbling down the path, moving faster on her bad ankle than most women do on two good legs. "Good luck, Tiger Wrestler," Ross whispered weakly. Hashti bowed her head in promise, and withdrew to give the doctor room.

# CHAPTER EIGHT

THE WORLD MOVED IN SLOW MOTION. HASHTI STOOD
helplessly by, ready should Anna ask assistance. But
there was nothing to do. Anna maintained a professional
calm as she tried to keep her husband from suffocating in
his own blood. She even managed to smile and kiss him
when, with his last shred of rationality, Ross looked up
at her and mouthed, "Goodbye." He died in his wife's
arms, there on the snowpacked path.

Anna broke into shrill keening. Hashti laid a tentative
arm around Anna's shoulders. Did Anna even feel it?

Meanwhile Sweat had staggered to his feet. Shards of
bone poked through his torn sleeve. Big Red looked
briefly at the tattered arm and dismissed Sweat into
Gay's custody. The boss sent two men for a sled. They
rolled Ross's body onto it. Anna rose to follow, but
crumpled again as her leg refused to support her weight.
Big Red scooped her up and carried her home like a
child.

Hashti's own grief, temporarily numbed by shock,
welled up as she walked back into the stable. Too dis-
traught to find her usual solace in small activities, she
paced the corridor. Hercules stretched his gray nose
over the divider and snorted at her. She shook her head
at him and kept pacing. She could not bring herself to
take off her blood-soaked clothes. They were her last tie

to the living Ross. To take them off would be to acknowl-
edge that he had really died.

She looked a pretty mess, then, when Lance came in.
He glanced diffidently away from her bloody clothes and
tear-streaked face. "The Boss wants to talk to you, Miz
Hashti. He's in the doctor's cabin."

Hashti tried to say, "Thanks for telling me." It disin-
tegrated into a case of hiccups. The absurdity of the re-
sulting sentence brought her to laughter.

"Are you all right?" Lance asked warily.

She rubbed the tears from her eyes. "I'll—hic!—I'll
be fine, Lance. I'm just—hic!—just a little—hic!—a
little upset. What happened—hic!—happened to Sweat?"

"Nothing, yet. His arm is broken a couple places and
I think some ribs are cracked. Doctor Anna just finished
sewing him up and settin' the arm."

Putting together the man who'd shot her husband? "I
hope she went light—" she hiccuped "—light on the anesthetic. Thanks for the message, Lance. I'll go right up."

He eyed Hashti uncertainly. "You should prob'ly
wash first. You look like you have war paint on."

She smiled shakily back. "I will. Can you keep an eye
on things down here?"

"No problem." He picked up a stiff brush and went to
work on Betsy's bur-matted tail.

Hashti scrubbed her face in water which had grown
icy, and put on clean clothes. Then, taking a deep breath
and squaring her shoulders, she set out. The snow lay
churned and bloody where Ross had fallen. Hashti
walked wide around the spot, fixing her eyes on the
silver-gray wood of his old cabin.

Big Red met her at the door. "Sweat's in the office,"
he explained quietly. "I need to talk to you before I talk
to him. Come in."

Reluctantly Hashti entered. On the couch in the clinic

room, to her left, lay Ross's body, a blanket thrown hastily over it. Anna, wearing a blood-streaked scrub gown, sat at the maple table in the center room, surrounded by surgical tools and scents of antiseptic and plaster. Her face was buried in her arms. She lifted it when Big Red laid a tender hand on her shoulder. "Hashti's here. You don't need to listen to this, Anna."

The dead man's wife acknowledged Hashti with a nod that was scarcely more than a fluttering of her eyelids, then looked back up at Big Red. "I'll stay. I have to know what really happened."

He sighed and shook his head. "Then let's get you properly settled." He swung Anna's chair to face Hashti, and hovered like a fussy nurse as the doctor propped her bandaged foot on a bench and packed it with ice bags. Only after he'd fluffed a pillow and tucked it behind Anna did Big Red turn back to Hashti, his face grim. "I've heard Sweat's version of the story. Yours had better be better."

Still standing just inside the door, Hashti shifted nervously. "What do you want to know, sir?" Even in good humor this was a man to be reckoned with. Hashti was afraid of him now.

It must have shown on her face, for he shook his head as if to clear it and motioned her to a chair. "Start at the beginning, but sit down first." He hesitated. "You want a drink?"

She did. Two exquisite crystal glasses stood on the shelf above the library terminal—Ross and Anna's pledge cups, Hashti thought a little wildly. Big Red filled them with mead from a flask in the corner cupboard. He seemed to know exactly where everything was. But of course he'd lived in this cabin during that first year of exploration. He handed one glass to Hashti and the other to Anna.

Anna set hers aside, untouched. Hashti sipped cautiously from her own. The mead bit her tongue. Red pulled an armchair around to face her. "Tell us what happened."

Hashti wet her lips. "He—Mister Ross—was down in the barn talking to me, when we heard Sweat shout. I was sitting in Betsy's manger; I couldn't see what was happening. But Mister Ross took off down the corridor, yelling at Sweat not to shoot. I followed as fast as I could. Sweat was standing thirty yards from the barn door. Khan was crouching by the two little blackpines. Sweat fired and missed. Ross tried to grab the gun, Sweat swung around—" She paused, words blocked by the lump in her throat. Big Red waited, his face unreadable. Hashti swallowed and went on, "—and the gun went off. I think it was an accident."

Anna had picked up her glass. Now she set it down, sloshing mead onto the table. Big Red balled his right hand into a fist and pressed it against the palm of his left hand. "What happened next?"

"Mister Ross tried to get up. I caught him as he fell again. Sweat was waving the gun around yelling that he didn't mean to do it. The tiger took him from behind and kicked the gun out of his hands. Khan was coming over to me when we heard everyone running down from camp. I yelled and Khan ran. I tried to stop Ross's bleeding but I couldn't. Finally Doctor Anna came—"

Hashti's interrogator lifted his hand and shook his head, silencing her. Anna had buried her face again. Her shoulders shook. Coals settled in the stove. Big Red spoke again, very quietly. "This tiger, Khan. He's the one you played with out at the Rock?"

Hashti nodded. Big Red must have heard the results of her trip. He watched her intently. "Why was Khan coming toward you, after he dropped Sweat?"

"He wanted to—" Hashti paused. She'd been going to say, "He wanted to see if I was all right." How did she know? It had all happened so fast!

The boss read her hesitation correctly. "We know you can't be sure," he said. "Give us your best guess."

Go with your hunches, Ross had said. "I think he was worried about me," Hashti answered, feeling foolish.

"Gaylord said the tiger was attacking you," Big Red countered.

"No!" Hashti flashed back. "He was—I don't know what he wanted, but Khan wasn't attacking. I've seen him attack. This was different." She glared defiantly at Big Red.

"I believe you," he said, his eyes still measuring her. "You agree with Ross, then, about the tigers?"

"I do," Hashti answered. "Khan's never hurt me. And he taught me some of his words."

Big Red's gaze didn't swerve. "You have to tell the camp that."

Hashti, still in shock from Ross's death, felt anything but ready to step into his shoes. "I'm just a horse trainer," she pleaded. "Can't you tell them?"

Anna listened quietly, drawing her finger along the rim of her empty glass. Big Red shook his head. "No. You were close to both Kevin and Ross. No one will think you don't care. And only you have played with a tiger. You have to tell them."

Her sense of inadequacy was irrelevant. There could be only one answer. "Yes, sir."

"Tonight at dinner. This has to be cleared up. Shooting intelligent creatures is not only wrong, but damn dangerous."

Anna cleared her throat. "Gaylord won't like it, Hashti."

Big Red nodded agreement. "You're the one person he might listen to."

Mead and apprehension mingled to give the young woman a sense of unreality. Inside she protested, what have I ever done to deserve this? Aloud she said, "I'll do the best I can, Mister Red."

He smiled grimly. "I know you will. So will I. And now I have to talk to Sweat. I'll see you tonight."

Hashti entered City Hall that evening with a racing pulse and sweaty palms. Ross's hastily erected bier waited in the square, though his body remained in the cabin. Sweat had been closeted with Big Red for two hours that afternoon and rumor said it had not been pleasant. Now the laborer was back on his bench, playing his injuries for all they were worth. An excited buzz hung over his table.

Company table was achingly quiet. Six folk had sat there last night—Big Red, Anna and Ross, Lael and Georgia, and the reclusive chemist Mister Jack. Now Ross was dead, and Anna sat vigil over him. Their absence weighed heavily.

Hashti took her seat at the guild table. Its occupants greeted her with the diffidence due a woman who'd embraced two fresh corpses in the last thirty hours. The puddle of tryp gravy in her bowl turned Hashti's stomach. Could she eat at all in her state of grief and nervousness? An academic question. The porridge had not yet come to her when Gaylord, who was not serving tonight, rose from his place. A hush whispered its way around the room.

Gay faced squarely toward the Company table. "Mister Red!" He did not wait for an answer. "Two men have died now." There it was, the plain fact. A mutter rippled outward. Gay hushed it with a move of his hand. "When do we start defending ourselves?" he asked.

The boss was alert, sizing up the challenge, but he did not deign to rise. "We'll discuss that after dinner tonight. There are complications."

Gay stayed on his feet. "There have been enough complications already, sir. Let's discuss it now."

Red's hands were folded quietly on the table in front of him. The softer his voice became, the more menace it carried. "Very well."

"It's time to shoot tigers," Gaylord said.

Hashti's chair tumbled to the floor behind her as she rose. "You can't do that, Gay!"

Startled, he half turned to face her. "Why not?"

"They're intelligent!"

He stared. "You still believe that? After your playmate tried to kill you this afternoon?"

"He wasn't attacking me. He wanted to see if I was all right." It sounded incredible, even to Hashti.

Sweat stood, dramatically favoring his sore ribs. "He wanted to see if we were all right," he repeated, tapping his cast. "Look how he checked on me! He'd have ripped you to bits, girl, if I hadn't given him such a scare."

Sweat thought he'd rescued her from Khan? It took Hashti two tries to find her voice. "If you hadn't been waving that gun around, he'd never have bothered you."

Sweat started to answer. Gay, aware that Sweat's support could cut both ways, intervened. "Ross had a theory that the tigers might be intelligent," he explained to the hushed hall, "although the First-In Circle spent a year here with no such suspicions." He challenged Big Red with a sideways glance. Big Red listened impassively. Gay went on.

"Hashti told me about it yesterday, just before Kevin was killed." Men stirred uneasily at Kevin's name. Gay smiled at Hashti as if to say he was really on her side. "I

knew that if the tigers were intelligent, we shouldn't
shoot them. So I checked into the matter." Lael's lips
curved slightly as Gay continued. "The Frontier Code
gives criteria for possible intelligence. The first require-
ment is manipulative ability. Tigers do not have it."

"Mister Ross knew that!" Hashti said. "That's why
the First-In team didn't suspect anything. But then Mister Ross and Doctor Anna dissected Kevin's tigress.
They found a smart brain and a nervous system wired for
speech, even though the tigers don't have hands or anything."

"According to Code guidelines, the tigers can't be
smart," Lael reemphasized.

"Maybe the Code lawyers weren't smart either," Big
Red growled.

Lael shot him a look of pure hatred. "You're our expert on other races," she told him. "Name an exception
to the Code rule."

"There's one on this planet."

"Not proven. Inadmissible evidence. Any other instance?"

"Not yet, but—"

"I rest my case," Lael said, smiling at Gaylord.

"No," Big Red said. "Check Section 17 of your precious Frontier Code. It gives First-In acting authority on
the frontier unless specifically countermanded by a duly
constituted treaty tribunal. I claim that authority. Effective now, anyone who shoots or otherwise picks trouble
with a tiger stands in violation of the Orion treaty."

Lael's eyes widened, then narrowed. "You can't do
that, Red."

"The hell I can't. I speak for the Circle."

"You haven't got a Circle," she said. "Only an interracial team qualifies. Your freak friends have all left. So

you, legally, are only a consultant contracted to Oldearth Company."

Hashti didn't understand the ramifications. Big Red clearly did. His face flushed to the color of his hair. "Then as adjustment consultant to Oldearth, I forbid the killing of tigers. In the interest of continued lumber production, of course."

Gay spoke. "Who cares about lumber production? It's a losing fight and we all know it. Let's do something that pays. Those pelts will fetch ten ounces apiece on Valhalla."

Red lost his composure entirely. "You can't!"

Gay lifted his chin. "We can. Forget the sweetsap wood. Oldearth skims the profit off that. On skins, Finder's Claim puts the profits in our own pockets. At worst, we'll make the woods safe for logging. More likely, we'll decide logging's not worth the bother."

"That's not what we're chartered for," Hashti protested.

Lael smiled. "No, but the company can't hold us responsible for more than our fare home. And store debts, of course. Both of which would be covered by the profit from a load of skins." Hashti had always assumed that Lael, as the Company's legal agent, favored its interests. But perhaps she hated it as much as everyone else did.

The men, prepared beforehand, were nodding. Hashti could smell their rebellion. To folk frightened of tigers and desperate to beat the Company's game, Gay's straightforward proposal sounded attractive. But Hashti knew he was wrong. "I tell you, the tigers can talk!"

"Lover's quarrel!" somebody stage-whispered. Scattered laughter broke out.

Gay himself frowned at the intrusion. In a gentle, affectionate voice he told the trainer, "We all know you have a magic touch with animals, Hashti. That's why

you're such a superb barn boss. If there's anyone who
could play with a tiger and walk away unscratched, it's
you. But the rest of us need to defend ourselves."

How do you fight someone who dismisses you with
compliments? Hashti raised her voice, careful not to
sound hysterical. "Khan's not an animal. He's been trying to communicate with me, and we're getting somewhere. Are you going to come in with guns blazing like a
cheap novel?"

"It will give your talking tigers something to discuss,
dear," Gay said. Men laughed again.

Hashti entertained a brief fantasy of throwing her
plate at Gay. But that would only play into his game.
Instead, she schooled her voice to coolness. "Kevin shot
two tigers," she reminded everyone. They quieted.
"Then the tigers killed Kevin. Do you think that was
coincidence?"

A nearly imperceptible shadow of doubt flickered
across Gay's face. For a moment, Hashti thought he'd
repent. Then the muscles in his neck stiffened. "Maybe
not. Ross said even animals know their enemies. We'd
better teach the tigers to respect us."

"That's a big lesson to teach with only twelve guns,"
Big Red said.

"There are other ways to kill animals," Gay answered. "You know them better than I. If you cared a rip
about this camp, you'd help us set traps or something.
But why bother? You're First-In. You're guaranteed
your pay." He turned his back on the Company table and
faced the commons. "The rest of us live or die on what
profit we can find here. I say there's more in tigers than
in trees."

An ugly mutter swept the room. The workers had respected Big Red. Man to man, none would defy him

even now. But Gaylord had rallied them, and Gay wasn't backing down.

Big Red made a final try. "Let Anna tell you what she found dissecting that tiger."

Gay had learned politics in a ruthless school. "That won't be necessary," he answered over his shoulder. "We know how First-Inners stick together." Anna's credibility evaporated with Big Red's.

"Hang yourselves, then," Big Red said. "But don't expect me to help." He walked out of the hall.

Hashti, too, made a last attempt. "Give me a week to talk to the tigers before you start shooting."

Gay shook his head. "No. Enough men have been attacked trying to defend you. You stay away from tigers."

Like Red, Hashti had had all she could stomach. She wanted no part in what would follow. Throwing her napkin at her bowl of congealed gravy, she headed for the door.

The First-Inner was gone when Hashti reached the entryway. Voices buzzed behind her as she pulled on her coat and rummaged through the pile for her boots. She was winding her scarf to protect her face from the bitter wind outside, when a hand fell on her shoulder. She started violently. "Where do you think you're going?" Gaylord asked in a voice more concerned than angry.

Still stinging from his jibes, she knocked his hand away. "Out to run off with the tigers," she told him. "I'm sentimental, you know. No sense."

He looked down. "I'm sorry, Hashti. But I can't let you destroy the camp."

"What?"

"You know the lumber operation has a snowball's chance of success. Oldearth rigged it that way. A third of the men in this camp are company debtors already. The rest will be, and you too, if we can't outsmart Oldearth. The tigers are our hope."

"You can't shoot intelligent aliens for skins!"

He held her at arm's length, his face in shadow, only his eyes catching the light as they searched her face. "You don't really believe that."

"How can I not believe it? Ross was convinced. So are Anna and Big Red. And they haven't even met Khan. I tell you, I talked to him! Gay, you can't start shooting now." A tear of anger escaped down Hashti's cheek.

Gay's fingers dug into her shoulders, reawakening the ache of her injury. "Snap out of it, Hashti! You've been through hell the last two days, but don't fly into a fantasy world! You heard what Lael and Big Red said. The tigers don't fit the criteria for intelligence. They haven't got hands and they haven't got tools. They're impressive animals, but they're just animals."

Gay was beyond persuasion. "Let go of me," Hashti told him. "I am perfectly sane and you are doing something that all of us are going to regret. I don't want to hear about it. Goodnight."

He took her elbow in an iron grip. "Are you going down to the barn?" he asked icily.

"Where else would I go?" She tried to jerk herself away.

He held tight. "Stay in the bunkhouse. Stay with Lael. Stay with Anna. Or I'll go to the barn with you, after the meeting. But don't go alone. I don't want to find you in the snow like we found Kevin."

"You think I want you in the stable with me? Forget it." She was glad to see him wince. "The tigers have had their chance to hurt me. They didn't. Now let me go."

Gay shook her lightly. "Damn it, you're crazy!"

Glancing over his shoulder at the door to the main hall, he continued more softly. "I can't stand here arguing with you. I've got to finish what I started. Will you promise to behave? Or do I have to put you under guard to keep you safe? I can and I will, Hashti."

It was no idle threat. Gaylord ran the camp now. The more Hashti fought him, the less her chance was of convincing him. "All right," she sighed. "I'll go to Anna."

Gay looked skeptically at her, doubtless thinking he had won too easily. "You promise?"

"I promise," Hashti said. Gay let her go, but stood in the doorway watching her until she turned the corner toward the doctor's cabin.

Hashti found Anna in her rocker, small and frail among her quilts, her foot propped up and cold-packed. Through the clinic door Hashti glimpsed Ross's body, washed and dressed for tomorrow. First-In's formal white silk partly counteracted the pallor of his face. Still, he looked very dead. Turning her eyes away from him, Hashti apologized for intruding on Anna's vigil. Then she came to the point. "I need your help."

Anna sat forward in her chair. "Gay fought you?"

"Fought and won," Hashti admitted. "They're going to shoot tigers."

"Where's Big Red?"

"I don't know. He walked out just ahead of me."

Anna leaned back in her chair. "He'll be here soon enough. What sort of help did you want?"

Hashti swallowed. "I need your pack and camping stuff."

Bright dark eyes assessed her. "Where are you going?"

"To find Khan. We've got to learn enough about tigers to make our case! At the very least I've got to get Khan away before he gets shot."

As Hashti finished her sentence, an urgent rap sounded on the door. Red entered without waiting for a response. He nodded briskly at the guildswoman. "Hashti! I should have guessed you'd be here."

"She wants to go out after Khan," Anna said.

Red's eyebrows went up. "So? Let's talk about it. But I have something to do first." He dug in his pocket and pulled out a fistful of metal parts, which he dumped on the floor.

"What are those?" Hashti asked.

"Firing pins," he answered curtly. "And so forth. Guns won't do Gay much good if they won't shoot. Anna, where's Ross's gun?"

"Peg in the bedroom," she answered.

Big Red strode through the doorway on Hashti's right and returned in seconds with a rifle in his hands. He pulled out a small tool and began disassembling the gun. Soon he had added another set to his pile of parts.

"All of them, Red?" Anna asked.

"All of them. If I leave even one," Big Red replied, "Gay will screw my thumbs to find out where it is." He fetched a hammer from a shelf, smiling grimly at Anna. "One thing First-In never taught us was sabotage. But it seems fairly easy." He stooped down and methodically smashed the parts, then scooped the mangled bits into a cloth pouch. "This ought to crimp a certain gentleman's plans. Now—what is Hashti proposing?"

"I've got to go out and find Khan."

For the first time Big Red really looked at her, surprise giving way to thoughtfulness and then approval in his eyes. "That's the best idea I've heard tonight! We can learn the language better on his turf. Are you sure we can find him?"

We? "He was looking for me this morning. I can't

guarantee anything, but I think if I go out and wait, he'll come."

"Is there anything special we need to take?" the big man asked, still squatting on the floor. "Anything that'd help us demonstrate good intentions?"

"Red," Anna interjected softly. "You can't go with her."

He frowned up at his Circlemate. "Why not?"

"Because you're boss of this camp."

Big Red shook his head emphatically. "Oh, no. I never asked to be boss of this circus. Gaylord wants it, he's got it."

Anna stood her ground. "You know better than that. Gay has the debtors in his pocket—they've nothing to lose. But first-timers will have second thoughts about jumping contract. Gay has to keep them occupied. You know he'll decide to continue logging, and tomorrow morning he'll ask your help with it."

Big Red smiled coldly. "But I won't agree. I'm playing all-or-nothing. Until he drops the skin business, Gay's in charge. He can handle the mice in the kitchen, the hole in the forge furnace, the cracker crumbs Joe dropped in Dak's bunk, Cy saying Lael jimmied the books, Bennie's snoring waking Luiz, Ivan's three-hour lunches, and the itch powder in the rinse water." His smile warmed as he ran through this catalog. "And meanwhile, Hashti and I will be in the bush singing to tigers."

Anna shook her head. "No. Gay lacks imagination, but he's competent. You leave him undisturbed, the camp will rally around him and a lot of tigers will die. You have to be sitting on your porch smirking, if we're going to keep things properly unsettled."

Big Red sighed. "You shouldn't violate a man's fantasies, Anna. I'd much rather leave the mess behind."

"Sorry. But I can't do it for you."

Reluctantly he agreed. "Back to Plan A, then. I stay here and subvert." His attention shifted to Hashti. "It was a good idea. But Anna's right, we can't go."

Hashti had listened with growing hope, but now she saw that she, too, was back to Plan A. "It's all right," she told Big Red, trying to convince herself. "Khan prefers meeting me alone anyway."

Anna jerked upright. "You can't go by yourself!" She glanced briefly toward the clinic where her husband's pet rabbit nosed curiously at his body. "Oh, Ross, we need you now!" Then Anna assumed her best didactic voice. "This is the frontier, Hashti. We're playing for keeps. However tired you may be of hearing it, this planet will kill you if you don't respect it. It was a good idea, but since neither Red nor I can—"

"Excuse me," Hashti interrupted. "I'm not asking your permission, Doctor Anna. I'm only asking your help."

Red smiled slightly, his eyes shifting from Hashti to Anna.

"We can't let her go," Anna told him. "You and I are trained in cross-racial communication and wilderness survival. Hashti's inexperienced on both counts. It's morally indefensible to send her out alone."

"You'll have to stop me, then," Hashti told her. "Gay's already offered to put me in custody. If you want to keep me here, you better get him to do it. Otherwise I'm going—with or without your help." She half hoped they would lock her up.

But Big Red grinned and nodded, with a mixture of amusement and respect. "All right, spitfire. If you're going anyway, you might as well be properly outfitted. Pull in your claws, and let's see what we can find for you."

Anna's brow was still furrowed. "This is madness, Red! She's not trained for it!"

"You've watched the woman," he answered coolly. "Admit she's got what it takes. You were the one who pulled her file—you know she's camped in the Carolina mountains. Coping with snow won't be entirely new to her. And she obviously knows how to deal with tigers. Furthermore you're ill positioned to protest. I know what madcap tricks you and Ross pulled when you were old enough to know better!" He locked gazes with her. "You're just jealous because you can't go."

Anna smiled briefly at Big Red's allusion to her past. "Maybe. Or maybe she reminds me too much of myself. For God's sake, Hashti, be careful out there."

Red glanced anxiously at his beacon. "I'd better get out of here. As soon as they finish talking, Gay will look for his gun. Then he'll look for me, and if I'm not home, this is the next place he'll come. I don't want you implicated in my initiative with the firing pins, and we certainly don't want Gay to find Hashti with a pack on her back." He frowned at Anna's bandaged foot. "Can you two manage packing? Or should I come by later?"

"We'll be fine," the doctor answered, reaching for her crutches. "Get you gone."

He paused long enough to give Hashti a bear hug. "Good luck, friend. Anna's right—be damned careful. I don't want anything more on my conscience than I've already got."

"I'll be fine," Hashti assured him, wishing she believed it herself. "Just keep Gaylord off my back."

Red winked conspiratorially. "Gay will have his hands full of other things, I assure you."

As Red left, Anna summoned Hashti into the clinic. Hashti barely noticed her anticopper injection, unnerved as she was by the corpse on Anna's examining couch.

Ross's earring was gone. Anna must have kept it as a memento.

The doctor, her face twisted with tears, rummaged in the cupboard above the body. "Don't lose these," she warned, handing Hashti a small red packet and a blue one. "Blue's pure tryp, take one a day if for some reason you decide to eat local food. They're big but they go down easier than gravy." Thank heaven for small favors, thought Hashti. "Red's a chelator. If you're out after your shot expires, take one pill with each meal of native stuff."

Anna slammed the cupboard shut. "Everything else is in the bedroom. Let's get out of here before I crack."

They spent the next two hours gathering and packing equipment. The testers scurried and chattered, upset by a stranger's presence. Anna talked nonstop the whole time, explaining the uses of each item, giving tips on comfort and survival. Hashti could barely lift the final package.

Anna eyed it unhappily. "This is a minimal outfit, Hashti. But we've got to keep it light or you'll exhaust yourself, and then you've had it."

Hashti looked again at the minimal outfit. "Could I take the motorsled?'

"Not if you've never driven one. It takes practice to handle the thing. It can't go through dense brush, and it's easy to flip on a hidden log or crossing a ravine. Besides, the whole camp would hear you leaving, and we don't want Gay knowing you're gone."

"How long do you think you can keep it from him?"

"If you get out of camp without being seen, and beyond the logging area, I can promise at least a day and a half. I'll tell folk you're here. They'll be too busy to look further. By the time Gay finds out, maybe he'll listen to reason."

"What if somebody finds my trail?"

"I don't think they'll notice it, since they aren't looking for it." Anna took a deep, disciplined breath. "Let me worry about covering for you. You concentrate on talking to tigers. Go ahead and get dressed."

Hashti exchanged her outerwear for lighter, tougher, explorer's equipment. Anna watched in silence, intervening only to steady the pack as Hashti struggled into the harness. Hashti pulled her knit cap down over her ears. "Ready?" Anna asked.

Hashti nodded.

"Come here, then." She led Hashti back to the clinic room. "Take off your beacon."

Hashti obeyed. Anna reached gently across Ross's body to unclip the First-In beacon from his sash. "Usually a Circle beacon goes to the pyre with its maker. But you need this far more than Ross does." She cradled it in her hand, showing Hashti how to operate it. "It has two-way voice transmission with a range of about forty miles. You won't need to go nearly that far. Just get beyond reach of Gay's hunters, then make yourself a base camp. The beacon has a finite power supply, so don't use it for idle chatter, but do call whenever you need our help. Once we can prove the tigers' intelligence, we can overrule the Guidelines, bring you back, and work from here." She handed Hashti a second small object which clipped onto the beacon. "This is a data condenser. Use it to record all the words you learn, and anything else important, right away. That'll help fix it in your mind. Transmit your results to us each evening. That way, if—" Anna hesitated, then went on. "If you don't come back, we'll have something to work with."

Soberly Hashti pocketed the beacon. Anna planted a benedictory kiss on her forehead. "The camp's quiet now. Good luck, Hashti. Don't let the tigers trip on you."

With unexpected tears in her eyes, Hashti returned her adviser's hug. Then, stomach fluttering, she stepped out into the night.

# CHAPTER NINE

❧❧❧

BOTH MOONS WERE UP, ONE NEARLY FULL. THE TEMPER-
ature had dropped again, and snow squeaked underfoot
as Hashti hurried to the stable, seeing Gaylord in every
shadow. She groped through her dark room for the few
personal items she needed. Getting her "minimal kit" on
again was a trick. Hashti couldn't lift it with one hand.
Finally she stood it on her bed and backed into the
shoulder straps. She wondered how she would accom-
plish this maneuver in the woods.

Back in the corridor, Hercules whinnied a greeting
and stretched his nose towards Hashti. "Quiet, big fellow," she told him, holding out a wisp of hay. "Somebody might wonder who you're talking to. Wish me luck,
and tell Lance to take good care of you." He slobbered
over the hay as if it were an oatmeal cookie. Hashti gave
his ears a final affectionate rub, then slipped through the
big double doors. She strapped on her skis, double-
checked her load, and took the sleigh road north.

Gliding along a firm surface with no awkward ob-
structions, she made good time. But two miles from
home the road ended. Now she had to fight her way
through virgin forest. Brambles and crusty snow dragged
at her feet, making her long for a pair of homely,
dependable snowshoes. Skis held no advantage for a
lone traveler breaking trail in the dark. Only when she

143

made a base camp and confined her travel to established trails would skis come into their own.

It was a long way from here to there. Hashti had gotten out of Swamp City undetected. Could she make it through these woods without blinding herself on a protruding branch? Could she locate Khan? No. Would he locate her? A blue glint flashed at the edge of her vision. Hashti's head snapped around. Two sapphire disks blazed in the moonlight. Eyes!

They moved up, then down, in a wide arc. The young woman heard a stirring, just a whisper of motion in the night. "Khan?" she called tentatively. The eyes froze. Hashti tried a whuff.

Snow crunched, branches rustled, and the eyes disappeared. Noise betrayed the animal's progress, and finally she glimpsed its fleeing silhouette in a snowy clearing. A deer!

Hashti tried to explain to her pounding heart that she had only imagined threat. What was she doing out here? Was she ready to encounter the wild in the wild? So far, she'd thought only about her hope of meeting Khan. Did she really want to? What had he intended as he dropped Sweat and turned toward Hashti? Whatever it was, she'd responded by shying a snowball at him. Where did she stand with the black-faced tiger?

Fear, having entered her mind, took over. What about the other tigers who roamed these woods? Did Sabra, the champion pouncer, lurk in wait? Or the huge male with the scarred foot who'd jumped Kevin and dragged his slain body to the road? Had his bloodlust been slaked by the murder? When would she meet *that* tiger?

The hours dragged on, and so did Hashti. Every drop of snow from a branch sounded like a paw-fall. Every icicle catching the moonlight seemed to be a tiger's eye. She had a continual sensation that something was following her, but could never confirm it. Ross's beacon told her that in the weary six hours since she'd left the road, she'd put only four additional miles between herself and the camp. Then, an hour before dawn, the encounter she'd been fearing befell her.

Eyes again, a pale emerald color. They were off to her right, at a distance unguessable in the dark, swinging steadily from side to side. Hashti told herself it was another deer.

Her brain envisioned a tiger walking toward her, head weaving to balance the motion of the great forequarters. It superimposed the vision on the green disks—a perfect fit. Hashti froze. So did the eyes. Time suspended itself for a long frosty moment. Then the eyes dipped, wavered, and accelerated directly toward Hashti.

Encumbered by her skis, she could not jump aside. Desperately she shrank to a crouch, hands flung over her face as if they could protect it. At the same time, a deafening roar exploded behind her. Snow showered her as something hurtled by on a collision course with her attacker.

The two animals hit head-on twenty feet away, in a snarl of twisting shadows and flashing teeth. They rolled through the drifts, clawing and spitting, then separated and faced off, heavy tails still lashing. Rapid singing echoed through the woods. Hashti stayed crouching, terrified.

The tiger to the left leaped sideways, toward her. Almost simultaneously the other tiger jumped to block him. Both had trouble moving in the deep snow. The second tiger took a stand directly in front of her, facing outward. At this distance, even by starlight, Hashti could see a familiar black mask. How long had Khan been following her?

Ears flattened, the opposing tiger snarled and sang.

Khan bugled a short, fanfarelike reply, repeating it twice. The attacker lowered his head, chattered a few notes, and began to back away.

Hashti stayed squatting, and Khan stood guard, until the other tiger turned and trotted off into the blackness. Then Khan, his eyes still glowing an eerie green, turned and whuffed in Hashti's face. Almost hysterical with relief, she whuffed back and sang his name. She wanted to throw her arms around his neck, but caution forbade it. What if he took the action amiss?

Khan himself initiated closer contact, rubbing his head against Hashti's side, then sliding his whole body past her, purring. "Twinkle little star," he hummed in her face. At that she did hug him. Then she stood up and shifted the pack, which weighed painfully on her shoulders. According to her beacon, she'd drifted forty degrees west of the northern bearing she wanted. "Let's get moving, Khan. Things will be even more unpleasant for you than for me if Gaylord finds us here."

He chirruped something, and they struggled on through the snow. Khan, traveling a tiger's length ahead of Hashti, veered left. Well, one direction was as good as another, so long as it was away from camp. She followed her guide to a game trail. Even with its abrupt twists and turns, it made for more rapid travel—the disturbed snow had frozen into bridges which easily supported the diffuse weight of Hashti's skis. Khan, despite his wide paws, sank deeply at each step. As the east brightened toward a pale northern dawn, the tiger sat down, breathing hard, and looked at the woman. Hashti was exhausted too. She'd come eight miles—a more than respectable distance, under the circumstances. "Where do we camp, old boy?"

Khan flicked his ears and sang something. It meant no more to her than her words had to him. She yawned, stretched, and feigned going to sleep. "Sleep. Rest. Where?"

He crooned something and duplicated her charade, peeking comically at her from beneath a supposedly closed eyelid. He must be giving her his word for sleep. She echoed the motif, trying to imitate a purr of assent.

Khan shook snow from his feathers and moved forward again. When the sun was half a diameter above the horizon, Khan paused by a cedar. It resembled the one that Ross and Hashti had taken refuge in, except that it stood on a hillside, sheltered by a rock face on the north.

Southeastward, toward Swamp City, a smudge of smoke marred the clear dawn sky. "Dust does not forget the dream that stirs it," Hashti whispered, caressing her beacon as if it were a talisman. Had Ross ever dreamed she would be here now? Khan's whiskers wiggled questioningly. Hashti dropped her pack and hauled out the tent, shaking her head at the tiger. "Someone special died to save you. You better be worth it."

If she was exhausted from physical exertion, grief, and fear, her feline companion seemed equally drained. Eager as Hashti was to begin language lessons, she and Khan both needed rest. She shook out the tent, anchored it under the sheltering limbs of the cedar tree, and sat down on the entrance flap to pull off her boots.

Khan, who'd been packing himself a bed in the snow, yowled and jumped backward. He landed in a crouch, tail switching, ears laid back, pupils dilated.

Hashti paused, startled, one shoe on and one shoe off. "What's wrong, Khan?"

He said something, but of course she couldn't understand it. What had gotten into the animal? She reminded herself that he was articulate and possibly as rational as herself. Hashti tried to see the scene through Khan's eyes. He'd watched her take off her boot—she burst into laughter. "No, silly, I didn't take my foot off. It's just clothes!"

She presented the clumsy work boot for inspection. Khan slunk forward for a wary sniff, then sniffed her stockinged foot in like manner. He investigated the second boot. Hashti pulled it off. Khan compared it to the first. He licked it experimentally. He tried to put his own foot in. It didn't fit. He pushed the boot back at Hashti. Meanwhile, she had dusted herself free of snow. Collecting her footgear, she backed into her tiny tent and pulled the bedroll in behind her. She sang the sleep tune, adding, "I'll see you in a bit, friend." Laying her head down, she thought snow had never been so soft.

Hashti wakened two hours later, when the climbing sun found its way through a gap in the branches to illuminate the dark green fabric of the tent. Opening the entrance flap, Hashti saw the depression in the snow where Khan had lain. The tiger himself was gone. Hashti suffered a flutter of anxiety. Would he return? Perhaps he watched from hiding even now.

If so, he stayed hidden. Hashti puttered about her tiny camp, changing socks and underwear, setting damp clothing in the sun to dry. She pulled out her beacon and recorded the word she thought meant "sleep," a description of the night's encounter, and what she could recollect of Khan's fight song.

Would Anna be back in her cabin by now? Hashti fumbled with the First-In beacon's unfamiliar controls, relieved when it responded. Anna answered on the second blip, her voice hoarse and strained. "Hashti! We've been waiting for word from you."

"I'm eight miles northwest, and I've found Khan. Or he found me. He fought off another tiger that attacked me."

"Oh Lord," the doctor responded with quiet intensity. "Do you want to come back?"

Hashti realized, to her surprise, that she didn't. "I think we'll be all right. The fight was during the night. Afterward Khan showed me a trail, and we made better time. By dawn we were both pooped, but I learned the word for sleep. Do you want the recording?"

"Please," Anna answered. Hashti transmitted it. "Is Khan with you now?" the doctor inquired.

"He was gone when I woke up. But he's obviously keeping track of me."

"I hope so. Have you eaten?"

"Not yet."

"Damn it, Hashti, are you trying to kill yourself?" Anna's vehemence startled the younger woman. The First-Inner herself seemed surprised by it. "Sorry. I'm on edge. But you've got to be careful. Don't push yourself so hard. You're burning calories faster than your appetite can respond. Eat now, as soon as you're done talking. You should go another five miles or so before you set up permanent camp, but don't hurry. There's a light snow coming, to cover your tracks."

"Does Gay know I'm gone?" Hashti asked.

"Not yet. He wondered why you weren't at the funeral. I told him you'd sat up all night with me, and were sleeping it off. Tomorrow you'll help me sort through Ross's things. Beyond that, we'll need Lance's cooperation."

Would Lance lie to Gaylord on Hashti's behalf, Hashti wondered? She didn't envy him the task, but there was little point worrying about Lance. She had problems enough of her own. So did the doctor. "I saw the smoke. I'm sorry, Doctor Anna."

Anna's voice was faint. "So am I. Now you've got to

do his job." The First-Inner cleared her throat and increased her volume. "Anything else?"

"Not really."

"Go eat, then. Keep us posted. I'll be around most of the day."

Putting the beacon away, Hashti realized that she'd forgotten to tell Anna about Khan and the boots. Never mind. She'd do it on the next call.

Anna's mention of food brought Hashti's stomach to full alert. She wolfed a candy bar as she rolled up her sleeping bag, and downed a second bar as she folded the tent. Then she bit into a stick of dry, salty meat, relishing the concentrated nutrition. Would she grow tired of these as the days wore on? Hard to imagine.

But she ought to conserve her instant rations, she thought, and besides, she needed to occupy herself. Good as the bars were, a hot meal would be better. Hashti strapped on her skis and went foraging for firewood.

As she arranged tinder around the kindling, Khan trotted up. A fluffy feathered body hung from his mouth. A rabbit! Did tigers bother with such small game? Looking hugely pleased, Khan laid it at Hashti's feet, as stable cats had sometimes done with their mice. Hashti patted the tiger's head. "Very good."

He waited expectantly. Hadn't she made a satisfactory fuss? Hands behind her back, she appraised the carcass again. "You're an accomplished hunter, Khan."

He laid one paw on the dead rabbit's head, sank his teeth into the flank, and yanked, tearing off a goodly hunk of skin and casting it aside with a toss of his head. His sharp teeth struck twice more, slashing the oddly colored meat into fine strips. Hashti regarded him warily.

He dumped the corpse on her boot, looked up at her, sang "twinkle little star," and licked his lips.

Was he threatening to treat her as he'd just treated the rabbit? Did "twinkle little star" mean "lunch?"

Don't be silly, Hashti, she told herself. You deserve to be treated like a rabbit if you panic this easily. Reminding herself that Khan was no animal, Hashti tried again to look through his eyes. How did she begin befriending animals? Food. Now the tables were turned. Khan was trying to win her trust.

He wanted her to *eat* this tattered blue-bloody mess? Hashti's hunger vanished.

Khan processed the kill a little further, laid a bloody gob in front of her, then withdrew, as if thinking his presence might frighten her. It did, she reflected wryly.

Hashti had read enough frontier novels to know that refusal of food is a deadly sin in most cultures. She could hardly ignore this overture of friendship. She picked up the gob.

Khan purred.

Hashti shut her eyes and nipped off a token piece of the meat. Its coppery-tasting blood seared her tongue.

Khan beamed approval and began to clean his paw.

Hashti quelled a gag and considered her options. She couldn't eat this rabbit! Its copper based enzymes and oddly balanced proteins were poisonous to her! No, she admitted, she had means to deal with that. Her objection rose at a more basic level: raw ungutted flesh turned her stomach. But that, too, she had means to correct. Turning back to the fire she'd laid, she held her igniter to a curl of paperbark. A thin, acrid stream of smoke, blossoming into flame, rewarded her efforts.

Khan had stopped washing to watch her. Now he flattened himself to the ground, spitting. Hashti looked about for enemies, but saw none. The fire! That was the source of Khan's distress. In his world fire came in only one form—forest fire. Hashti understood his dismay.

But he would have to get used to this if they were going
to travel together. "Sorry, buddy. This is the way humans
do things. It's called a 'campfire.' I promise not to let it
loose."

By the time Khan quit snarling, Hashti had inexpertly
cleaned and spitted the bunny. The tiger watched warily
as she roasted her lunch. Once she scraped the ashes off,
it tasted fine. She'd eaten gamier meat in Town Hall, and
this at least was unsullied by well-intended gravy.

Khan, although still distressed by the fire, rumbled
approvingly as she ate. Hashti wanted their relationship
to be as reciprocal as possible. She sliced off a hunk of
the roasted meat and held it out to the tiger.

Don't be ridiculous, she told herself. He brought it to
you in the first place! But Khan accepted her offering,
although he retreated several yards from the fire before
turning his attention to it.

He bit into it. He spat it out.

He nosed at it, took it in his mouth again, and spat it
out a second time. Golden eyes fixed inquiringly on
Hashti as Khan's whiskers waggled in distaste.

"Go ahead. Cooking makes it easier to chew, and kills
the bugs. And *you* don't have to take pills with it."
Hashti bit off a chunk of the rabbit leg in her hand.

Khan tried the meat a third and final time. Then,
snorting with disgust, he dropped it on the snow and rose
to his feet. He scraped with his huge paws until the tidbit
was buried. He sniffed once more, assuring himself that
the offending morsel was truly gone. Then he moved
away and washed himself most fastidiously.

Hashti watched, suspended between indignation and
hilarity. So this was what he thought of her food? They
might have a wider cultural gap to surmount than she
thought, if he buried good roast rabbit like feces!

When the meal was finished they moved north, traveling four miles in as many hours. Khan paused frequently to discuss the scenery. He taught Hashti terms as varied as "beaver lodge" and "waterfall." The more she learned, the more frustrated she became. What use had she for the nouns of the forest? She needed interrogatives and abstracts. She needed to ask, "What are your people like?" "What do you talk about?" "How do you live?" Would she ever be able to fulfill her mission?

But she couldn't learn everything in a day. And even if she'd had the vocabulary, she lacked the breath for steady conversation. Between stops she trudged quietly, not gliding on her skis, just walking as if on snowshoes. Khan, by contrast, hummed steadily. He mentioned her name occasionally, and something about beavers.

He was rehearsing an air about seven minutes long. It grew more complex as he practiced. He introduced rhythmic variations, melodic rhymes, and grace notes. The song acquired a haunting weirdness, sounding more and more like the one the spotted tiger had sung at the Rock.

Memory of that spotted giant unnerved Hashti. She'd had her fill of traveling in the dark. Tonight she wanted to settle in before sunset. "Sleep?" she asked Khan, mimicking the turning motions he used to pack his bed.

"Sleep," he sang back, adding more that she did not understand. She started to take off her pack. Khan hissed, pressed against her legs, moved on down the trail, and whistled briskly back at her. This must mean "Come on." Hashti granted him fifteen minutes.

Just when she grew ready to rebel, Khan stopped by a fallen blackpine. The giant had rooted in soil only a couple of feet thick. When a high wind finally toppled it, its roots pulled free of the dark granite bedrock, bringing most of the soil with them. A second and much smaller tree had fallen across the mass of roots, forming a cozy shelter walled by earth and roots on one side, with the second tree's branches providing roof and two more walls. The tiger and Hashti fit in with just room left for her pack. "Lodge?" Hashti asked, using a term Khan employed for beaver houses, rabbit runs, and bird nests.

He snarled, repeating her word along with an exclamation that might mean "no." He butted the fallen tree's roots with his head and sang a new word.

"Shelter," Hashti tentatively translated it, as she spoke it to her recorder. What, she wondered, was the difference between a lodge and a shelter?

Khan ducked under the branches and began to circle. Hashti stayed outside, surveying the place critically. "Very good. But I can make it better." She spent fifteen minutes with her hatchet, lopping limbs and rearranging them while she puzzled over Khan's distinction. Was a "shelter" natural, a "lodge" constructed? If so, her improvements had changed this place's status. "Lodge," she said as she crawled into it to put away the hatchet.

"No. Shelter!" Khan answered.

Large snowflakes spiraled lazily from the sky, as Anna had promised. The temperature lingered in the high teens. Hashti would need no tent tonight. She padded the shelter's floor with a tarpaulin and branches, so that cold rock would not suck away her body heat. Then she went outside, seated herself on the fallen tree's trunk, and triggered her beacon. Big Red's wry, deep voice answered. "How's it going, Hashti? Settled in for the night?"

She answered affirmatively and gave him her bearings, than began to quiz him about events at his end of the line. "Where's Doctor Anna? Has Gay found out I'm gone?"

The ex-Boss snorted. "Anna's asleep, and needs it. Gaylord hasn't had time to eat, let alone go looking for you. You should have seen his face when I handed him that bag of smashed firing pins! How's your tiger vocabulary coming?"

"Slow," she answered. "I did find out what tigers call us. 'Hill beavers.' I suppose it's because we cut trees and build cabins. Here, I'll give you my report."

Big Red chuckled heartily over the rabbit story. "He doesn't like your cooking, huh? If that's your worst misunderstanding, you'll do wonderfully. Shall I tell Anna you'll call this time tomorrow?"

"I'll try to. Tell her not to worry about me."

"It's good for her. Gives her something constructive to think about. Keep up the good work."

"I'll do the best I can." Hashti hated to terminate the contact, but she had nothing more to say. "Good night, Mister Red."

"Skip the Mister. We're partners now. Goodnight, Hashti." She heard a soft click as he cut transmission, then only a faint hiss of static.

It was five in the evening. Snow crystals dropped gently through the gathering darkness. Hashti caught a big one, three-eighths of an inch across, on her wrist. Its lacy latticework drooped and puddled as her hand's heat seeped through her mitten. Khan waited silently, a dark shadow on the snow. The world was quiet, quiet, quiet. Snowfall muffled even the normal cracks and pops of the forest. The last milky glow faded from the sky, cut off by the looming height of mature blackpines. Hashti rested a few more moments in snowy peace, then roused herself to crawl into the tree-root cave. She barely made it into her sleeping bag before she fell asleep.

Khan slept in the snow cave with her, a warm and comforting presence, although he grumbled whenever she changed position. Shortly after midnight, Hashti woke wondering if Khan had fleas. Fleas—and probably their New Lebanese counterparts—were a specialized bunch, she knew, and any of Khan's would probably ignore a human. The thought made her itch, just the same.

She awoke again just before dawn. Khan was gone. Fourteen hours of sleep had improved Hashti's outlook and freshened her appetite. She drained her last half bottle of lukewarm tea, then built a wood fire. The little blaze produced a distressing amount of smoke, perfuming her hair and clothing. As she set a pan of snow over the fire, Khan arrived, a limp deer carcass in his mouth. He laid it down, sixty feet away, and called coaxingly. "Twinkle little star!"

"I'm busy, friend." She scooped another handful of snow into the pot, added another stick to the fire, and blew hard. The smoke vanished in a clear bright blaze.

Khan paced back and forth several times, wanting her attention but reluctant to approach the fire. Finally he twittered in disgust, returned to his deer, and cleared the thick coat of feathers from its haunch. He bit with tiger gusto, seizing and tearing and shaking, ripping the meat into slices small enough to be swallowed. Hashti tried to ignore it all.

Then she heard an odd squishing sound. In spite of herself, she looked over her shoulder. She wished she hadn't. Khan had bitten the deer's intestine off just below the stomach, and was consuming it as a child slurps a spaghetti noodle. He squeezed it between his teeth as he sucked it in. The contents, in varying stages of digestion, dripped out the other end. Warm steamy piles accumulated on the snow.

Hashti looked away, disgusted. This was an intelligent creature?

"Living with aliens is tough. Crazy little things, like the way they eat their food, can bother you more than you'd ever imagine." Hashti told herself to be fair. Customs vary. But she still rebelled at the sight of Khan slurping the poor gaunt deer's intestines. Had she really slept beside this creature last night? What would her mother think? She doubted her mother would understand.

# CHAPTER TEN

HUNGER HAD CAUGHT UP WITH HASHTI. EVEN KHAN'S intestine sucking could not put her off for long. When the tiger gave her meat, the woman ate gladly.

Her small fire flickered and snapped. Snow seemed to take forever to melt. But at last the fluffy white mass collapsed into liquid, and Hashti drank a pint and a half straight from the pan, ignoring ice chunks still floating in it. She made tea of the next two cups. Her thirst gave new and frightening reality to Anna's warnings about fluid depletion. Hashti continued feeding the fire and melting snow until she'd refilled all her canteens.

By this time Khan had turned away from his greatly diminished deer carcass, yawned, and settled in a sunny spot atop the blackpine's trunk. He laid his head on his paws and fell asleep.

Hashti, eager to keep busy, heated more water to wash her underwear. Knowing better than to wet her hands in this ten degree weather, she simply dumped her laundry into the kettle and stirred. Everything came out looking dirtier than before. Hashti rinsed the garments anyway and hung them in the sun to dry. They froze stiff.

Khan opened one eye, stretched, and came down from his perch to investigate. The soap bar interested him greatly. "Little star! Little star!" he sang.

"What?" Hashti asked, startled. Khan's word sounded like part of her name.

Khan laid his ears back just a touch, sniffed at the soap, and repeated, insistently, "Little star."

"Little star?" the woman sang back, confused.

"Little star," affirmed Khan, nudging the soap bar with his muzzle. He came over to sniff at Hashti. "Little star." He sat back, watching her. "Twinkle little star." Was there some connection between her name and the soap word? Hashti sniffed at a loose strand of her hair. Beneath the reek of woodsmoke remained a faint scent of rose. Did "little star" refer to the smell of her soap? What, she wondered, did "twinkle" mean?

Khan licked the soap, then backed away shaking his head, his lip curled. Hashti laughed aloud.

Khan glared, fanned the feathers of his ruff, and stalked to his perch atop the fallen blackpine. He yawned elaborately—with half an eye on Hashti, she thought—and went back to sleep in the sun.

Disappointed at losing her companion, Hashti straightened up after herself, set venison in the pot to simmer, found a comfortable spot, and tried to follow Khan's example. She wasn't sleepy. Pulling out her carving knife, she began shaping a chunk of root into a toy horse.

Absorbed in the task and memories of Carolina, she didn't hear Khan until his shadow fell across her. He nosed at her creation, singing. Could this word be "horse"? She pulled a charred stick from the fire and, with it, sketched a horse on a piece of bark. Khan confirmed its identity. What a way to work on vocabulary!

She spent the entire afternoon drawing pictures, miming, straining her voice to achieve the pitches of tiger speech, and drawing some more. She built a log cabin with sticks. "Hill beaver lodge," Khan said. She set her

tiny wooden horse beside the structure, added a hastily
constructed two-legged figure with a wisp of cloth
around it. "Horse," Khan told her, his eyes never swerv-
ing from the miniatures. "Twinkle little star!" Shifting
position, Hashti formed a double handful of snow into
something approximating a snowbird. Khan sang the
name for her.

His habit of decorating final notes with trills, quavers,
and tremolos complicated Hashti's task. She thought
these endings might differentiate "a blackpine" from "the
blackpine" or "blackpines in general," but the variations
were too numerous and complex for her to distinguish,
let alone duplicate. She finally ignored them, supplying
articles as needed in her translations, and omitting them
from her own speech. Khan, for his part, seemed pleased
that she could speak at all. One could not expect a
beaver to pick up all the nuances in a day!

Hashti had never before encountered an alien language, but she'd learned half a dozen human tongues
common among Carolina's patrons. She knew, through
experience, the basic rules of language learning: guess
meanings from context; try using words yourself; record
everything, it'll help you remember; don't worry about
mistakes. With these techniques and the tips Anna had
given, Hashti learned rapidly. For every lexical success,
she encountered a dozen words she did not comprehend,
and as many more that she wanted to ask about, but
could not phrase the questions. Still, she felt well satisfied that evening. "I spent the day discussing pictures
and models with Khan," she reported to Anna. "I can
say 'yes,' 'no,' and 'what's this?' Tigers call themselves
'speakers,' though of course it sounds better in their language. There's another word for tiger that sounds like
this—" Hashti paused to sing.

"I hope you recorded that," Anna commented.

"I did, it's all in my report," Hashti assured her, ignoring the fact that if it were in the report, she need not tell Anna now. "Khan's own name has something about beavers—I think it might be 'Beaver Teacher.' I told you they call us 'hill beavers.' 'Big' and 'little' are a couple of notes each, tacked onto the name of the thing you're describing. My name's put together that way. It means 'Soapy Baby,' or 'Flowery-smelling Cub,' or some such."

Anna laughed as Hashti paused for breath. "I know Gay likes the way you smell, but I never thought Khan would care."

"Does Gay know I'm gone?"

"Not yet. Lance lies very creatively. One would think he'd had practice. Tell me more about tigers."

"Khan has a word for 'horse,'" Hashti answered, jumping to the subject she knew best. "So he must know about the wild ponies here."

"He can't have seen them himself," Anna muttered. "They're too far away. There must be communication between tigers in various places. Interesting! Have they any sort of government?"

"I don't know," Hashti confessed, suddenly discouraged. "I'm still learning housekeeping talk. Parts of the body, kinds of food—it's in my report. What's happening in camp?"

Anna's voice turned glum too. "Logging's called off until they find better protection than skunk. Jack's working on a contact poison. In the meantime Gay got three tigers with poisoned bait. The men are thrilled. Can you warn Khan?"

"I'll try," Hashti promised. But Khan only listened in patient puzzlement. After all the day's successes, Hashti's communication with him remained frustratingly inadequate.

Monday, Khan refused to discuss pictures. He paced the snow-packed paths about their camp, then returned to nudge Hashti with his head. "(Let's go?)!" he insisted.

Hashti's body ached at the thought of leaving her cozy camp and wandering through the snow. But, utterly dependent on Khan as she was, she could scarcely defy him. Perhaps he had something special to show her, she thought, as she detached the belt portion of the First-In pack. This part contained such heavy but indispensable items as a first aid kit, tarpaulin, and emergency hotbottle. Hashti strapped it around her hips, added a clumsy but lightweight roll of dry clothes, lashed her boots to the skis, and followed Khan into the forest.

He moved at a relaxed pace, slower than that which Ross had set on the trip to the Rock. Hashti found that without a full pack pressing her into the drifts she enjoyed skiing. Just as he had on the way to the fallen blackpine, Khan sang. Despite the song's ornateness, Hashti recognized a word here and there. Khan mentioned the camp, himself, and Hashti. With breath to spare at this gentle pace, and eager to improve her language skills, Hashti tried singing along. Khan stopped and stared. "You speak my (?)?" he asked, in a key conveying amusement.

"What (?)?" she asked back, uncertain of the new word.

"I am a speaker," he explained. "Beaver Teacher is my name. This is my (?)."

Hashti hummed the explanation to herself, trying to make sense of it.

"Name, (?)," said Khan crisply.

Hearing the two words juxtaposed, Hashti understood. The word she'd translated "name" was compound, beginning with the "small" prefix. The new word, the one she'd asked about, used the same stem with a "big" prefix. That stem, she now saw, derived melodically from the verb "speak." She stared at Khan, her lips moving silently as she tried to put it all together. "Beaver Teacher is your small-speech, your song was your big-speech?" she asked in English.

Khan's left ear swiveled backward ever so slightly, a sign of irritation. He hated it when she lapsed into her own language. He warbled something fluently and, for Hashti, unintelligibly.

She tried without success to decipher the paragraph. "Again?" she finally pleaded.

Khan dropped to a sphinx's crouch, as if to say he knew this would take a while. Patiently he repeated his remark, phrase by phrase. "Beaver Teacher is my (name/small-speech). I spoke my (big-speech). You (too?) spoke my (big-speech). Speak not my (big-speech). Speak your own (big-speech)."

What? Hashti frowned. Perhaps she should stick with her original translation "name" for the noun. She ran again through Khan's words. "Beaver Teacher is my small-name. I spoke my big-name. You too spoke my big-name. Don't speak my big-name. Speak your own big-name." This made more sense!

"Rose Cub's small-name Rose Cub?" she asked.

Khan blinked. "Yes!"

"What Rose Cub's big-name?" she asked.

It took her a moment to decipher his answer. "Are you not a tiger? Speak your own big-name!" No, wait. That word for tiger meant speaker, or perhaps namer. "Are you not a speaker?" Khan had asked.

"Rose Cub not (tiger/speaker/namer)," Hashti answered.

Khan's right ear cocked sideways in a manner that reminded Hashti of a mother shaking her finger at a child. "I am Beaver Teacher. I will teach you to speak."

He rose, shook lightly to shed the snow sticking to his feathers, and resumed his northward course, humming as he plodded.

Just as familiar names catch one's ear in an otherwise unintelligible conversation, the few tiger terms Hashti knew jumped out at her from Khan's monologue. Bit by bit, as Khan repeated the song, Hashti pieced together a translation. "I, Rose Cub, (now?) speak my big-name. I am a cub of the hill beavers, (like?) (soap? a rose?) I smell—"

Hashti scurried to catch up. "What sings Beaver Teacher?" she asked.

He sat down, nose twitching. "I sang your big-name, cub. (Now?) speak you your big-name." He watched expectantly.

How could Khan expect her to repeat a song she had heard only a few times? "What Rose Cub's big-name? Again?"

Khan lay down. "I, Rose Cub, now speak my big-name."

"I, Rose Cub, now speak my big-name," she repeated.

Khan's ruff lay smooth, a signal of calm. "I am a cub of the Hill Beavers," he prompted.

"I am a cub of the Hill Beavers," Hashti sang.

"(Like?) a rose I smell," Khan said, then rippled off an additional phrase which was gibberish to his companion. Hashti echoed as accurately as she could.

Khan gave her another, even longer phrase.

This would never do. Hashti had trouble enough with phrases she understood. She could never master these strings of seemingly random notes. "Again?" she asked Khan, as she switched on her data condenser. "I, Rose Cub, now speak my Name—"

The composition was about five minutes long. "Let's

go," Hashti suggested when she had satisfied herself of the recording. They continued down the trail, Hashti replaying the song again and again, stopping frequently to repeat phrases.

The horse trainer normally spoke tiger with a "lisp," because her voice had a smaller range than the cats'. Khan had pitched this tune in a range she could reach. Even so, it gave her trouble. The five-minute song had no verses; its melody and rhythm varied continuously. By noon, she'd only half learned it. "(Very good?)," Khan purred, but his ruff lifted as Hashti faltered midway through a phrase. "She is only a hill beaver," Hashti imagined him reminding himself.

"I should make you memorize the Orion treaty," she told him in her own language.

"Sing not (like?) a hill beaver," he scolded.

She thumbed her nose at him.

Cross-country skiing, even at a relaxed pace with a light pack, is hungry work. Hashti's stomach demanded compensation. "Rose Cub hungry," she told Khan, glad to be using familiar words again. "Where eat?"

"Warm rocks (ahead?)," he answered. "Good for your eating—and my napping."

To each his own! With the temperature at zero, Hashti found even the coziest boulder a poor bed. But she trudged obediently behind Khan, who led her to a clearing as promised. Even the hardy cedars could find no purchase in this thin soil, and naked bedrock protruded in several places. Hashti happily shucked her pack and dug out lunch. Khan wrinkled his nose and shook his paw. "Eat you your beaver droppings," he said. "I go to hunt."

Very well. Hashti settled into a rock niche. She slurped venison stew from a canteen, then hauled out the data condenser to resume practice on her "Name." An hour later her voice gave out, and her patience with it. Even a song about oneself is boring if one understands only a fifth of it! Hashti pulled on an extra sweater, wiggled as far out of the wind as she could, and dozed. Waking, she checked her beacon. Two o'clock. It had taken three hours to get here. The return trip would go faster, since the trail was already broken. Still, only two and a half hours remained before sunset. If she did not leave soon, Hashti would be caught by darkness.

Khan had not returned.

Which was worse—being caught by night, or caught without her guide and protector? Hashti fretted another ten minutes, straining for sight of a tiger. No luck. She decided to head for home. Khan ought to know where she'd gone. He'd certainly shown his ability to track her. With a last hopeful, fruitless glance around, she slipped her wrists through the loops on her ski poles.

The sun still lay in thin red streaks across the treetops when Hashti reached the fallen blackpine. Warm happiness surged through her as she sighted the ungainly, snowbanked knot of roots. Home! In the security of this familiar place, her supper fire already laid and awaiting the touch of her kindler, she hardly worried about Khan's absence.

He arrived an hour later, angry. He butted her over, and growled in her face. "Are you a tiger"—(not speaker/namer, but the alternate term)—"or a beaver?"

"Rose Cub hill beaver," Hashti replied, with as much dignity as she could muster.

"(Act not like?) a leaf eater," Khan said scornfully. "You spoke your Name. Speakers sleep not in lodges."

They had been here before. "Not lodge. Shelter," Hashti corrected.

"Lodge," Khan said, with a little hiss of disgust. He stalked to the tree root den and demolished it with a few blows of his forepaws. Hashti shrank from the animal's power.

No, she reminded herself, Khan was a person. In his eyes, she was the animal. Animalness had something to do with lodges.

Khan looked around to see how she'd reacted. She glared at him. He bit at a bur in his tail, then stretched. "No lodge. Let's go."

Hashti ground her teeth in frustration. She didn't want to spend another night on the trail. What was wrong with sleeping here? For the past two nights the blackpine's roots had been a "shelter," and Khan had been happy enough to share it with her. Now suddenly it was a "lodge," or had been, and sleeping there made one less than "tiger."

But whatever weird notions Khan harbored about tigerhood, Hashti had to live up to them. Sullenly, she rooted in the wreckage of the shelter for her sleeping bag and pack.

Khan shook himself. "(Bring?) not the little-lodge." Thus he normally referred to her tent.

She straightened, hands on her hips. It was hard to be authoritative when she agonized over every word, but she did her best. "Beaver Teacher feathers. Rose Cub, no feathers. Little-lodge, Rose Cub's feathers. It comes."

A heavy tail-tip twitched in amusement. "You have (?), Rose Cub, (although?) you (act like?) a leaf eater. (Bring?) the little-lodge, then. You have a Name. We will go to the speaking (place?)."

Heavily weighted and seething with rebellion, Hashti followed Khan into the darkness. She nourished her anger, for if it died, fear would take its place. What was a speaking place? Evidently one did not go there until one spoke one's Name. To whom did one speak it? She re-

membered the scene she'd watched with Ross at the
Rock. Had the spotted tiger spoken his Name? Was the
Rock a speaking place? Was that where they were going
tonight? Who would be there?

One moon hung high above, a fingernail crescent. The
other had not yet risen. The milky pulsating light of the
aurora reflected any which way off the snow, illuminat-
ing but casting no shadows, making it impossible to pick
out the bumps and dips of the trail. Hashti slipped and
tripped, fighting to keep her heavy pack from overbal-
ancing her. A small lake with blessedly level footing provided relief. At the foot of the hill on the far side, Khan
turned to Hashti. "(Know you?) your Name?"

She surprised herself by singing it without mistake.
Khan scratched his cheek on her leg. "Well spoken. We
go to the speaking place."

Hashti shivered. Should she have sung less well?

Near the top of the hill lay a clearing, forty feet wide,
bounded on the far side by even higher rock. Against
that far wall rested a tigress with two cubs, probably
from last winter's mating.

"Come!" Khan said, perfectly relaxed, heading toward a huge sweetsap tree.

The tigress rose, snarling. She was small, as tigers go,
but quick and strong. Pairs of bold black stripes streaked
her pelt, the brightness of its orange showing even in the
half light. The tigress's cubs were less vividly hued, but
they had inherited their mother's double stripes. The
larger cub crouched, forequarters low, hind legs tucked
beneath her, eyes fixed on Hashti. At nine months, the
cub weighed twice what Hashti did. And the cub looked
ready to spring.

Khan faced the cub, his lips stretched, back straight,
tail stiffly bent. A deep rumbling growl erupted from
him. "Stay!" he commanded.

The cubs' mother moved forward, eyeing Hashti. "What is that leaf eater?" she asked. "Is that a hill beaver?" The tigress spoke rapidly. Hashti could barely follow, though she knew all the words.

"It is a hill beaver," Khan affirmed. Hearing him talk to his own people, Hashti realized how he'd been slowing and simplifying his words for her.

The tigress swiveled her ears in disapproval. "The speaking place is for tigers. A leaf eater (may not?) enter."

Khan licked his forepaw, then cocked his head. "The hill beaver has a Name. She will speak."

The tigress hesitated to quarrel with a male who outweighed her by three hundred pounds. She sat back and looked at everything but the newcomers as they approached the big sweetsap tree.

Khan sniffed its bark, leisurely and thoroughly. Hashti waited, watching the other tigers from the corner of her eye. Khan backed against the tree, tail high, and splashed his scent on it. He looked at Hashti. "Pee on the tree, Rose Cub."

"The hell you say," she growled under her breath. "It's five below zero out here." Khan didn't understand the human words, but he knew the tone of insubordination. His lips parted warningly.

What could she do, Hashti wondered? She was not designed to urinate on trees. She'd end up with wet legs —dangerous!—and a dry tree. Yet she must act like a tiger. The penalty for failure could be death. As she fumbled reluctantly with her belt, inspiration struck.

She loosened her pack straps. Khan knew this was not how she lowered her pants. "You are a speaker, Rose Cub. Pee!"

"Wait," she told him. With fingers made clumsy by tension, she dug out her soap. She spit on the bar and

raked the tree with it. "Rose Cub hill beaver," she reminded Khan. "This Rose Cub's pee."

Khan knew it wasn't strictly true, but he got her
meaning. He sniffed the tree and blinked in satisfaction.
"The hill beaver has left her (urine/scent/mark?)," he announced to the other tigers.

The female cub bounded forward to confirm the report. She was a sturdy, well-built animal with broad,
bold stripes and a saucy air. She smelled the soap and
sprang back three paces, lips curled and tongue sticking
out. "Little star!"

Her mother shouldered her aside. "I will smell." She
stuck her own tongue out. "Yes, the hill beaver smells
like roses!"

Khan fluffed his ruff. "Her name is Rose Cub. I call
myself Beaver Teacher. I taught the hill beaver to
speak."

"I call myself Tree Walker," the tigress said.

Khan asked her something, his words recognizable as
a question by the preceding marker and a slight alter-
ation of scale. It must have concerned Tree Walker's
name, because for answer, she leapt at the sweetsap
tree. She clung six feet off the ground, looking proudly at
Khan, then climbed another six feet. "You (climb?)
well!" he exclaimed. Most tigers were too heavy for such
feats.

"I call myself Tree Walker," the tigress repeated
smugly, pushing herself away from the tree to land neatly
beside Khan. He whuffed at her face. She whuffed back,
then they rubbed bodies in full-fledged greeting.

The second cub had crouched on the far rim of the
clearing. Now he crept toward Hashti. He was smaller
than his sister, and stepped oddly. Hashti saw, as he approached, that his paws twisted inward. Despite the de-
fect, he had a bright, appealing face with an intelligent

look. Black crescents above his wide-set eyes made them look even larger than they were, glowing green in the light of the aurora. Hashti smiled and extended an empty hand for him to sniff. "I call myself Rose Cub."

He whuffed gently, scarcely more than a loud breath, and spoke his own name. It took Hashti a few moments to recognize the passive form of the usual introduction. "I am called Big Eyes."

If Khan had taught Hashti anything, he'd taught her tiger greeting customs. She whuffed back at Big Eyes, and they rubbed faces.

When his sister saw that Big Eyes came to no harm, she shouldered him aside, whuffed in Hashti's face, and rubbed her with much gusto and little restraint. Hashti braced herself against the tree in time to avoid being toppled.

The smaller cub sat with luminous green eyes fixed on the woman. "Have you (really?) a Name?" he asked.

"Yes," she told him.

"Speak it," the larger female cub ordered.

Should she comply, Hashti wondered? Fortunately Khan had an ear turned toward the group. "Have you a name?" he asked the bold baby tigress.

She shook herself lightly, so the aurora's light glanced off her double stripes. "I call myself One-Who-Gets Rabbits," she announced.

"One-Who-Gets" was a form of Khan's favorite verb, "Gotcha!" What did the name really mean? The cub's haughty air suggested something like "Suave Chaser of Hares." Hashti translated it, privately, as "Bunny Pouncer." Meanwhile Khan's ears flipped in what Hashti had come to recognize as amusement. "Speak," he commanded the cub.

Hashti scrambled for her recorder.

The youngster gathered herself and sprang to the top

of a large boulder. "I, Bunny Pouncer, now speak my
Name," she announced, hanging a multitude of little
grace notes on the ritual formula. She launched into
song, a performance plainer than Khan's, closer to ordinary speech, but fluent far beyond Hashti's halting efforts. The finer points of the narrative escaped the
woman, but the culminating episode concerned a hunt.
"I saw the bunny, the bunny saw me." Bunny Pouncer
perched beside the boulder, ruffled her neck feathers,
pricked her ears, and stamped. Then she reshaped herself in tiger form and sprang, landing with paws cupped
around an imaginary prey, jaws poised to bite. "I, Bunny
Pouncer, pounced the bunny. It (?) between my paws.
And then it ran." For a few brief moments she became a
rabbit again, fleeing in terror across the speaking place.
"(Thus?), I call myself Bunny Pouncer." Tail waving
proudly, the cub marched back to Tree Walker.

Hashti wondered if she had heard correctly. Did the
rabbit get away? Why brag about that?

"Rabbits are fast," Khan said. "One (needs?) quick-
ness, to pounce them. You will hunt well." The half-
grown tigress purred. So did her mother. What a
politician Khan was! He turned to the second cub.
"Have you a Name?"

The little male shrank down. "I am called Big Eyes,"
he answered, with a swift glance at his misshapen paws.

"He is too slow to hunt," Bunny Pouncer said, with
big-sisterly superiority.

Big Eyes hissed at her. "(Soon?) I will kill. (Soon?) I
will speak."

Bunny Pouncer opened her mouth to reply, but Tree
Walker intervened. "Speak your name, Beaver Teacher."

Khan needed no second invitation. Jumping atop the
rock, he stretched and ruffled his feathers. "I, Beaver
Teacher, now speak my Name," he announced, using an

even more intricate form of the formula than Bunny Pouncer had employed. Hashti wished fervently for video pickup on the data condenser. Khan's acting was magnificent, and his actions helped Hashti follow the story. His ears went back and his hackles rose as he told of a fight with another tiger. He rolled contentedly as he described a lakeshore retreat. He described a very fast horse he had killed.

What? The camp wasn't missing any horses. And Big Red said the nearest native horses were five hundred miles from here. Hashti frowned. Once again she must have heard wrong.

Thirty minutes later, Khan reached the melody he'd practiced on the trail, describing the lodges of Swamp City. With striking accuracy he depicted the posture and motions of a workhorse straining to haul a large load. Then he knocked Hashti sprawling in the snow and stood serenely over her, describing their first encounter. He demonstrated the effects of Gay's skunk gun, and gave a tiger's eye account of Ross's death. He sang of last night's lodge—only now he called it a shelter again—in the roots of the fallen blackpine. Finally he declared that Hashti had a Name. With chin drawn in and tail curved high, Khan gave an ear-shattering roar. "(Thus?), I call myself Beaver Teacher," he proclaimed.

Tree Walker looked dubious. "The hill beaver (must?) sing. It speaks, or dies." She employed the neuter pronoun that denoted an animal, and the verb which described the fate of prey.

Khan's tail twitched. "Speak, Rose Cub."

Heart pounding, Hashti walked over to the boulder. Its sides were slippery with ice. She tried to climb, and slipped back. She tried again. Not until the third try did she find a crack in which she could hook her fingers to haul herself up.

Bunny Pouncer sniffed. "The hill beaver climbs (poorly?)."

All too true, but Hashti was stuck with herself. Climbing was the least of her worries. She took a deep breath. "I, Rose Cub, now speak my Name." Only an hour ago she'd sung for Khan. Now the stakes had risen. She forced herself not to think about stupid errors or simply forgetting her lines. Her voice grew stronger as the minutes passed. When she reached the end she threw her arms wide and sang jubilantly, "I call myself Rose Cub, (companion? pupil? pet?) of Beaver Teacher."

Tree Walker looked respectfully at Khan. "Yes, the leaf eater speaks. Your Name is large indeed, Beaver Teacher!"

Khan smirked.

Her heart still pounding, Hashti slid down from the rock. She'd done it! She'd sung her Name! She was a speaker!

# CHAPTER ELEVEN

❧❧❧❧

AN HOUR BEFORE DAWN, STIRRING TIGERS WAKENED Hashti. "I go to hunt," Big Eyes said.

His mother licked his nose. "Hunt well, my cub. (May you return?) a speaker." He padded away across the snow, leaving a trail of crooked pawmarks. Tree Walker watched him go, her expression unreadable. Only when he was out of sight did she stretch and yawn. "I too will hunt." Bunny Pouncer bounded to her side, begging to join the chase.

The tigress batted affectionately at her daughter. "Yes, but you must (?) from the bushes. Hunt you, Beaver Teacher?"

Khan rolled over, scratched his back against the rocks, and swayed lazily onto his feet. "I come. Rose Cub, stay."

That was fine with Hashti. She knew how little use she would be to a team of tigers on the hunt. She sought the shelter of a bushy blackpine sapling and crawled into her sleeping bag.

The low winter sun hung in the southwest when the shrill voice of her beacon wakened her. Had the dead-man switch activated itself? No, she'd reset it before she went to sleep. Someone must have triggered the beacon from camp. She fumbled inside the sleeping bag and finally silenced the offending noise. "Hashti here," she spoke into the small instrument. "What's up?"

"This is Red. Sorry to bother you, but we needed to know if you were OK."

Tension clawed at her. "Why did you wonder?"

"Two men got killed checking bait lines this morning. A third came back mauled but alive. Anna's in the clinic reassembling him."

"Is Gay all right?" Gay had forfeited any right to her worry, but old habits die hard.

"All in one piece," Big Red assured her, "but having trouble holding the camp together. The men got mad when Gay used good meat for tiger bait. Now they've got two new deaths to think about. And some of them are wondering why they haven't seen you. Gay's got his work cut out for him."

"Is he ready to give in?" Hashti asked.

"Not yet," Big Red answered grimly. "The majority are still behind him. But it won't be long. Ready for more good news? The barometer's dropping, which probably means a blizzard."

Hashti blinked at the deep blue afternoon sky. "How soon?"

"Twelve to forty-eight hours. Can't tell exactly, with no satellite. Might not hit us at all, but better safe than sorry. I'll fetch you with the sled if you want to come home."

Ross and Hashti had sat out a storm with minimal preparation. Certainly she could do better now, with Khan's aid and plenty of warning! "The equipment you gave me can stand up to a blizzard, can't it?"

Big Red hesitated. "Sure. But blizzards are touchy, and since you're alone—"

"I've got Khan, and I've got your advice. I'll be all right." Hashti was tired of listening to the camp's problems. She had good news to share. "Listen to what I did last night!"

She knew, without Big Red saying so, that she'd made a major breakthrough when she communicated with tigers other than Khan. Just the same, it was nice to hear his praise. "You're getting us what we needed, Hashti—a glimpse of their culture. Khan really said he'd killed a horse?"

"I thought so."

Red whistled. "That tiger's traveled, Hashti. Hundreds of miles. But it fits with everything else. Anna and I dug out the First-In linguistic analysis manuals. Working over your reports, we found the meaning of your second word for tiger."

"What does it mean?" Hashti asked.

"Those-who-do-not-lodge. Lodgeless Ones."

"So that's what Khan was storming about!" Hashti told of the tiger's sudden aversion to their base camp. "When I went back, he asked me if I was a tiger or a leaf eater! But why did a shelter suddenly become a lodge?"

"You stayed there too long."

Hashti thought about it. "Mister Red?"

"I told you to drop the Mister. Yes, Hashti?"

"Do the tigers have homes at all? Or do they spend their lives wandering from speaking place to speaking place?"

"You're the one who's living with them." He hesitated. "My guess would be they travel forever. They've got a pure information economy, or nearly so. No money, no warehouses of food, no fancy toys. No way to carry any of that. Instead they trade in stories—where they've been, what they've done. As money means power in our world, an impressive Name means power in theirs. You said the smaller cub had no big-name?"

"He didn't speak one. I think he might have to make a kill before he can speak."

"Ordeal," the First-Inner said thoughtfully. "But not for mating. He's nowhere near old enough, if he's from last year's litter. I suppose—a mother can't afford to waste years on a physically unfit cub." He paused. "Don't get too fond of him, Hashti."

She found this turn of thought disturbing. "I don't know if I'll ever see him again. Khan hasn't told me where we're staying next. *Sheltering*, that is."

Red sighed. "Just be sure it's warm and protected from the wind. Wish I could help you dig in."

"You sound like Doctor Anna."

"How's that?"

"She's always fussing about my safety."

"For good reason. She's seen what happens when folks get careless. Sure you don't want to come back?"

"I'll be OK. If I go back now, Khan will think I'm a leaf eater." Surprising, how that thought upset her.

Big Red chuckled. "Heaven forbid that Khan should think you a leaf eater. Regardless of his opinion, you find a good lodge tonight."

Hashti promised, but the sky was still clear and she felt no pressure to move quickly. An hour later, Khan, Tree Walker, and Bunny Pouncer returned, bellies bulging. Bunny Pouncer bounded happily about, reenacting the hunt. Khan, rather than dozing as he usually did after a big meal, paced the speaking place and finally butted his head against Hashti's legs. "Get your little-lodge, Rose Cub. We go."

"Why?" she asked. She enjoyed Bunny Pouncer's antics.

Khan shifted his weight. "A (storm?) comes. Cold. Big wind. We must not sleep (here?)."

"Beaver Teacher and Rose Cub go blackpine shelter?" Hashti asked, without much hope.

Khan snarled. "I am no leaf eater."

Big Eyes returned as Hashti checked the balance of her pack. He'd been less successful than his mother. Even with his feathers fluffed out to provide insulation against the wind, Hashti could see the flatness of his sides. How long since Big Eyes had eaten? Why couldn't he share his mother's kill as his sister had, and refresh his strength? But Hashti had no chance to ask. Everyone was moving on. Tree Walker and her cubs bade farewell with much sniffing and rubbing.

"Go big away, get hunted things good," Khan said to Tree Walker. Or so Hashti heard. But the ornamented melody and ruffling of Khan's neck feathers suggested an elegant, ritualized farewell. More likely he'd said, "May you travel widely, and forever find fine hunting."

"Get many quarry and good drinks," the tigress replied.

Hashti hiked with Khan to a small river about a mile away. Snow had drifted deeply against the southwestern bank, nearly covering the tops of the whipbranch bushes. Khan scrabbled a hole between the bushes and the overhanging bank. Hashti buried her tent so that it faced Khan's burrow. Drifted snow and the sides of the ravine would protect them from almost any wind. Hashti sharpened a long slender stick with which she could poke an airhole, should the drifts cover them completely.

She had discovered that winter campfires, at best, roast one side of the body, while the other side develops goose bumps. Hashti now used fire only for cooking and melting water. Tonight, she inched out on a boulder and dipped her drinking water from a hole in the ice of the swift-flowing stream. She wondered briefly about the presence of open water at this temperature. Did a hot spring empty into the stream somewhere nearby? She would have to ask Khan, if she could. A bath would be wonderful. In the meantime, she eased carefully to shore with her water. Combined with trail rations and frozen roasted meat from two days back, it made a fine supper. She swallowed a tryp tablet with the final bite. Anna was right. Pills went down far more easily than gravy.

Kevin walked her dreams that night. He stood on the road outside the stable, his gun leveled at Tree Walker's cubs. Hashti shouted at him not to shoot. When he obeyed, lowering his gun, the tigress sprang and broke his neck with a single well-placed bite. Big Eyes watched from the bushes, hunger in his gaze, ribs protruding.

Then the tigers turned on Hashti, growling that she was an imposter, a leaf eater. Likewise the men of the camp searched for her, sure that she had murdered Kevin. Gay called her name. She huddled silent in a snowbank, scarcely breathing. Just when she thought she'd escaped, her beacon burst into frantic beeping. Gay grabbed her wrist to haul her out of the drift. She fought back. Eventually she woke enough to realize she'd been dreaming. Her arm was confined only by her sleeping bag. The beacon still chirped.

Again? Hashti dug it out of the pile of clothes in the foot of her bag. A tiny indicator light confirmed that the alarm had been triggered by a signal from camp, and had responded by broadcasting her coordinates. It was seven-thirty in the morning, half an hour before sunrise. What prompted Big Red and Anna to disturb her at this hour?

Anna sounded brisk and alert as always. "Good morning, Hashti. You ready for the blizzard?"

"Snugly camped and sound asleep," Hashti answered. "At least I was a few seconds ago."

"Sorry," Anna replied, with what might or might not

have been genuine remorse. "I forgot you're on sun time. But I do have a reason for calling. We had more excitement after we talked to you last night."

"Gay found out I'm gone," Hashti guessed.

"Right. Lance sent him three different places in a row to find you, and when you weren't at any of them, Gaylord put two and two together. He knew where to come with his questions, too." Anna's voice held a lilt of amusement. "It's the first time in years anyone's decked Big Red."

Gay must indeed have been angry. Red stood a full foot taller than he, and the big man was not delicately built. "What happened then?" Hashti asked. "Is everyone all right?"

"Red's cheek is pretty tender and Gay acquired a bloody nose on the return round, but they both deserved what they got. Men that age ought to know better. When Gay settled down enough to listen, we played him your reports, and suggested he talk to you this morning and hear from your own lips that you're all right. He was still mad, but he said it sounded like a good idea. I should have known he was too agreeable."

"Why? Where is he now?"

"On his way to talk to you. In person. The motorsled roared out about two hours ago."

Hashti swore. No more sleep this morning. "How soon will he be here?"

"Maybe an hour. Maybe three. Depending how rough the traveling is and how well Gay drives. When he gets close he'll have to trigger your beacon again for a more exact location." Anna paused. "Hashti, if you want to come home with him, do it. Tigers can be ugly, and so can blizzards."

"I'll think it over," Hashti told the First-Inner. She switched the beacon off, and lay awake in her little co-

coon within the snowbank. She would not return to
camp. There was still too much to learn. Running
seemed pointless. The coming storm might hide her for a
while, but at best, it would delay the reckoning. Sooner
or later, Gay would find her.

Best face him now, and make clear her reasons for
refusing to go back. She hoped she could convince Gay
to accept her decision. What were her options, if he did
not?

The beacon screeched again an hour and a half after
sunrise. Khan flattened his ears and growled. Perhaps he
had reasons of his own for disliking the noise. Perhaps it
irritated him only because it agitated Hashti. She slapped
the shutoff switch, but the beacon broadcast her complete location before it subsided into silence.

The young woman turned to Khan. "Hill beaver
comes—Barroom, barroom!" She imitated the raucous
noise of the sled. "Rose Cub sings to beaver. Khan
stays. Rose Cub comes back."

Khan's ear swiveled. "I will go with you."

"No! Hill beaver hunts Khan. It has—" Hashti
paused. "It goes *bang bang!*" she finished. It would actually go *squirt squirt* with a gun full of contact poison, but
she'd not yet succeeded in explaining that to Khan.

Khan knew what guns could do. "Will he not (shoot?)
*you*, Rose Cub?"

"No *bang bang* Rose Cub. Hill beaver sings to Rose
Cub. Khan stays."

This offended Khan's pride, but he had sense. "I will
stay (here?) (while?) you sing to the hill beaver."

Hashti planned to go no farther than the next bend of
the stream, but Anna had drilled her well—never go
*anywhere* without equipment. By the time Hashti had
loaded the fanny pack and belted it on, she could hear
the alien drone of the motorsled's engine breaking the

snow-clad silence of the hills. She listened hard, hoping she had imagined it. No. Gay was near at hand.

She headed south to meet him, keeping the ravine between herself and the gradually increasing noise of the sled. Her beacon went off again as Gay took a corrective reading. A quarter mile from her tent, she sat down on a dry rock to wait. A low and leaden cloud front cut off the sun. She hoped she could finish this before snow began. The noise grew louder. The sled roared into sight on the opposite bank of the ravine.

Gay drove. The cook sat behind him, alertly scanning the forest, his stance suggesting he held a weapon of some sort. A skunk gun loaded with contact poison? Hashti was glad she'd left Khan behind. She waved at the visitors. "Over here!"

Forest silence dampened the offensive echoes as Gay switched off the motor. The cook kept watch from his perch on the vehicle while Gaylord dismounted and hurried to the lip of the ravine. An absurd clench of desire stirred in Hashti's belly. She stilled it.

"Hashti!" Gay called across the stream. "You're safe! There's a big storm blowing in. I came to take you back."

She stayed sitting. "I'm not going back. I've got a snug camp and plenty of food. The storm won't be a problem."

He set his jaw. "You're not safe. Tigers killed two more people yesterday. Sooner or later, one will attack you. You won't survive unarmed."

"I'm doing better unarmed than you are with your guns. I've already met strange tigers. We rubbed faces and spoke Names. I have a Name, you know. I'm not a leaf eater anymore."

The cook glanced over his shoulder at her. His comment was meant to be private, but Hashti could hear quite clearly across the snowy gorge. "Has she gone crazy?"

"Heaven only knows," her lover muttered. He raised his voice. "Look. Can't you talk to tigers from camp? Wouldn't this whole project be easier with hot food and a warm place to sleep?"

Hashti steeled herself against temptation. "Not if you're killing tigers. Besides, they don't believe in lodges. They'd think I was just a beaver."

The cook shook his head. A hard round snowflake bounced off Hashti's nose. Gay glanced apprehensively at the sky. "I can't spend all day here, Hashti. Get in the sled."

"Did you hear anything I said?" she asked. "I'm not going back to camp."

"I can't afford to leave you here," Gay said with angry honesty. "Too many wild rumors. Your absence makes me look bad. I have to take you home."

"Will you quit shooting if I come?"

"No. The tiger pelts are our chance to beat the Company. We have to get them now, before the men lose heart. I can't drop everything to accommodate your whims."

"Gay, those are people you're shooting!"

He shook his head again. "You're kidding yourself. Words aren't intelligence. Lael read up on feline communication. She says even house cats have special noises for special situations—one for 'rat' and another for 'mouse.' If your tigers are so smart, where's their technology? Where's their governmental structure? What are they doing with those alleged brains?"

"That's what I'm here to find out."

"It's a wild goose chase. Khan's been good to you so far, but you don't know when he'll turn on you. Or when his friends will."

"Gay, what do I have to do to convince you they're smart?"

"Show me a centrally heated tiger den. Get them to build a bridge across the Merrywater. Have one explain integral calculus to me."

"They don't have that kind of culture! Their bodies aren't built for it! Khan doesn't need central heating."

"So what's left that you call intelligence, if all they do is hunt and make weird noises?"

"Those weird noises are speech!"

Gay sighed impatiently. "We're going in circles. Look. If you're so goddamn fluent in tiger talk, tell them to stay away from Swamp City. Then you won't have to worry about me killing them."

"I can't tell them that from the back of your motorsled."

A veil of little white dots swirled between them. "Storm's here," the cook muttered.

Gay nodded aknowledgment and raised his voice. "We'll talk about it later, Hashti. Right now, I'm taking you home. Will you cooperate?"

Would she ever get another chance to meet Khan on his own ground? "No."

"I gave you your chance." Gay muttered something to the cook. Then he plunged feet-first down the bank of the ravine, creating a plume of snow which dispersed rapidly in the wind. He really meant to drag her home against her will!

He'd have to catch her first. Hashti braced her pole tips in the snow and pushed, launching herself north along the ravine.

Whipbranch, brambles, paperbark, and young blackpine grew thickly here where sunlight, in kinder weather, pierced the break in the forest canopy. The lush understory hindered Hashti's flight, but it would also shield

her from Gaylord's eyes, if she made good her head start
while he fought his way across the stream. Snow, pelting
from the sky and streaming off the trees, provided a second protective screen. Hashti paused, panting, three
hundred yards upstream. She peered cautiously back
from the cover of a young blackpine. Surely Gay had
clambered up the east bank of the ravine by now! But
she saw no sign of him. She had skis and Gay did not.
Perhaps he had given up the chase.

Her beacon squeaked for the third time this morning.
Hashti punched angrily at it. "Shut up!" Evading a radio
trace required action more drastic than she wanted to
take.

But already she heard the sled's motor again. Gay or
the cook must be pursuing along the opposite bank.
Hashti stood in the whirling snow, fingering the beacon.
Ross's beacon. Hashti's lifeline. How much did the
tigers mean to her?

The sled emerged through the thickening storm, its
engine noise blending with the wind's roar. Gay dismounted, cupping his hands to his mouth to help his
voice carry through the storm. "We'll catch you sooner
or later. Come now, and make it easier for all of us!"

She bit her lip, so hard it bled. "No. I'm staying. Give
this to Big Red and Anna!" She hurled the beacon at
him.

It thudded into the snow at his feet. He glared helplessly. "Hashti! You can't stay without this!"

She fled.

The sled's motor revved for the chase, but the wind
had gusted again. Blowing snow obscured Hashti's view
of Gay, and his of her. Soon, she knew, even her tracks
would vanish. Trembling with an aftershock of fear and
excitement, she pushed north toward her tent. If she
could evade Gay even a little longer, he'd never find her.

The gale pummeled her as she moved upstream. She leaned into it, struggling for balance, fearful lest she slide down onto the icy rocks below, equally fearful of leaving the stream, now her only guide. Driven snow stung like sand on her face. Envying the cook his thick beard, she pulled her scarf up to cover her mouth and nose, and tugged her knit cap down over her forehead. Then she drew her windjacket's hood tight over all, leaving only a narrow tunnel for breath and vision.

Fifteen minutes later she stopped. What little she could see, through her clothing and the storm, looked unfamiliar. Had she missed the tent? She saw no old footprints, but snow filled her tracks nearly as fast as she made them. Worse, her left hand was numb. Crouching to protect herself from the wind, she investigated. Sure enough, as she floundered along the bank, snow had worked its way into her elbow-high mittens. The hand was raw and red, with several dead white spots. Frostbite! Cursing her carelessness, she opened her jacket enough to slip her hand inside. Tucked into her armpit, the fingers thawed quickly. Hashti gritted her teeth against the burning pain. The teeth would not stay clenched. They clattered against each other.

"What are the signs of hypothermia?" she heard Anna's voice asking. "Shivering, irrationality, clumsiness, drowsiness. Ways to avoid it? Dress right, stay dry, eat well, avoid exhaustion. Treatment? Get out of the cold, hot liquids, dry clothes, warm bodies."

Frightened, Hashti considered her options. The tent was the place to be, but she didn't know where to look for it. The search would keep her warm for a while, but the longer she kept moving, the more tired and cold she'd be when she stopped. Why, oh, why had she abandoned the beacon? And where, oh, where was Khan?

The temperature dropped every minute that she stood

there. She had to do something. "Get out of the cold, hot liquids, dry clothes, warm bodies." She'd stop where she was. Thank God for the emergency pack.

She wrapped herself in a thin, windproof tarpaulin, and sat in the deepest snowbank available. She wriggled down so that her head was out of the wind. Vaguely she remembered that the head was a major source of heat loss. She pulled the tarp up over her hood.

What next? "Hot liquids, dry clothes, warm bodies." Warm bodies? She thought longingly of Gaylord's sturdy frame. But Gay was gone. So was Khan. Dry clothes? She'd brought spare socks and mitten liners, but first she'd have to strip off the ones she was wearing. She couldn't bring herself to do that, when she was finally getting hands and feet warmed up. Hot liquids?

She took a self-heating bottle from the pack. Just pull the tab and wait three minutes. She was shivering too hard to get a firm grip. Angry, she tore the tab out with her teeth.

Three minutes. Her timekeeper lay in Gay's motorsled. But minutes can be counted. One one-thousand, two one-thousand, three one-thousand...where was Khan? Ten one-thousand, eleven one-thousand...Still waiting patiently in that cozy snowbank? Or had he gone looking for Hashti? Forty-six one-thousand, forty-seven one-thousand. Had he run afoul of Gaylord despite her warning? Fifty-nine one-thousand, sixty one-thousand! Had she counted two minutes, or three? Better be cautious. She started the third minute's count over again. At fifty-nine, doubt swept through her. Was she really that far into the count? Or had she skipped from thirty-nine to fifty? She counted out an extra ten, to be sure.

The bottle held a warm syrupy concoction. It burned her tongue. She spat it out. She didn't need it anyway. She'd stopped shivering. Only her toes were still cold.

She dumped snow into the bottle, cooling its contents to the temperature of a hot bath, and poured the liquid into her boots. Her toes had been happier cold. They screamed with outrage as circulation returned.

Vaguely Hashti remembered Anna telling her that after drinking the liquid, she could use the bottle with its chemical mixture as a heating pad. But it was really too hot to feel good. She set it in the snow.

Wind whistled outside. She leaned back, congratulating herself on her arrangements. Too bad Gaylord wasn't here to see how comfortable she was! She had just one worry—that strange tigers might come. She needed something outside to scare them away. She stood up, stripped off her outer sweater, and dressed a broken sapling with it. Not bad. She stuck the discarded bottle on top as a head. Even better. But her scarecrow needed fingers, to show that it was intelligent. All intelligent creatures have hands, that's what Lael told everyone. Hashti tried to tie some twigs to the ends of the sleeves. It was an impossible job, with the clumsy double-layered mittens she was wearing. She took them off and tried again. Then, above the howling of the wind, she heard the very thing she had been fearing: a tiger call.

The tiger, with a black-masked face, stood not six feet from her. "Rose Cub! What are you doing?"

She made a shooing motion. "Get away from here," she told the tiger in clear English. "You'll attract the bad guys."

Instead of leaving, he came closer to sniff at her. She slapped his nose. He shied back and looked at her. "You (?) shelter, hill beaver cub. The wind is (fierce?)."

She began laughing. A hill beaver, was she? Not any more. She'd just pitched her beacon at a hill beaver's feet. He was unlikely to want her in his lodge. She was a speaker now. As soon as she had her property marker erected, she would take a nap in true tiger fashion.

The tiger moved a few steps away, squinting against the wind. "Come, Rose Cub."

She gave up on the fingers of her scarecrow. She'd tie them on after the storm. "No," she told the tiger. "I'm fine where I am." He looked as if he didn't understand her. Well, never mind. She sat down in her snowbank.

She should have finished her scarecrow. Perhaps it would have kept the tiger from attacking her. As it was, he fished her out of the snow with his paws and bit her in the back of the neck. Fortunately he was confused by her layers of clothing, and ended up with only her jacket between his teeth. He pulled. She twisted around and kicked him. "Put me down, you brute!"

He shook her. Her head snapped painfully. Frightened, she kept quiet. Her hood in his mouth, her body trailing between his front legs, the big cat dragged her along. Her boots left an interesting furrow in the snow. This was undignified and uncomfortable, but Hashti was too tired to think of a way to free herself. The world faded in a white blur.

# CHAPTER TWELVE

✴✴✴✴

HASHTI WOKE IN BLINDING, BURNING AGONY. SHE
floated in pain-wracked darkness, every muscle bathed
in flame. She tried to lash out. Suffocating fire invaded
her nostrils, while the world heaved in a seasick sway.
Some great unseen force twisted her head as she gasped
and choked. Had she died? No, she was still breathing.
She groaned, longing to lapse back into oblivion.

Instead, she suffered a slow return to consciousness.
Her name was Hashti, and her last memories were of a
cool, restful world of ice and snow. Khan had been dragging her somewhere. Where had he brought her, and
when had sleep been overtaken by pain? Tiger song penetrated the roaring in her ears. "Sing, Rose Cub," it
commanded.

The resonant voice was real, and close at hand, although it echoed in a way that made it difficult to understand. "Khan?" Hashti whispered into the darkenss.

"She wakes," a voice sang on the other side of her.
"She (should?) drink." A massive object shifted at the
periphery of Hashti's vision. Suddenly she could see
again. She lay on her back in a warm pool, her half-sub-
merged head resting on the rocky bottom, her feet drifting in deeper water. The underside of a huge boulder
formed an ice-caked ceiling just four feet above her.
Twisting around, she saw that the cave was about fifteen

feet deep and seven feet wide, with water filling the rear half. Tree Walker lolled beside Hashti, guarding her from turning her face underwater. The two cubs sprawled at the water's edge. Khan had just moved aside from the frost-rimed entrance, allowing light and a frigid swirl of snow to enter the cave. Beyond its icy mouth, Hashti saw only blank blizzard whiteness.

Khan waded over to nose at Hashti. "Drink!" he ordered.

Drink? She blinked stupidly. Drink what? The tiger's motion sent tiny ripples lapping at her face. Ah yes— drink! Hashti rolled onto her side. She came up spluttering. She tried again, more carefully. The water, slightly warmer than body temperature, slid smoothly down her throat and blotted out the screaming of her limbs. She let her head drop back against the rock bottom, took a deep breath to be sure her nose was above water, and fell asleep.

Darkness greeted her again at her second waking. Her body, so recently abandoned to the storm, still protested its recall to service. But other sensations penetrated the pain. She smelled tigers around her, warm and comforting. She felt the gentle sway of water as she shifted position. She cupped her hand, drank, and slept again.

Morning had come when she woke the third time, now lucid enough to understand what had happened. Too little sleep, too much difficult travel, and the stress of the flight from Gay, had left her vulnerable to hypothermia. The blizzard's bitter cold and high winds tipped the balance. She'd had warning: frostbitten fingers, uncontrollable shivering, clumsy inability to grip the tab on the hotbottle, desire for sleep. But the most deadly symptom, irrationality, had blinded her to what was happening. She winced as she remembered her stubborn struggle to erect a scarecrow. No wonder Khan had been nonplussed by her behavior!

But the tiger had refused to let her slip into icy death. He'd dragged her here, to this rocky shelter with its warm spring, and persuaded Tree Walker and her cubs to share their hideaway. Sprawled in the pool surrounded by tigers, Hashti had warmed back to life.

It seemed a mixed blessing. Her feet ached and itched from frostbite. She was weak. The pool which had saved her life had also soaked her clothes. Without dry garments, she'd relapse into hypothermia as soon as she left the cave. Hashti slid along the slimy bottom into deeper water, stripped, and washed and wrung her soiled clothing.

Khan must have told Tree Walker's family about the hill beaver's removable feathers, for they showed no alarm at her actions. They did stare curiously. Hashti had never been more aware of her body's smallness and helplessness. Bunny Pouncer flicked her ears disapprovingly. "The hill beaver is very (thin?) (without?) its feathers." The cub pointedly used the pronoun for an animal rather than a person. "It would have (died?) if we had not warmed it."

How dreadfully true, Hashti thought, as she clambered out of the water and spread her dripping clothes on rocks near the entrance. The hill beaver would also die if no one fed it. She was ravenously hungry. Khan customarily went several days between gorgings. Having eaten the day before yesterday—(how long had she lain unconscious?)—Khan was unlikely to hunt until the blizzard ended. Just as well, Hashti's soberer judgment decided. Her pills were back by the stream with the rest of her emergency equipment. Without them, the tigers' largesse would soon poison her. She glanced again at the snow whirling outside, then retreated shivering into the water.

The hours dragged less than they might have, for the cubs, bored by inactivity, turned all their curiosity upon the hill beaver who shared their cave. They themselves were still learning their language, and they loved to show off for someone who knew even less. Also, they had less difficulty than adults in distinguishing the sounds of human speech. The cubs and Hashti began working out a pidgin: part tiger, part English, part mime, and part frustration. Hashti talked with Big Eyes and Bunny Pouncer until her throat hurt.

Conversation did not assuage Hashti's hunger, nor could she fool her stomach by filling it with warm water. "Rose Cub hungry," she complained to Khan a few hours later, with little hope of satisfaction.

"Cubs are (always?) hungry," he grumped.

"I'm not hungry," Bunny Pouncer boasted, eager as always to assert her adult status.

Hashti was desperate beyond pride. "Rose Cub hungry," she persisted.

"Small cubs must be fed (often?)," Tree Walker remarked. She rose from her spot in the pool and shook herself, spraying fine drops of water over Hashti. Then the tigress padded softly to the water's edge. She looked back at Hashti. "Come, Rose Cub."

Wondering if she'd understood correctly, the woman followed the tigress out of the water.

Tree Walker lowered her head at Hashti's feet. The tigress's sides heaved briefly. A reeking mess of nearly-digested moose meat spewed from her throat. She sat back, licking a few stray drops from her lips. "Eat, Rose Cub."

Hashti stared for as long as it took the smell to reach her nostrils. Then her own body spasmed to add a new sour-bitter contribution to the puddle on the floor. The woman fought to calm herself. She breathed deeply. The stench sent her stomach heaving again, although she had nothing left to throw up. She plunged back into the pool and rinsed her mouth, staying as far as possible from the steaming pile beside which Tree Walker sat, ruff raised.

Bunny Pouncer stepped briskly over to nose the pile of tiger and human vomit. She lapped tentatively at it. Hashti fought down her bile and closed her eyes. Now the tigers were all talking at once.

"Stop!" Tree Walker chided Bunny Pouncer. "The (vomit?) is for Rose Cub."

"Rose Cub (wants?) it not," Bunny Pouncer retorted.

"(Why?) eat you not?" Khan asked. "(Vomit?) is good for cubs."

"(Maybe?) Rose Cub is not a cub," Big Eyes speculated. "Hill beavers are small. Perhaps it is (?)."

"Come, eat," Khan ordered.

"No," Hashti said. "Rose Cub eats not (vomit?). Bunny Pouncer eats, yes. Big Eyes eats, yes. Rose Cub eats not."

"(Vomit?) is good for cubs," Khan insisted.

Hashti clapped her hands over her ears, her sign that she needed a chance to catch up with the conversation. Cubs! Cubs ate vomit! And Khan thought Hashti a cub. She'd gone along with the misidentification, feeling it gave her leeway for inexperience, social blunders, and just plain weakness. Now it caught up with her. Cubs ate vomit.

Hashti took her hands off her ears. "Rose Cub no cub," she explained as emphatically as possible. "No cub. No eat vomit."

"(I told you so?)" Big Eyes fluted. "Rose Cub is (a female?), (that is why?) she is small."

"True?" Tree Walker asked. "You are (a female?)?"

Hashti hoped she had understood the conversation correctly. She pointed to the mess on the floor, swallowing her gut's protest. "Yes. Rose Cub eats not vomit. Rose Cub *makes* vomit. Feeds cubs."

Tree Walker, confused by Hashti's refusal to partake despite the woman's need, eyed her dubiously. "Shall Bunny Pouncer eat the vomit?"

"Bunny Pouncer and Big Eyes eat vomit, yes!" Hashti assented.

Bunny Pouncer moved in. Big Eyes watched wistfully. Hashti noticed again how thin the male cub was. "Big Eyes eat vomit," she suggested.

Tree Walker growled—briefly, but a true working growl. "No. Big Eyes is (?). He (must?) kill (in order to? before?) he eats."

Hashti frowned. How could Big Eyes' own mother refuse food to the starving cub? Bunny Pouncer, large, healthy, and capable of killing for herself, lapped freely! But Hashti herself was too hungry, weak, and now nauseated, to argue. She sank back into the pool and tried to ignore Bunny Pouncer's slurps.

By next morning, the stench of vomit was gone, and Hashti's clothes had reached a state approximating dryness. Her hunger had only sharpened. She dressed, crawled to the mouth of the cave, and peered out at the whirling snow. Khan's whiskers twitched disapprovingly. "Go back to the water, Rose Cub."

She shrank from the bitter wind. "Where Rose Cub's little-lodge?"

"Under the snow, (silly?) cub. The wind blows (fiercely?). Stay in the water where you will be warm."

"Beaver Teacher go little-lodge. Rose Cub go little-lodge with Beaver Teacher." Hashti crawled beyond the overhanging ledge of the cave entrance, looking back to be sure Khan followed, hoping he would lead her to the tent. But when she tried to stand, blood drained from her head and the blizzard dissolved in red swirls before her eyes. Thrown off balance by the wind, Hashti fell back onto hands and knees. Head drooping, she waited for the dizziness to subside. She could never travel through deep snow in this condition. Defeated, she crawled backward into the cave.

Big Eyes watched curiously. "What were you doing, Rose Cub?"

"It (knows?) not," Bunny Pouncer answered. "It is a (silly?) hill beaver."

Hashti slumped against the wall of the cave. She had to have her pack, soon, and she could not retrieve it herself. "Rose Cub no feathers," she reminded Khan. "Little-lodge Rose Cub's feathers."

"Feathers are not a lodge!" Bunny Pouncer protested. Khan, sensing Hashti's seriousness, glared at the young tigress. Bunny Pouncer held her tongue.

"Little-lodge Rose Cub's feathers," Hashti resumed. "In little-lodge Rose Cub warm." She wet her lips, concentrating on the notes, struggling to pronounce the causative form of "come" which meant "fetch." "Beaver Teacher fetches Rose Cub's feathers."

But in Khan's experience, one did not carry feathers. One's own feathers came along automatically. Prey feathers were waste, an indigestible portion to discard. Khan answered with a long-suffering shake of his tail plumage. "No lodgeless one fetches feathers."

Hashti understood that something about the notion of fetching feathers bothered Khan. She tried again. "Little-lodge Rose Cub's shelter." She had the frustrating feeling that she'd been here before. "Beaver Teacher fetches Rose Cub's shelter."

Khan stared blankly back at her. One did not carry a shelter. One found a shelter, slept in it, then left it and moved on. "No lodgeless one fetches shelter," he told Hashti. "Lodgeless ones fetch (only?) meat."

All right, then! "Rose Cub's meat in little-lodge. Little-lodge Rose Cub's meat. Beaver Teacher fetches meat, fetches little-lodge, fetches Rose Cub's meat!"

Khan glanced towards the entrance. "It is (bitterly?) cold. Snow (falls?) (thick?), and wind roars."

Hashti laid her head against her knees in discouragement. "Rose Cub hungry. Little-lodge meat. Beaver Teacher fetches Rose Cub's meat."

Khan rose and paced to the entrance, wrinkling his nose in distaste as a gust ruffled his thick pelt. He looked reproachfully back at her. "You (want?) me to fetch your little-lodge?"

"Yes!"

"All right," he said, using the special interjection which preceded an unpleasant task. "Stay with the cubs." He disappeared into the whiteness.

Hashti gazed after him into the storm. It looked as if she might survive. She wondered if Gaylord had. He was experienced, capable, and had the cook to help him. The First-In motorsled surely carried generous emergency supplies. Still, the wind blew so fiercely, and it was a long journey back to camp. Gay, however mixed his motives, had tried to help Hashti. Angry as she was at him, she did not want responsibility for his death.

Finally Khan returned, dragging the tent so gently that its fabric suffered no tear. The cubs clustered round. "What is that?"

"A little-lodge," Khan replied, shaking the snow off his coat. "Rose Cub sleeps in it. It is (something like?) feathers." He sounded disgusted.

Hashti was too relieved to be bothered by his mood. She scrambled for her pouch of rations, yanked out a stick of dried fruit, and bit off as large a chunk as she could chew.

She finished the bar, filled her mug from the pool, drank, and pulled out a second ration stick, jerked meat this time. Big Eyes padded over with a wistful sniff.

Hashti stroked his side and felt ribs beneath the down. This food was hers to give. Would the iron in it harm the cub? There was iron in the water he drank. He probably had a fair tolerance. She held out the bar.

"STOP!" Khan streaked across the cave, knocked the bar from Hashti's hand, and watched snarling as she picked herself up.

"What?" Hashti asked, confused and frightened.

"Feed not Big Eyes, you (stupid?) leaf eater. He is (?). He must kill for himself."

Don't get too fond of him, Hashti. Mothers can't afford to spend years on physically unfit cubs.

Big Eyes, who'd been shoved away from Hashti when Khan plunged between them, returned to her side, stepping carefully and pointedly around the meat bar. "I am small," he said, "but I sing better than Bunny Pouncer. When the snow stops, I will kill, and I will speak. Feed me then. (Perhaps?) I will call myself One Who Eats with Rose Cub."

Khan's ruff rose. "I taught Rose Cub to speak," he warned. "The hill beaver is mine."

Tree Walker, ill at ease throughout the incident, smoothed her cub's flank feathers. "Kill soon, my son, or you will die."

Bunny Pouncer, uncharacteristically, held her tongue.

Hashti retrieved the partly-eaten meat bar which had caused all the commotion, but it stuck in her throat as she eyed the cub's twisted front paws and sunken sides. *Could* he kill? She wished she could help him, but could think of no way. He must pass this ordeal on his own.

Bunny Pouncer paced. Tree Walker growled softly when anyone approached her. Khan took over the baby-sitting. "Come," he said to the cubs. "We will teach Rose Cub to (?)."

They tumbled over each other to cuddle up by him. "Come, Rose Cub!"

She took her place at Khan's side. What awaited her now?

He asked Big Eyes some question about lodgeless ones in the cave. Big Eyes answered. Khan asked the same question with respect to the cub's paws. Same answer. Khan inquired about something Hashti did not recognize. Same answer again. He snorted four times. Yet the same answer. Hashti frowned, concentrating. What did tigers in the cave, paws, and snorts have in common?

She held up four fingers. "Four!" everyone hollered. "Very good, Rose Cub! Four!"

Hashti felt slightly miffed. How dare they think this such an achievement? She knew numbers, she just needed the vocabulary! Arithmetic proved more difficult than she anticipated, for tigers counted in sets of four, but Hashti held her own. Then Khan moved to trigonometry.

Abashed, she heard him ask the cubs, "What's (the angle?) between my front paws?" and "From that white rock to the (?) your mother's tail to Rose Cub's eyes, what's (the angle?)?"

They answered to the nearest forty-eighth of a circle.

Then Khan said, "I go down three days and sleep by a lake." Hashti shook her head slightly. Khan's use of the verb "go down" for northward travel always unsettled her. "I turn to the sunset," he continued, "and travel four more days. I come to (?) rocks speaking place. Tell Rose Cub how to go to the speaking place. What (direction?) shall she go?"

"One twelfth (of a full circle) down from sunset," answered Big Eyes, who made his mind compensate for his twisted paws.

Hashti couldn't have figured that, even with a calculator. She'd have had to draw and measure. Big Eyes, by whatever method, had done the problem in his head. "Have one explain integral calculus," Gaylord had challenged. The speakers might be able to.

Khan licked the cub's ear. "Good. (How many?) days of travel?"

"Five," Big Eyes said. "If you started (together?), Rose Cub would (arrive?) two days ahead of you."

"It would not," Bunny Pouncer said. "The leaf eater would (get lost?)."

Khan's ears swiveled back one twelfth of a full circle from their normal position. "Rose Cub knows (numbers?)," he reminded Bunny Pouncer. "She is no leaf eater. She is a speaker. If you call her a leaf eater again, I will pounce you in the snow."

"It is a leaf eater!" Bunny Pouncer repeated, in an excited staccato.

Khan growled and rose to his feet. Bunny Pouncer streaked out into the blizzard. Khan flew after her, ducking to get through the iced-up entryway. Even storm winds failed to cover their growls and squeals as the two wrestled in the snow.

In ten minutes they returned, snow-covered and breathing hard. Tree Walker grumbled some maternal imperative, perhaps "Wipe your feet before you come in."

Bunny Pouncer gave herself a mighty heave, her whole body wriggling. Then she trotted to Hashti's side. "You are a speaker. I will not call you a leaf eater. Although you are a hill beaver," she added, eyes on Khan.

He did not challenge her. Disappointed, she pounced at Big Eyes' tail.

He twitched it away. Bunny Pouncer growled and nipped his shoulder. He swatted at her. She ducked nimbly out of range. With a classic kick-the-dog reaction, Big Eyes turned to Hashti and snarled.

Twisted paws or no, Big Eyes weighed half again what Hashti did. Peaceably she patted the floor beside her. "Lie here, Big Eyes."

He seemed relieved that she had refused the invitation to fight. Whuffing politely, he lay down by her leg. She scratched under his chin. He laid his head across her lap, purring. The warm body felt good alongside her own. If only it were not so thin!

On the third day the storm withdrew, leaving a crunchy-cold, dazzlingly white world. The sun shone once again, although the temperature still hovered thirty degrees below zero. A crisp breeze sent bright crystals skittering along the drifts. Hashti's clothing crackled when she moved.

Tree Walker stretched and sniffed the cold air. "I go to hunt," she announced, and vanished into the trees.

"I too will hunt," Big Eyes said. He headed in the opposite direction.

Hashti needed to recover the rest of her equipment. The tent, which Khan had fetched, contained food, shoulder pack, and some spare clothes. But the most crucial items, like first aid kit, knife, and igniter, had been in the hip pack when Hashti went to meet Gay. They'd been left in the ravine when Khan rescued her.

She had no idea which direction to go. "Where is the river?" she asked Khan.

"What river? There are many rivers."

"The river where I was cold.

"Hill beavers are always cold. Your feathers are (inferior?)."

An action is worth a thousand words, especially when you lack those words. Hashti hung her spare shirt on a stick. "*Scarecrow*," she said in her own language.

Khan looked wary. "You made one of those (during?) the storm."

"Where?" she asked. "Take me to the *scarecrow*."

Twenty minutes' clambering over windpacked drifts brought them to the bank of the ravine. There was no scarecrow. "You brought me to the wrong place," Hashti wanted to tell Khan. But before she could sort out how to say it, a flash of bright color caught her eye.

An orange fabric marker, the kind used for blazing logging trails, fluttered from a broken paperbark sapling a few yards back from the opposite rim of the ravine. Hashti squinted against the glare of sun on snow. Two stubs of branches jutted out from the sapling just below the point where it had broken off. Arms. Hashti looked more carefully at the crushed bushes on her own side of the stream. Broken. By a motorsled's passage.

She crossed the stream, climbed the far bank, and examined the erstwhile scarecrow with its vividly colored flag. Gay must have followed her tracks on foot through the storm, trying to rescue her from an overconfidence which seemed simple madness to him. Even as he followed her, she'd been proving herself unfit to travel without a beacon. By the time Gay reached this spot, Hashti had succumbed to hypothermia and Khan had dragged her away. Gay had found—what? A scarecrow. A hole in the snow. And tracks of a tiger, hauling away a heavy, unmoving object.

Gripped by the simple, irrational feeling that the spot of her death deserved some marker, he'd left this blaze. He did not believe her still alive. If he'd thought there were any hope, he'd have left her sweater and hotbottle. Thank heaven she had spares!

Hashti winced under a new fear. Had Gay left anything at all for her? Her nest in the drift had been a few paces upstream, she thought. Hurrying to the spot, she pawed frantically, tossing aside large brittle chunks of windpacked snow. Nothing. Nothing. Something! A different shade of white amidst the white—the heat-reflective emergency tarpaulin, starred circle glittering on its corner. In the tarp was the hip pack with its valuable supplies. Gay had not noticed it, buried as it was, and had not thought to search for it. For all he'd known, it had still been on Hashti's body.

Her skis, carelessly discarded in the confusion of hypothermia, took longer to find. A tiny round dot of frostbite blossomed on Hashti's cheek as she searched. Only when she finally spied a smoothly shaven ski tip jutting out of the snow, a neat little drift behind it, dangerously close to the lip of the ravine, did Hashti dare believe in her survival.

The final report in the data condenser had warned that Hashti might find it necessary to ditch the beacon, that she was still with Khan and prepared to weather the storm. But Gay's news would supersede her message. Anna and Big Red must now believe her dead. She wished desperately that she could tell them otherwise, but with the beacon gone, she had no means, short of a forest fire, of signaling. They'd know she was alive only when they saw her.

How *would* she get home? The camp lay southeast. She might follow a river to the big lake, but which way to turn when she got there? Would she recognize the mouth of the Merrywater, having seen it only a few times, in other seasons? "This is the frontier," she could hear Anna saying. "We're playing for keeps. This planet will kill you if you don't respect it." Hashti respected it now, from the bottom of her heart. But respect had come too late. Only the tigers could lead her home now, and she had only a limited amount of time with them before nutritional problems caught up with her.

Chastened by her helplessness, she followed Khan back to the cave. She built a fire and made moose stew from her share of Tree Walker's catch. The adult tigers and Bunny Pouncer lazed about with full bellies, watching her. Big Eyes returned very late and very quietly, his muzzle feathers unbloodied.

As he rose in the black of night to resume his hunt, Tree Walker stopped him. "I am (tired?) of this place. We will go down." She warbled a rapid-fire set of directions, concluding, "Find us there. But hunt first. You must kill before hunger (weakens?) you further." Then she drilled him on technique: "(Choose?) an (?) animal, or a cub. (Let?) it come very close. If you jump (too soon?), it will run. (?) hindpaws on the ground (as?) you strike, to move with your (quarry?). Bite behind its ears. You will know (how?)."

Big Eyes blinked, gravely attentive. He knew his time was running out. But he bade farewell to his mother with a cocky flip of his tail, promising, "I will return a speaker."

Hashti could not fall back asleep. Curled in the warmth of Khan's belly, she pondered Big Eyes and his fate. A lodgeless one, it seemed, must kill to become a speaker. Only then could one say "I call myself" instead of "I am called." Only then could one sing one's Name in speaking places.

One killed and spoke—or died. Big Red saw it as a matter of practicality. "A mother can't afford to spend years on an unfit cub." But how could Tree Walker let Big Eyes die? He was markedly brighter and more artic-

ulate than his sister. Why not give him a year or two to
learn to compensate for those twisted paws? Why did
everyone, even Big Eyes himself, so unquestioningly respect the unwritten law of the ordeal?

The matter had implications for Hashti, as well. Khan
had taught her the adult formula, "I call myself." She
had a Name and had sung it at a speaking place. Was this
a special dispensation for an amusing leaf eater? What if
her speakerhood were challenged?

Finally dawn rescued her from troubling thoughts.
Khan purred approvingly at Tree Walker's plans. "Rose
Cub and I will travel with you. The hill beaver learns
well from your cubs." Hashti did a rapid mental tally.
Her First-In rations were nearly gone, but she had a
week's supply of tryp and chelator pills, and several days
beyond that before any symptoms of poisoning developed. It was true that she learned well from the cubs,
and the more she learned of tiger language and culture,
the more effective an ambassador she would be on her
return. Yes, she would travel another week with Tree
Walker's family before she asked Khan to guide her back
to camp.

The tigress led them to a sheltered ravine a half day
north. "Many deer (herd?) in the swamp sunsetward,"
she told Khan. Hashti thought of Big Eyes, seeking his
kill.

The adults went their own ways; Hashti and Bunny
Pouncer stayed near the ravine, seeing who could throw
sticks furthest. Hashti enjoyed the game—her body was
designed for throwing sticks. Bunny Pouncer's was not.
The cub finally quit in favor of a nap in the sun. Black
and orange glistened behind Hashti. "Rose Cub! Come
with me." It was Big Eyes, using the slow plain diction
Hashti understood best.

She stared in surprise. "Me? Rose Cub? No Tree Walker, no Beaver Friend?"

"Yes, you, Rose Cub," he said.

Hashti hesitated. The adults were nowhere in sight. Bunny Pouncer opened her eyes slightly. "Take no hill beaver. You must kill!"

Big Eyes laid his ears back. "Rose Cub, will you come?"

"In a second," she muttered, checking the straps of her belt pack.

Bunny Pouncer closed her eyes again. "(As well?) take a rabbit." The drumming of those notorious pests ruined many a tiger hunt.

Ignoring his sister, Big Eyes led Hashti into the forest. What had he in mind? Surely Bunny Pouncer was right —the swishing of skis would spook the deer! Hashti said as much, softly.

Big Eyes paused behind a cedar tree to explain. "Deer feed below us, in the swamp. Go around them, six twelfths. Stay on the hill, (frighten?) them not. Then descend by the big stump sunsetward. Make much noise. Now, stick your head in the snow!"

Hashti started. "In the snow? Now?"

Perfectly calm, he repeated the ludicrous command. "Yes. Stick your head in the snow!"

She hesitated. Then, slowly, she knelt on her skis and put her head to the drifts between them—

"Rose Cub? (What troubles you?), Rose Cub?" Big Eyes' nose nudged the back of her neck as he sang the soft inquiry tigers used when a companion showed distress.

"Rose Cub sticks head in snow," she said, stumbling as she tried to conjugate the unusual verb.

He stared at her in puzzlement. "The snow is deep, I told you!"

"Oh, no!" Hashti crumpled in laughter. Just when she thought she'd learned the language! Big Eyes hadn't said "Stick your head in the snow"! He'd said "Beware the very deep snow!" Never again would Hashti forget that depth measurements took the preposition "in."

The snow was not only deep, but cold on her unprotected nose. Hashti wiped herself off and declared herself ready to go. She did not ask Big Eyes about his own plans, but she was fairly certain he would be lying in wait when the herd bolted. His strategy impressed her, and she was glad to take part, even if she'd been chosen for her clumsiness. She circled wide around the swamp, as instructed. Big Eyes had been right about the snow. It had drifted over bushes, leaving pockets of air which collapsed when Hashti crossed them. Again and again her skis sank beneath her. When she tried to climb back to the surface, her ski tips snagged on the snow crust. She had the full attention of the deer.

Finally she reached the stump, and charged towards the herd, yelling. Startled, the deer barked and ran. Big Eyes broke from cover to jump at a fleeing doe. She dodged. He followed, rising on his hind legs to sink his teeth in her shoulder. He pulled. She stumbled and fell. He struck again, higher on her neck.

Fascinated by these events, Hashti forgot to watch her footing. The crooked branches of a fallen paperbark tree embraced her ankle, and she pitched headfirst into the drifts.

Her body sank. Her feet, buoyed by the skis, stayed on the surface. She tried to sit up, pushing with her hands. Her arms only sank deeper into the yielding powder. She remembered Ross's advice for such a situation. "Try your pole. If that doesn't work, you'll have to take the skis off."

Here in the swamp, snow depth exceeded the length

of her pole. By the time Hashti righted herself, dusted off, and got her footgear back in order, Big Eyes stood proudly over his first kill. He had not escaped un-scathed. His second bite should have gone into the doe's neck from above, severing her spine. Instead, he'd gripped from below, hanging on until the constriction of her windpipe strangled his prey. She'd had time to slash at him with her dainty-looking hooves. Big Eyes had lost some blood.

But he had killed nonetheless. Bright-eyed with triumph, he raised his voice. His roar echoed proudly.

Tree Walker and Khan responded from the far side of the hill. Big Eyes bellowed directions. The adults arrived as he dragged the liver from the deer's belly. Bunny Pouncer bounded close behind, struggling not to pant.

Tree Walker saw her son, his own and the doe's blue blood smeared across his bright feathers, and the victim on the snow. "You have killed," she said, her ceremonial formality failing to hide her delight. "Speak, my son!"

Big Eyes, hungry as he must have been, left the liver untouched on the ground in front of him. Spreading his ruff, he declared, "I call myself, He Who Hunts With Rose Cub."

Silence. Hashti's proud smile faded as Tree Walker and Khan stared at her, ears flat. What was wrong? Shouldn't there be a celebration? Big Eyes had made his kill! Why did the other tigers act as if something terrible had occurred? "(When?) came you here, Rose Cub?" Khan growled. He looked back at Big Eyes. "Why call yourself He Who Hunts With Rose Cub?"

"Rose Cub (helped?) me kill," the cub answered.

Tree Walker's tail slashed furiously, tumbling snow from a small blackpine behind her. Bunny Pouncer had shrunk down on her belly, feathers pressed tight to her body as if she were in pain. Khan stepped stiffly for-

ward, ears swiveled backward, his gaze shifting from Big
Eyes to Hashti. She faced him, frightened.

"Yes, Rose Cub?" Khan asked. "(Helped?) you with
this cub's kill?"

Too terrified to sing, she nodded. Khan recognized
the gesture. Feathers raised to full loft, he snarled.
"Knew you not the (ordeal?)? (Wished you?) to die,
Rose Cub?"

Her heart thumped furiously. The life-earning kill
must be made unassisted. Even she, an ignorant, half-ar-
ticulate hill beaver, had understood that much. The cub's
own mother would let him starve rather than violate the
ordeal. What had possessed Hashti to interfere?

Khan's body dropped just slightly, preface to a spring.
"(Helped?) you with the cub's kill?" he demanded again.

Big Eyes, stiff and crooked-tailed as Khan himself,
stalked to Hashti and stationed himself by her knees,
raising his voice in a trumpeting call like the one which
Khan had sung over Hashti that first night in the forest.

Khan growled again. "You may not sing the (fanfare?)
over the hill beaver," he told Big Eyes. "You are no
speaker. You know the (?). From the (first?) snow of
your (first?) (?), no lodgeless one may help you. You
must kill (alone?). You have (?) the ordeal."

Big Eyes feathered out his ruff and even dared a slight
hiss. "Rose Cub is no lodgeless one," Big Eyes said. "I
(violated?) not the ordeal."

Bunny Pouncer raised herself slightly from the snow.
"Rose Cub speaks."

"Yes," a reluctant Tree Walker said. "No leaf eater
speaks. (Only?) lodgeless ones have Names."

Hashti, having tried so hard to establish herself as a
tiger among tigers, now listened, panting, and prayed
they would declare her an animal.

"The hill beaver speaks," Khan reflected gravely,

"but Big Eyes sang (truly?)—she came from a lodge, and sleeps in her little-lodge (still?). She is a speaker, but not a lodgeless one. (Applies?) the ordeal to speakers, or to lodgeless ones?"

Bunny Pouncer lifted herself a little farther, to a nearly normal crouch. "My ordeal (applied?) to Big Eyes, who was then a lodgeless one but not a speaker. It is for lodgeless ones."

Khan pondered for long moments. Then his feathers relaxed and his tail straightened. "Yes," he said. "It is for lodgeless ones. Rose Cub, (being lodged?), (violated?) it not."

Bunny Pouncer's feathers lofted back to their usual position. Hashti drooped, tears of relief smarting in her eyes. She wasn't sure she understood it all, but the tigers' posture told her that the crisis had passed. Their decision might have been different had the question been raised in advance. But presented with a *fait accompli*, they had given her the benefit of the doubt. Big Eyes' gamble had paid off. Tree Walker approached the cub, purring, and licked a spatter of blood from his face. "Speak, my son!" she said for the second time.

"I call myself, He Who Hunts With Rose Cub," he repeated, cocking an ear toward Hashti.

Hashti took a deep breath and lifted her head, determined to meet this occasion with true tiger ceremony. "My name shall sing of He Who Hunts With Rose Cub."

# CHAPTER THIRTEEN

❦

BIG EYES' KILL, PROVING HIM A SPEAKER, FREED HIM TO become a cub again, sharing his mother's kills, spending his days in play. Tiger cubs, like youngsters of any species, rehearsed the skills of adulthood in their games. Big Eyes and Bunny Pouncer expected Hashti to follow suit.

In every suitable clearing, they played speaking place, strutting about and bragging of their exploits, practicing tuneful twists on their childish explanations. Hashti, observing the mime that always accompanied Names, began dramatizing parts of her own story.

In more active interludes, Big Eyes and Bunny Pouncer spent hours tossing sticks with their teeth and batting them with their paws, trying to equal Hashti's range.

When the cubs seemed close to success, Hashti improvised a sling. "That (thing?) makes you throw further!" Bunny Pouncer complained.

"Here," Hashti said. She was finally learning to conjugate verbs and pronounce articles. "Take the (thing?). Your turn!"

Bunny Pouncer tried valiantly to use the tool. She succeeded only in entangling herself. Her anatomy could not accommodate a sling. A win for homo sapiens, thought Hashti!

Small victory. She could throw further than Bunny

Pouncer, but the cub could catch rabbits and the woman could not. Hashti's education had not included spearmanship or bow making. She tried to set some snares. No luck. Ross could have managed. Perhaps, with broadcast instructions from Anna, even Hashti could have done it. But the beacon was gone. She swallowed her pride, gave thanks that the tigers shared their kills, and hoped no one would think to put her through the ordeal.

Another storm blew in a week after the first. Hashti and her companions were nestled securely in a brush-sheltered cave when snow began to fly. The tigers, who'd gorged earlier in the day, lay purring with distended bellies, sometimes dozing, sometimes preening, sometimes chatting.

Big Eyes and Bunny Pouncer begged for stories. Khan and Tree Walker responded with heroic sagas, the Names of tigers long dead. They told other stories with even more ornate melodies, pitched in scales distinct from those of ordinary speech. Hashti, whose listening comprehension far outstripped her speaking ability, concluded from the fantastic nature of the events described that these were the fairy tales of the tiger world. One "fairy tale" told of a tiger who ate stars. He went to live in the sky, where he fed on the tiny lights to his heart's content, but they weren't filling enough. He wasted away until only his eyes—New Lebanon's two moons—remained, blinking slowly at the world.

Another legend concerned a tiger who followed the sun around the planet—they knew their world was round!—but could never quite catch it. Finally he turned and went the other way, hiding behind a mountain and ambushing the sun as it rose above the peak. The sun pleaded for mercy. The tiger let it go, but ever after, the sun wobbled in its orbit, coming up at a slightly different place on the horizon every day to avoid ambush.

Bunny Pouncer yawned and laid her head on her paws. "That is a (boring?) story. I would have bitten the sun," she said.

"Well," Khan said, "(as a matter of fact?), Sun Catcher did take a bite of his quarry. But the sun (is embarrassed?), and (hides?) his haunch. Only every few (years?) does he (forget?) and show the bite."

"That's silly," Big Eyes said. "A bite from the sun (means?) a moon walks before it."

"Right," Khan said. "That's why Sun Catcher's Name is a (fairy tale?)." Gay thought these were animals? Hashti knew folk in her own spacegoing society who were less matter-of-fact about eclipses.

The tigers loved taxonomy, and their stories were full of plant and animal names that Hashti did not understand. Many turned out to be archaic terms for creatures such as New Lebanon's horses. Big Eyes told her to listen carefully to one such story. "This gave me (the idea?) for our hunt."

A dozen tigers had surrounded a herd of horses and stampeded them, driving six over a cliff to provide a feast for every tiger in the area. Ross had said that tigers hunted alone, Hashti remembered. It seemed this was not always true. "Why hunt you horses thus, but not deer?" she asked.

Khan shrugged in a very human manner. "Deer live in the forest, where a (hunting group?) makes much noise, and one cannot see what one's (partners?) do. Alone, one can creep close to the deer, (unless?) one's paws are (twisted?). But where the horses live, one (sees a long way?), as does the quarry. Hunting is (easier?) with (partners?)."

"You know that," Big Eyes said. "Other beavers stalked the horse you killed."

The what? "I killed no horse," Hashti said, proud of her mastery of the complex rhythm of the first-person conjugation.

"You tell it in your Name," Big Eyes responded.

Bunny Pouncer lifted her head. "Is your Name a (fairy tale?), Rose Cub?"

From the way Bunny Pouncer asked, Hashti could tell it was an audacious question. Khan's lips lifted away from his teeth. "Rose Cub's Name is no fairy tale. I watched her kill the horse."

Big Eyes saw that the conversation had, as usual, left Hashti behind. He hummed a snatch of the Name Khan had composed for Hashti, the Name she'd so painstakingly and uncomprehendingly memorized at the beginning of her sojourn in the forest. This was one of many sections she'd never understood, though she knew it had something to do with horses.

Her expression told Big Eyes she was still lost. He sang the snatch again, without the grace notes and trills.

With her improved vocabulary, she understood. The hill beavers stalking, the horses taking flight, running down the hill, standing at bay on the ice. Rose Cub, seizing the fallen quarry by the throat, spilling its blood on the snow. So this answered the riddle of her status! Poor Hero. Poor, poor Hero! She'd never dreamed, sitting there with his head on her lap, that she'd just shown herself to be a speaker!

The stories kept coming. "Long, long (ago?)," Tree Walker said, "there were no speakers, nor any other (creatures?). The world had only one cub, a fine young rock. The rock went to his mother the world and said, 'Tell me a story!' She replied, 'I will give you a (sib?) to tell you a story.' And she (gave birth to?) a sweetsap

tree, who spoke its Name to the little rock. But the
sweetsap tree, although tall and far-seeing, traveled not.
Its Name was (boring?). The rock said, 'That is a very
(boring?) Name.' He went to his mother. 'I want to hear
a better story.' So she (gave birth to?) a rose. But the
rose lived only a few days. Its Name was (boring?), too.
'That is very (boring?) Name,' said the rock. He went
back to his mother. 'I want to hear a better story!' So she
(gave birth to?) a rabbit.''

The world produced every imaginable kind of creature, hoping that one could tell interesting stories to the
infant rock. But each time, the storyteller did not travel
widely, or had too short a life, or was too stupid to de-
scribe its adventures. "Finally the rock went to his
mother and said, 'There is not a single (interesting?)
story anywhere. Make me someone with a *large* Name.'
Then the world (gave birth to?) a speaker. The speaker
traveled far, climbed high, and swam (deep?). She
(always?) knew whence she had come, and how far. Her
golden feathers (were bright?) as sunshine, her stripes
black as night, and her belly white as moon and stars and
(?) on water. She lived long, and had a (beautiful voice?)
for singing her Name to the world's cub. She was mother
of all the lodgeless ones (that have ever been?), and she
had many cubs, so that the world's babies never (lack
for?) stories.''

"That is why there is a rock in (every?) speaking
place,'' Khan added. "The world's cubs still (love to
hear?) our Names.''

"What about hill beavers?'' Big Eyes asked. "Why
told they no stories to the baby rock?''

"Hill beaver Names (are far inferior?) to speakers','''
Bunny Pouncer said.

"No,'' Tree Walker said, looking puzzled, "that's not
(the answer?). There were no hill beavers, in those days.

There has (never?) been a hill beaver in our world, not in any fairy tale nor in any (ancient?) name, until (now?)."

The cub's wide golden eyes turned to Hashti. "Whence came you, Rose Cub?"

She was tempted to tell them that the baby rock had grown tired of tiger Names, and petitioned his mother for a new and more interesting species of storyteller. She shoved the impulse aside. "I (was born?) beyond the stars," she told the tigers.

To them, it probably sounded more ridiculous than the world-cub explanation. Certainly it sounded like something from a poorly written frontier novel. But Hashti's companions considered the answer gravely.

"That's a fairy tale," Bunny Pouncer decided. "Every one knows that when you climb the (?) gets (weak?) and cold. If you climbed to the stars you could not (breathe?). And you would (freeze to death?)."

"That is why we have lodges and fires," Hashti answered.

Bunny Pouncer had never understood lodges and fires. She was ill positioned to argue.

Even Hashti's hunting partner, Big Eyes, looked skeptical. "How got you to the stars? You are not Star Eater. You know not how (to fly?)."

She tried to explain about shuttles and starships. No engineer would have recognized the result. "There is a very large rock with a cave in it, where we make our lodges. When fire burns under the great rock, it flies."

The whole thing sounded absurd, but the tigers had no better explanation. Khan, who had seen human technology, gave Hashti the benefit of the doubt. "Hill beavers fetch sticks that thunder and kill deer at four-cubed paces. And I saw a small rocklike thing make loud noise and run swiftly across snow. It is said in speaking places that in the (past?) two (years?), three very large hot rocks fell into Bluewater Lake, and sprang up again. When the rocks fell, hill beavers (appeared?). Rose Cub has not sung a fairy tale."

Big Eyes stared eagerly at her. "Could a lodgeless one enter the burning rock?"

"Yes," Hashti answered.

"And fly to worlds beyond the stars, with meadows and forests and enormous horses?"

"Yes."

He snuggled against her. "Take me to the burning rock. I will go the stars and have a greater Name than any cub on this world."

Bunny Pouncer jumped to her feet. "Not you. I will go."

Big Eyes snarled. "I am He Who Hunts With Rose Cub."

Khan looked warningly at them. "You are only cubs. I, Beaver Teacher, will go. But not (until?) the wind stops."

Disappointed, they lay down. Big Eyes' thoughts were still beyond the stars. "Why speaks not your Name (of this?)?" he asked.

It wasn't in Hashti's Name because Khan had composed her Name and he'd known nothing about her coming from the stars. She wasn't going to admit that in Bunny Pouncer's hearing. Instead, she announced, "I shall respeak my Name."

This was a project even more interesting than fairy tales. Adults composed their own Names. For cubs and hill beavers, a community effort was allowed. While the blizzard bellowed outside, tigers crowded around Hashti to help her modify her song. The tiny niche in the cliff echoed with excited suggestions. She wondered if her hearing would survive intact.

Her new Name was beautiful, and this time she understood every line—well, nearly. She began by telling of Carolina's light gray mountains and the tall horses of the grasslands. Then she described the mountainside house she'd been born in.

Next she told how the puny hill beaver cub with the long black ruff pounced horses. "Pounce," she had learned, was a technical term for encountering prey in a position that would yield an easy kill, then springing away without harming the victim. A pounce was more difficult and dangerous than a kill, since one could be seriously injured while disengaging. It proved one's skill and daring, without wasting prey. It was the ultimate prestige feat.

Tigers, seeing Hashti work with horses, were awed by her ability to touch the top of the animal's neck, the spot of utmost vulnerability, the spot where a tiger would land its killing bite. They saw the simple act of haltering a horse as a masterly pounce. When Hashti continued to stand by the horse, she displayed unheard-of daring. Her survival was glory!

Thus she boasted, in a key that speakers understood. Next she described the space voyage. Khan calculated the distance in tiger measurements, but counseled her not to include it. "Lodgeless ones will think it is a fairy tale." Instead Hashti characterized her journey as motion through New Lebanon's sky, beginning in the circle constellation—the "Unblinking Eye," which the tigers saw emblazoned on all her equipment—and ending with the shuttle splashdown in Bluewater Lake.

She emphasized her surprise at the tigers' ability to speak and gave Khan due credit for teaching her the language. She concluded with her own version of the hunt with Big Eyes. "Be sure to say that the ordeal (applies?) only to lodgeless ones," Khan cautioned. "Since you come from a lodge, you did not violate it."

Tigers judged a Name in part by the gusto and realism of the accompanying mime. This low cave barely offered room to sit upright. Hashti could not practice her gestures here. But she thought hard about them. She would strip off her jacket as she explained her changeable feathers. She would hurl a snowball with her sling as she expounded the strange hunting techniques of beavers. She would split a branch with her hatchet when she mentioned her silver claw. Most impressive of all, she would pull out her igniter as she spoke of the fire that propelled the burning rock. Tigers always paid attention when she handled fire!

Yes, it was a marvelous Name. She could not sleep at all that night. She burned with eagerness to go to a speaking place.

As if to oblige her, the storm lasted only two days. Hashti had left camp fourteen days ago. Today, Middleday, dawned clear, so cold that dry snow rose in powdery swirls at the slightest puff of wind. Tiny flakes of condensation glittered as they drifted from a cloudless sky. Khan soon trumpeted that he had pulled down a deer. Divided amongst four tigers and Hashti, it made a reasonable meal, satisfying but not enough to deter them from traveling.

Smacking their lips, the group turned westward. Their destination, to celebrate Big Eyes' kill and Hashti's own redrawn Name, was a famous speaking place called "Cub of the Great River." Hashti, who had only four days' worth of chelator left, told herself she'd ask Khan to escort her home after this visit. The sun had nearly set when they arrived. Majestic blackpines cloaked the hills around a small lake. On the south it flowed into a marshy river. Hashti's dim recollection of New Lebanon's geography suggested that this river's mouth lay thousands of miles away in the tropics. It drained the entire center of the continent.

The river began as a small warm spring, running from a cleft rock north of the lake. Khan and Tree Walker gave the spring a respectful berth and sternly warned the cubs and Hashti to stay clear of it. The speaking place proper lay just west of the spring, higher on the hill. It was empty, but already since the blizzard someone had floundered through the snow to mark rocks with his or her scent. Hashti's friends did their own sniffing and marking, and Hashti raked her soap across the stone. Everyone settled back to await the stranger.

As the sun kissed the horizon, the strange tiger returned, a magnificent female in the prime of her life, with bold black stripes curled into question marks. Sabra! Khan, who'd been wrestling half-heartedly with Bunny Pouncer, rolled over to watch as Sabra sniffed the rock. She grimaced at the smells and sauntered toward Hashti's group. "Why smells the rock like a rose?" she asked. "And why is that hill beaver here?"

Khan twitched his shoulders just a little to show off his stripes. "She calls herself Rose Cub. She left the scent. You will hear more when she tells her Name. I call myself Beaver Teacher."

Sabra rubbed back and forth against a great-grandfather blackpine, purring deeply as she whuffed at Khan. "I call myself Moon Chaser. I have seen hill beavers, but they smelled very bad. They were little fun to pounce. Does this one (really?) speak?"

Hashti whuffed. "Yes, I speak. I call myself Rose Cub."

Sabra nudged Hashti politely, then turned back to Khan, giving him another full-scale body rub with a wiggle thrown in. "The hill beaver does speak. Yours must be a great Name, Beaver Teacher."

Big Eyes could restrain himself no longer. He
bounced up, whuffing with an enthusiasm that rivaled his
sister's. "I call myself He Who Hunts With Rose Cub. I
have killed a deer. I will speak my Name!"

Tree Walker herded him back to the other side of the
clearing. "Your (turn?) will come. But not yet."

Sabra purred benevolently. "He seems a fine cub. I
have birthed five cubs myself, four who (passed?) the
ordeal to speak their own Names. I am (ready?) for
more."

Khan sniffed again at her and curled his lip in the
idiotic grimace which meant he liked something. Sabra
rubbed her cheek on the ground, looking coyly up at
Khan. He leaned against the big blackpine, purring rap-
turously.

Hashti wouldn't have thought twice about such behavior between a stallion and a mare. But Khan was a
person, and *persons* should court with more circumspec-
tion. The woman blushed furiously. How could Khan
carry on this way with a female he'd never met before?

They crouched alongside each other and hummed
sweet nothings. Bunny Pouncer came over to Hashti, the
cub's solemn golden eyes assessing the adult pair.
"Moon Chaser is (?) and looking for a (?)."

The words were strange but Hashti knew exactly
what they meant. Sabra was in heat and looking for a
mate. Bunny Pouncer huddled next to her, biting unhappily at a sliver of ice wedged in her paw. "Surely she will
(choose?) Khan. See him sniff her!"

Instead Hashti looked at the little tigress beside her,
wondering why she sounded so disgruntled. Did she
have a crush on Khan? Bunny Pouncer laid her head
morosely on her paws. "Mother says it will be five years
before I come into heat. By then I will have a Name

(worthy of?) Beaver Teacher. But how will I find him? We will leave him when he mates Moon Chaser."

Hashti forgot Bunny Pouncer's problems in the face of her own. How long did the mating season last? She had come to think of the group as a big happy family, but Khan was utterly unrelated to Tree Walker and her cubs. They were chance acquaintances, temporary traveling companions. What would happen to Hashti if they moved on while Khan was besotted with this interloper?

Hashti turned her back on the flirting couple, and went to sit by Tree Walker, who was preening Big Eyes' coat. Tree Walker stretched her head out so that Hashti could scratch the tigress's ears. Perhaps, in her agitation, Hashti rubbed a bit too hard, for a few minutes later Tree Walker opened an eye to peek at her human friend. "What troubles you, Rose Cub? Are you, too, in heat?"

Hashti's throat was tight with fear and resentment. It took four tries to get her question out. "When Beaver Teacher mates, will you travel?"

Tree Walker looked puzzled. Hashti could see the tigress reminding herself that Hashti was an ignorant hill beaver. "Of course. Beaver Teacher will be (too busy?) to play with the cubs. He will mate with Moon Chaser for five or six days at least. Maybe eight. They are an exceptionally fine (couple?)."

Eight days. Eight days with no tiger to hunt for her, and not enough medication to compensate if he did. Hashti stole another glance at Khan. He was licking Sabra's ear. "Will you take me to the hill beaver lodges, Tree Walker?"

Big Eyes looked up, radiant. "We will hunt together again!"

Tree Walker nudged Hashti with her black-tipped nose. "Big Eyes would like that. But Beaver Teacher would be angry. You are his (companion? pet?)."

But if she starved to death in the meantime? Or was eaten by a strange tiger? "Tell him where we go. After mating, let him come to us."

Tree Walker blinked. "Ask Beaver Teacher."

Big Eyes knocked Hashti over and straddled her, licking her face. She twisted away from the sandpaper tongue, but her spirits rose as the cub told her, "I will show you how to hunt moose."

Bunny Pouncer, rejoining them, laid her ears back. "You know not how to hunt moose. How can you show Rose Cub?"

Before Big Eyes could answer, a heavy growl rolled across the clearing. An enormous male tiger with a distinctive ringed pattern erupted from the woods. Hashti gaped. It was the tiger that she and Ross had seen at the Rock.

He did not notice her. He sniffed regally at the scent rock, and what he found there interested him. His tail lashed as he turned toward Khan and Sabra. With dreadful economy of tune, he announced, "I call myself Killer."

Her forequarters pressed to the ground, tail raised in obvious invitation, Sabra whuffed at him. "I call myself Moon Chaser."

Khan strutted toward the newcomer. "I call myself Beaver Teacher."

"Beaver Teacher?" Killer scoffed. "Only leaf eaters (befriend?) beavers."

Khan's eyes narrowed and his own tail began to sweep the ground. "I taught a hill beaver to speak."

"I speak not to hill beavers," the huge old male said. "They are leaf eaters. I killed four of them."

Hashti's stomach dropped. What was going on at Swamp City? How would Killer respond to her own presence?

Big Eyes stepped forward, his small back very straight and the plumage along it raised. "I call myself He Who Hunts With Rose Cub. I travel with the hill beaver. Although she comes from a lodge, she has a Name."

Until now, Killer had had eyes only for Sabra and Khan. When Big Eyes spoke, the spotted tiger became aware of the rest of the group. His ears swiveled menacingly as he stared at Hashti. "Leaf eaters may not enter a speaking place."

She stood up, knowing that although the tiger far outweighed her, her height gave her a certain impressiveness. "I am a speaker. I call myself Rose Cub."

The big male stiffened, obviously startled and just as obviously determined not to back down. Tree Walker seemed amused by his discomfiture. "The hill beaver has sung," she observed. "Rub noses with her."

"I rub noses with no leaf eaters," he hissed.

"And I rub noses with none who kill hill beavers," Hashti bluffed. What if he sensed her fear?

Sabra had had enough of this shift in the center of attention. She sauntered across the clearing and rubbed languidly against the marking rock, midway between the male tigers. "The sun is gone," she observed. "I am in heat. Let us speak. Have you Names?"

"Yes," they answered simultaneously.

She stretched lazily. "I will hear you both. But first, I, Moon Chaser, will speak my Name."

They yielded the floor to her.

She sang well, with a complex, urgent rhythm. Her name feat had been a nocturnal swim, following the silver trail of the moon across Bluewater Lake, but she boasted many other accomplishments, including three successful litters. "I seek new cubs to swim with me," she concluded. "Who will (father?) them?"

One didn't need language to tell that Khan and Killer vied for the honor. They had listened intently, nostrils flaring, glancing sidelong at one another. Now they faced off, tails bent sharply toward the ground, ears swiveled sideways, heads at an angle, eyes locked.

Killer's tail twitched. "I will speak."

Khan hissed, took a step forward. "No. I will speak."

Sabra purred seductively, in full command of the situation. "Beaver Teacher shall speak first. Sing well, handsome one." Suddenly Hashti felt more warmly toward the tigress with the curly stripes.

Killer stared off into the woods. Hashti huddled with Tree Walker and the cubs, listening entranced as Khan posed and began his song.

His artistry had impressed her when she had barely known the language. His Name impressed her more as she understood it better. It reflected his intelligence and inquisitiveness, the questing passion of his spirit. He touched only passingly upon his physical prowess—his lush feathers and rippling muscles spoke for themselves. Instead Khan boasted of the breadth of his travel and the variety of his experience, each anecdote glittering in gem-bright melody. High adventure alternated with blissful repose, unabashed romanticism was leavened by wry commentary.

Tonight, lust lent extra resonance to Khan's strong voice. Clarion vibrancy gave way to a scherzo lilt when he related his first visit to Swamp City. Even Hashti laughed at his portrayal of the odd, inept hill beavers, and their clumsy but spirited cub who dared strike at a speaker. Then Khan's tone grew sonorous as he led them through the dramatic discovery that within the beaver cub's awkward body lived a soul that could sing. "Thus I call myself Beaver Teacher, for I taught Rose Cub to speak." He looked straight at Sabra. "I will (father?) cubs with tongues like quick-running water."

"Your Name is boring," Killer spat. It was the second worst insult a tiger could offer.

Sabra, ignoring the interruption, purred up at her friend, her eyes slitted. "Indeed you would father fine cubs. But first Killer must speak. Sing your Name, Spotted One."

This Name, too, Hashti had heard before, but only as the mysterious performance of a large animal. Now she saw a grand old man of the forest, confident of his supremacy, asserting his claim to the lady he wanted. Killer sang in a simple, straightforward style, scorning the complex caesuras Khan favored, relying on simple grammatical rhymes. The style suited the content. This was a boast of raw power. This tiger never pounced. He only killed. Unaided, he had pulled down a bull moose. He had dragged an eagle from her nest in the high mountains. He had killed two rivals in mating fights. Here he paused, eyeing Khan and Sabra to be sure they understood the implications.

Most recently, Killer had heard that new and dangerous prey lived north of Bluewater Lake. "It was said in the speaking places that hill beavers smelled like (skunks?), but it was also said that two tigresses had died. A hill beaver killed them with (thunderclaps?). I, Killer, went forth. I found the beaver. He was no mighty prey. His flesh was (soft? spoiled?). His bones were too (weak?) to clean my teeth. I spat him out. I left him by the lodge of the great horses."

Hashti's heart thumped harder. Kevin!

"I killed, and killed again. Hill beavers die easily, they do not fight. They add (nothing?) to one's Name." He glared again at Khan. "I left them for the cubs. I seek (worthier?) prey." He posed for Sabra and made his final pitch. "I call myself Killer. The cubs I (father?) will never hunger. They will be strong and fast. Killers, like me."

Tree Walker remained at the very rim of the clearing. The cubs and Hashti had crept forward for a better view. Scarcely breathing, they awaited Sabra's decision.

She stood and stretched, lengthening the suspense, enjoying her moment of power. But the vocal duet had aroused her, and desire demanded fulfillment. Her eyes, blazing green now in the moonlight, fixed on Killer. "You are bigger than Beaver Teacher." The spotted tiger swelled. "You are stronger than Beaver Teacher. You are probably faster than Beaver Teacher."

"But," she continued, looking at Khan, "even leaf eaters have size, strength, and speed. Those are (?) of (animals?). A speaker's (?) is speech. Since the days of the world mother and her cub, only one (creature?) has spoken. Now you have taught a new (creature?) to speak. Your Name will be (remembered?). I will bear cubs to (carry?) your (gifts?), Beaver Teacher."

Khan paced triumphantly to her side.

Killer stepped closer, feathers raised. "Your Name is a fairy tale." It was the worst insult a tiger could offer.

Khan whirled, snarling. "And your Name is less than a leaf eater's. Hear the hill beaver speak. Sing, Rose Cub!"

Oh, no. Oh, no! Hashti wanted no part of this confrontation. But her cause lay with Khan's. She must prove his Name, or be killed. She cleared her throat twice, stepped forward, and declared, "I, Rose Cub, now speak my Name."

"Silence, leaf eater!" Killer thundered, unable to tolerate proof of his defeat.

Khan jumped away from his lady and stood with teeth bared. "Let Rose Cub speak."

"No leaf eater speaks here!" Killer repeated. He sprang at Hashti.

Khan jumped at the same time, tackling his spotted opponent. They skidded together through the snow. Bunny Pouncer fled to her mother. Big Eyes stayed bravely by his hunting companion.

Khan and Killer separated, circling each other. Killer's ear bled. Khan was unharmed, so far as Hashti could see. He growled, far down in his chest.

Killer feinted sideways, then reversed to rush at Hashti. Khan hit him in mid-charge, knocking him to one side. Unfortunately, Hashti had dived in the same direction. Big Eyes, a huge ball of fluff with flashing claws, interposed himself between the woman and the big male tiger. Killer slammed into the cub. Furious, he picked Big Eyes up by the neck and tossed him aside.

Khan portrayed himself as poet and discoverer. His stance now, as he stationed himself over Hashti, proved that he was also a fighter. He was smaller than the spotted veteran, but younger, and inflamed. He sang the fanfare, the song of protection.

Killer hesitated. Khan had drawn blood once already, and showed no sign of backing down. Big Eyes lay crumpled where he'd fallen. Needing salve for his pride, Killer turned on the youngster.

But before he could reach the cub, Tree Walker shot at Killer, her knife-sharp claws unsheathed. She raked at his sides as he turned and fled. Howling with anger and dismay, he vanished into the woods to the west, Tree Walker close behind.

Trembling, Hashti wiped the snow off her face and looked around. Sabra, moaning softly, pressed herself against Khan. He nuzzled back with equal interest. Big Eyes lay quiet. Bunny Pouncer poked at him, mewing oddly. Hashti went to the cubs. "How is my hunting partner?"

Big Eyes was dead. Intentionally or otherwise, Killer had snapped his neck.

Frosty stars glittered above, unmoved by the passions sweeping the speaking place. Starlight, moonlight, aurora, reflecting off fresh snow, illuminated Big Eyes' body with unwelcome clarity. A deep crack like gunshot swept the lake as ice settled. Tree Walker returned, trotting anxiously toward her cubs. Hashti backed away. The tigress nuzzled Big Eyes, calling softly. She shook him. His head lolled backward at an angle horribly reminiscent of Kevin's. Feathers nearly perpendicular to her body, Tree Walker turned sunsetward, growling into the forest shadows, shifting her weight as if ready to charge any tiger that appeared.

Bunny Pouncer, who had backed away when Hashti did, paced nervously around the clearing. Hashti herself stood staring at Big Eyes, trying to breathe around the tightness in her throat.

Tree Walker returned to her son and lay with his body between her paws. Rumbling the deep purr of pain, she smoothed the feathers that she had preened so recently.

Sabra teased Khan, crouching invitingly in front of him, dashing away when he tried to mount. As if to spite her, he went to Big Eyes, nosing gently. "(I am sorry?)" he sang. Sabra edged in front of him, nearly on top of the cub's body, then sprang away. Frustrated and eager, Khan chased after her. They disappeared into the trees.

Hashti stared furiously after them. Khan's stupid rut had started this all. Big Eyes was dead, a casual victim of the courtship, and what was Khan doing? Screwing! Screwing a bitch tigress he'd met not four hours ago! Hashti sank to a crouch a few feet from Tree Walker, face pressed against her knees, shoulders heaving with dry sobs. Things could get no worse, or so she thought. Then she heard a wet champing noise, and looked up. Tree Walker was eating her dead cub.

Hashti made it to the edge of the clearing before she threw up. Bunny Pouncer, curious as always, followed her. "You have no cubs to feed. Did you eat (bad meat?)?" she asked.

"No!" Hashti yelled, tacking on a string of very human curses. Bunny Pouncer pulled back, whiskers twitching. "Are you angry with me?"

"I am angry with your mother," Hashti answered. "She's eating Big Eyes."

"You should eat, too," Bunny Pouncer said. "You helped Big Eyes earn his Name."

Hashti had adjusted to the tigers' boasting, intestine slurping, vagrancy, even the cruelty of the ordeal. But eating Big Eyes' body? Hashti gagged again. With the horrible bitter taste of bile still souring her mouth, she stumbled away from the speaking place, heading south. It was time to return to her own people.

# CHAPTER FOURTEEN

❧❧❧❧❧

BY THE TIME SHE REACHED THE FIRST DARK THICKET,
Hashti's sense of self-preservation clamored that she
was making a mistake. She slumped against a tree and
tried to think. She'd come to this frozen wilderness for
the sake of the tigers. Convinced as she was of their
intelligence, she could not let Gaylord shoot them. She
now had evidence to force him to stop.

But she'd assumed that her species, in general, could
outfight Khan's. Now she remembered the misgivings
that Ross and Big Red had expressed: "The last thing we
want to do is up the ante," and "Shooting intelligent
creatures is not only wrong, but damn dangerous."

The First-Inners had spoken more truly than they
knew. Killer's tale confirmed that tigers posed a signifi-
cant threat to the humans' poorly equipped camp. Hashti
did not want her friends and coworkers slaughtered. She
had to get back.

Yes, Hashti? What will you do when you get there?
It's no longer a question of getting humans to leave tigers
alone. How will you convince tigers to leave humans
alone?

Ross was right. Tigers attacked for two reasons: because they wanted to eat you, or because they found you
a threat. Skunk, rigged baits, and the iron content of
offworld meat had combined to dissuade tigers from din-

ing on people or their horses. But the humans' desire and ability to defend against attack made them interesting prey. Pouncing, even killing humans had become an elaborate prestige game. How to halt it?

Hashti's people must swallow their pride, play on their weakness. Look how puny a hill beaver is. Consider its small size and lack of speed. Killer himself had stated the answer, as he described Kevin's murder. "He was no mighty prey. His flesh was soft. His bones were too weak to clean my teeth. Hill beavers die easily. They add nothing to one's Name." Let that get trumpeted in enough speaking places, and tigers would have done with attacking humans!

Gay wouldn't enjoy trading on his helplessness, Hashti knew. But Gay wasn't going to enjoy any of what she'd say when she got back.

First she had to get there. She had two days' food, and only a vague notion of direction. A wilderness of trees, hills, rivers, and lakes yawned between her and the camp. In that wilderness roamed tigers—not all of whom, she'd discovered, wanted to talk to beavers. Wandering off on her own was simple suicide. Disenchanted as she was, she still needed Tree Walker's help. Hashti started to return to the clearing, then thought better of it. Let Tree Walker finish her loathsome funeral rites first.

Shining eyes blinked, thirty yards away. Hashti braced herself for a charge. Khan would not protect her this time. Then the tiger approached, chirping, "Why did you leave me, Rose Cub?" With immense relief, Hashti recognized Bunny Pouncer.

"I must return to the lodges of the hill beavers."

"Not yet. You must help eat Big Eyes."

"Go to hell," Hashti said.

Fifteen minutes later, Tree Walker herself came looking for the hill beaver. The tigress was angry. "You were Big Eyes' hunting partner. Why did you leave?"

"Why did you eat him?" Hashti countered.

Tree Walker got even angrier. "He was my son, a speaker! Should I leave his liver for wolves? He sang of you in his Name. Come back, or *I* will eat *your* liver!"

Tree Walker meant it, thought Hashti. Resentfully she rose and trudged back to the speaking place. Somewhere in the distance, Khan and Sabra sang a tender, hauntingly harmonized duet, *con amore*. It was beautiful. Hashti did not appreciate it.

Tree Walker had gutted her son. She stalked up to Hashti with intestines trailing from her teeth. "Eat, Rose Cub."

"No."

"Are you a speaker or a leaf eater?"

"I am a leaf eater."

Tree Walker's paw lashed out in a slap that knocked Hashti from her feet. "Big Eyes died (defending?) you. Is this your answer? Your Name is so small one cannot hear it!"

Would Big Eyes himself have wanted this? Hashti took the intestines from Tree Walker. They stuck to her cold leather mitten. "Eat," the tigress commanded.

Hashti couldn't. In her travels with the tigers, she had done a great many things she thought she could never do. But she couldn't eat Big Eyes.

Tree Walker and Bunny Pouncer waited.

Think, Hashti. How can you honor Big Eyes? She could not follow tiger custom, but perhaps she could introduce her own. She licked her lips and started singing. "When a hill beaver dies, fire eats its body."

Tree Walker started in horror. "Fire burns."

"The beaver turns to smoke," Hashti countered. "The

smoke rises to the stars. Big Eyes wanted to go to the stars. Let us send his smoke to them."

Tree Walker cocked her head at the woman, tail twitching. Twice she started to speak, and let the comment trail away in a low growl. Finally she decided. "You helped him (win?) his Name. Do as you will."

Hashti gathered wood for a small blaze and laid the cub's intestines atop it. Bright orange flames sent eerie shadows dancing around the speaking place. Big Eyes' eager, affectionate face purred at Hashti from the fire, asking her to hunt moose with him. Tears blurred Hashti's vision. "Dust we are, to dust we shall return. But dust does not forget the dream that stirs it." How did one translate the Litany of Dust into tigersong? Hashti looked solemnly at Tree Walker. "See the smoke? It rises to the stars. It sings the Name of He Who Hunts With Rose Cub."

The tigress blinked. "Big Eyes will be happy."

Did tigers believe in immortality, Hashti wondered? She'd never asked. She would like to know, but now was not a time for metaphysical inquiry. A more urgent concern pressed her. "I must return to the lodges of the hill beavers."

Bunny Pouncer flattened her ears. "You heard Killer. Many tigers gather to hunt hill beavers. You are a poor fighter, Rose Cub. They will kill you."

All too true. But soon she would have to return anyway, and the trip would not become less dangerous. "I am a poor fighter," Hashti agreed, looking at Tree Walker. "But you fight well. Lead me to the lodges, and your Name will be great."

The tigress seemed doubtful. "Why go to the lodges of the hill beavers? You have already seen them."

"The hill beavers are my brothers. They are dying."

"Oh," Tree Walker said, as if Hashti had explained everything. "I see. You must eat their livers."

Hashti rolled her eyes at the moon, but did not correct Tree Walker's statement. Again she asked the tigress, "Will you travel with me?"

"Yes. I would like to see your hill beaver lodges. But we must tell Beaver Teacher."

Tell Khan? In his frame of mind? But to Hashti's surprise, the lovers responded to Tree Walker's call. Sabra lay beside Khan, licking his shoulder, while Tree Walker stated Hashti's intentions. Khan eyed his human protégé with disgust. "You are acting like a beaver again, Rose Cub. Why are you so fond of lodges?"

"My brothers are being killed," she reminded him. "I must go to them. Will you come with us?"

"No," he said. "Moon Chaser is in heat and I am eager to mate with her. I will find you afterward." He nipped playfully at his companion, and they skittered into the woods together. Hashti told herself she didn't care, but anger and loneliness washed over her each time she heard Khan's lusty roar.

Tree Walker and Bunny Pouncer led Hashti south at a slow but unrelenting pace, traveling quietly, each busy with her own thoughts. As Hashti got over the shock of Big Eyes' death, she found her "solution" to the tiger problem less satisfactory. Yes, humans could shame the tigers out of attacking by emphasizing human unworthiness. But that was not the relationship Hashti wanted. She wanted equality between the races, interaction based on mutual respect, a partnership rewarding to both sides.

Tigers had more to offer than pelts. She loved their language and their wit, their keen artistic sense and rich literary/musical heritage. Perhaps they would have contributions for mathematics and philosophy as well.

They'd exposed her to an utterly new milieu, where power rose from one's own physical and mental capacities, rather than from money and connections. Hashti had come away more appreciative, and more critical, of the technology her life depended on.

Tiger culture was not the stuff of great trade empires, but it had value. What could humans offer the tigers in return for their sharing of thoughts?

Precious little. To tigers, technology was proof of weakness, animalness. They scorned lodges and clothing. Weapons? Tools? Hashti remembered Bunny Pouncer's attempt to use her sling. What good were goods to a species which could not use or carry them? "A pure information society," Big Red said.

You are thinking like a beaver again, Hashti chided herself. You're stuck on the things your own society values. Try again, Rose Cub. Think like a speaker. What are the important things in life?

"The world gave birth to a speaker. The speaker traveled far, climbed high, and swam deep. She knew whence she had come, and how far. She lived long, and had a beautiful voice for singing her Name to the world's cub." Tigers, in their own eyes, had been created for travel and adventure, for seeking novelty and telling about it.

What did humankind have to offer them? The galaxy! Bunny Pouncer was preparing to ambush Hashti's left ski pole. The woman turned to the cub. "Would you like to go into the burning rock, and travel to fields beyond the stars, where great horses are born?"

Bunny Pouncer forgot about the ski pole. "Oh, yes! Although I dislike fire."

"You must sleep among hill beavers," Hashti warned. "And you must not pounce them. If you pounce them, they will push you out of the burning rock."

Bunny Pouncer bounded alongside Hashti, spattering
her with snow. "I will not pounce any hill beavers. I will
not even call them leaf eaters. When will we enter the
burning rock?"

"It will not come until the snow is gone," Hashti answered, hoping she had not raised false expectations.
There would be problems. The tigers had no government
and no formal law, so they must be negotiated with as
individuals. It would take them a while to understand the
constraints of human society. Hashti could just see
Bunny Pouncer getting bored and pouncing some hapless
spaceship crew member! She grinned as she imagined
the havoc the cub could wreak at a High Snows sleigh
party.

But Bunny Pouncers' enthusiasm confirmed that
Hashti had found the right bait for tigers. If the camp
could not grant all the tigers spaceship rides, it could at
least build a museum, a demonstration center where
lodgeless ones could sample the wonders of the civilized
universe. Yes, humans had a few things that would interest these cats!

But Hashti's happy scenario left Swamp City's original problem unsolved. The pioneers remained trapped in
Oldearth's snare. If logging had been marginal before, it
would be hopeless now that they had lost so much time
and so many people. Hashti's report would, she hoped,
permanently quash the pelt proposal. Was there any
other way to make a profit?

She could not envision one. Time was short. Once it
was established that tigers were a rational species, Company employees would be kicked off the planet and
First-In would take over. Initial negotiations with an intelligent race were delicate, not to be disturbed by un-
controlled commercial activity.

The First-Inners would come. Where would they live?

The Company employees had one asset. Swamp City itself.

Hashti tried to remember what Lael and Gaylord had said about Oldearth Company's franchise. The phrase "timber export rights" stuck in her mind. The camp buildings were the camp's, as long as they remained on the planet! First-In could buy the town from the loggers, rather than build a new one themselves.

Unless, of course, they wanted their base in a more temperate location. If so, they could hire the jacks to build it. The Circle's Core needed a new location. Wouldn't this planet be a good choice? Hashti slept happily the next two nights, dreaming of possibilities.

She woke the third morning to Bunny Pouncer's whuff. "Wake up, Rose Cub. We reach the hill beaver lodges today."

Hashti rubbed her eyes. "Where is your mother?"

Bunny Pouncer shook her ruff proudly. "She has gone ahead. There are many speakers here. Mama will sing with them while I lead you to the lodges."

It sounded like an excellent plan, if Bunny Pouncer could do her part. Hashti lashed her sleeping bag onto her pack. How she had struggled to don this load when she first left camp! Now, in one smooth motion, she hefted it with both hands, braced it on her right thigh while she put her right arm through the strap, then slipped her left arm in and swung the pack across her back. She followed Bunny Pouncer's black-tufted tail southward.

Hashti need not have doubted the cub's abilities. In less than an hour the pair emerged from the woods into a jumble of stumps and brushpiles. This area must have been logged some time ago, for the snow lay smooth and undisturbed. Tigersong echoed faintly through the trees.

Bunny Pouncer cocked her head to listen. "They are sunsetward of us. It is safe to go."

An unnatural silence hung over the familiar terrain. No saws. No horses stamping. No curses or shouts. Only the ever-louder singing of the tigers. When had these roads last been used?

As the woman and the cub entered the remnant of forest adjacent to the camp, a lone tiger roared somewhere east of them. Bunny Pouncer flattened herself to the ground, hissing. "Be still. We must wait until he joins the others."

Hashti cowered, trying to look like a stump. The tiger moved westward, still calling. Bunny Pouncer rose to her feet. "Come now. The lodges are just over the hill."

They crested the hill. Hashti stared. The slope had been stripped of its magnificent trees. The camp itself was now surrounded by a palisade of upright logs. The main gate opened to the east. Men were still at work on the southern, downhill edge of the barrier. Others had climbed the fifteen foot fence to peer westward at the woods where Tree Walker and her friends sang. No one had come out since the last storm. Snow lay smooth as glass over the denuded hillside.

Bunny Pouncer pressed against Hashti's legs. "Mother said I may not leave the forest. You must go by yourself from here. Run very fast down the hill. When the tigers see you, they will chase."

Three hundred yards of barren snow yawned between Hashti and safety. Whether or not she made it to the gate, she'd need camping equipment no more. She took off her pack. She took off her outer sweater, too. She'd be more than warm enough as she made her dash. She looked down at the arrogant, absurd little tigress who'd brought her here. With Big Eyes dead and Khan's attention turned elsewhere, Hashti and Bunny Pouncer had grown close. Hashti hoped to make good on her promises about the Burning Rock, but who knew what might happen to either herself or the cub? The woman's eyes filled with tears as she pronounced the farewell formula. "May your travels be wide, Bunny Pouncer, and the hunting good."

"May you find plenteous game and sweet water, Rose Cub," Bunny Pouncer replied, sounding very grown-up. Then she added, *vivace* as usual, "Run fast!"

Hashti took a deep breath and launched herself toward home. A mocking roar exploded behind her. "Stand aside, cub of the lodgeless ones. I will show you how hill beavers die!"

If Killer had attacked Hashti in the forest, he'd have had her. But he scorned so easy a kill. He intended to make a show of the woman's death. By the time he finished blustering at Bunny Pouncer, Hashti was thirty yards downhill, poling for all she was worth.

The slope favored her. She skimmed across its sun-hardened surface, knees bent, propelling herself with both arms. Her shoulders ached in expectation of Killer's fangs, but the bite did not come. Hashti stole a peek behind. The snow crust was crumbling under Killer's weight, forcing him to move in high, short bounds rather than the flat, ground-eating gallop a charging tiger normally employed. He sank to his elbows each time he landed.

Hashti plunged forward, her breath hard and short, her whole body burning with exertion. Oh, dear God, she had to make it! But she'd crossed only a third of the distance. She heard Killer's heavy breathing. Unwise in the ways of beavers, he lunged at the closest part of her—her right ski pole. It snapped in his jaws even as Hashti yanked her wrist free of the loop. She was moving too fast for poling now, anyway. She dropped into a

tuck, crouching over her skis, absorbing the unevenness
of the terrain with bent knees, elbows against her sides
to reduce wind drag.

A hundred fifty yards to go. People shouted. Killer
dropped her pole and continued chasing, angrier than
ever, but the deep snow hampered him. The tiger was by
nature a sprinter, unsuited for sustained effort. If Hashti
could maintain her pace, she'd win. Icy air seared her
throat as she gasped for breath.

Then, raising her eyes toward that wonderful, impos-
sibly faraway log wall, she saw new trouble. Two tigers
had emerged from the forest on the west. They angled
upward to meet her. A third streaked toward her from
the east. She eyed him desperately, wondering if she
could get to the gate before he intercepted her. "Run,
Rose Cub!" he called in a breathless whistle. She looked
again at the powerful body, the clean single stripes, the
black mask. Khan! She veered left, toward him. The
tigers from the west adjusted course.

They all converged fifty yards from the palisade.
Hashti was streaking due south, aiming for the gate.
Khan, heading west to intercept the other two tigers,
crossed just in front of her. Her skis snagged on the jum-
bled snow of his trail and slewed sideways with a sicken-
ing jolt. Somehow, she stayed on her feet. Behind her,
she heard the crash of tigers colliding.

Hashti hadn't time to look back. She was flying directly toward the palisade with no room to turn, moving
too fast for an elegant stop, especially with loose bind-
ings and clumsy skis. "You can always brake with your
bottom," she'd been told. She sat down, plowing up a
blinding plume of snow. With a heavy thud, but safe, she
hit the log wall.

On the other side, people shouted. "Here she is! Hold

on, Hashti! Can you make it to the gate? Someone get a rope!"

She wiped the snow from her eyes and looked back uphill. Blue blood spattered across the snow. One tiger backed away. Khan roared savagely and threw off the second. The stranger whirled and stood poised, facing Khan, ten feet away. Khan bared his teeth and roared again, but did not rise. A huge flap of skin hung from his shoulder. Beneath, Hashti saw torn muscle.

Eager to salvage some sort of victory, Killer plowed downhill toward Khan.

A head popped over the wall above Hashti. "Miz Hashti! Are you all right? Grab this rope!"

She stood up, still facing the tigers, holding her one remaining ski pole like a spear. "Beaver Teacher! What troubles you?" What a stupid, stupid question!

He spared a quick glance at her. "Killer is angry over Moon Chaser. Go to your brothers, Rose Cub."

The two tigers already bested by Khan watched silently as Killer approached. Khan struggled to his feet, his right foreleg trembling. Killer, still fifty yards uphill, paused to gloat. "You look no stronger than your Rose Cub, Beaver Teacher!"

Hashti's face twisted in fury. The skis dragged like lead, and it was hard to climb without her poles, but she climbed anyway, back up the slope toward Khan.

Voices rang behind the wall. "She's crazy! What's she doin'? Get back here!"

Killer glared at her. "Be gone, leaf eater. This is a matter for lodgeless ones."

Khan, hopeless, endorsed Killer's advice. "Go to your lodge, Rose Cub." The notes quavered.

She kept climbing, and when she got to Khan, she straddled his bloody body, shaking her pole at Killer, who stood hesitating twenty feet away. "Get out of here!

Get back!" In the tension of the moment, she spoke her own language.

Killer hissed. The other two tigers, the ones who had come from the west, snorted softly. "Go," Khan told Hashti again. "I will fight."

This time, Khan would lose. Even a hill beaver could see that. Something tugged at her mind, a song, specially made for situations like this. Khan had sung it the night she left camp, when she was assaulted in the darkness. Big Eyes had sung it over Hashti, the afternoon he won his Name, and Khan had sung it again three days ago at Cub-of-the-Great-River Speaking Place. Hashti took a deep breath, and gave her best imitation of the fanfare.

One of the observers, the one who had torn Khan's shoulder open, snorted in surprise. "The hill beaver does sing! Tree Walker's song was not a fairy tale."

Killer's tail whipped back and forth. "Sing not that song, leaf eater. Beaver Teacher is not your cub."

"No," Hashti answered, "but he taught me to speak, so I will sing. You call yourself Killer. What kill you? Hill beavers. Cubs. Those who cannot fight." She nodded at the frightened faces lining the top of the wall. "My brothers watch. Shall I tell them this is how lodgeless ones magnify their Names? Shall I tell them you are cub-killers?"

One of the strange tigers snarled. "Speakers kill no cubs."

"Killer does," she answered.

The spotted murderer gathered himself to spring. Hashti's listener raised a paw, claws extended. "Stop! Tree Walker told us of you. Rose Cub sang the (fanfare?) over Beaver Teacher. If you fight him, I will sing it as far down as the Great Ice and as far up as the Sea of Blood. Your Name will shrink beyond hearing."

Killer saw he could win no glory in this fight. "Are

you, too, a beaver (lover?)?" he asked. "Very well. Remain with the leaf eaters." With a look of utter disgust, he turned toward the woods.

"I go to my brothers' lodges," Hashti told the two strange tigers. "Beaver Teacher will go with me. Return to the forest. Tell Tree Walker I did not die."

They hesitated. "Go!" Khan sang. They obeyed.

Behind Hashti, the yelling stopped. A row of white faces stared at her. She forced her weary lungs into a shout. "Where's Doctor Anna?"

The faces stared silently back.

"Damn it, you fools, don't just gawk at me! Where's the doctor? Get her, or I'll come in with ten tigers and do it myself!"

A face resolved itself into Lance, waving. "Yes ma'am. I'll fetch her, Miz Hashti." He disappeared behind the wall.

# CHAPTER FIFTEEN

✦✦✦✦✦

WESTWARD, AT THE FOREST'S EDGE, A DOZEN TIGERS greeted the two who had witnessed Hashti's defense of Khan. Hashti saw Bunny Pouncer, unharmed, run to her mother's side. Their songs rose in discordant excitement. Behind the palisade, human voices buzzed in harsh monotone. Hashti and Khan stood alone between the worlds. The gaping wound on the tiger's shoulder terrified Hashti. "Can you walk?" she asked.

His whiskers twitched indignantly. "I can walk."

"Then come with me," she ordered.

Limping clumsily, he followed her toward the gate.

Of all the crowd, only Big Red and Gaylord ventured outside the wall to meet them. "Welcome home!" Red said, with a grin that stretched even his broad jaws.

"Thank you. Khan's hurt. Where's Anna?"

"On her way." Red cast an appraising eye over Khan's shoulder, then stooped so his eyes were level with the tiger's. "I call myself Big Beaver," the First-Inner sang with a passable accent, except that he used an incorrect definite article. "Big Beaver pleased that Beaver Teacher enters hill beavers' speaking place."

Khan, wide-eyed, whuffed back. "I call myself Beaver Teacher. Rose Cub did not tell me other beavers sang."

Hashti hadn't known. Big Red must have spent hours

studying her recordings, she thought, watching him rub faces with Khan. Gay, seeing the tiger's attention diverted, gripped Hashti's forearms with strong welcoming hands. "I thought you were dead! I found your sweater and—"

"I know," she answered, unwilling to deal with Gay just yet. "I'll tell you the story later. Let's get inside the fence."

As they stepped through the gate, Anna hurried to meet them, swinging expertly on her crutches. Lance, carrying her bag, trotted to keep up. The doctor's appearance shocked Hashti. Anna had aged ten years in the last two weeks. But her eyes burned into Hashti with as much intensity as ever. "You're back, and alive!" the First-Inner exclaimed. "Are you all right? They said you needed me."

Hashti gave the older woman an impulsive hug. "I'm fine. But Khan got hurt running interference. Can you help him?"

"Let's see," Anna answered, kneeling down.

The crowd had shrunk from Hashti as if she were a ghost, but now men pressed close to see what was happening. Khan, nervous among so many beavers, snarled. They stumbled over each other to give him room.

Anna flinched but held her ground, fishing a small wooden tube from her pocket. "I can't carry a tune in a bucket," she explained, with an apologetic glance at Hashti. She lifted the tube to her lips, her slender fingers dancing over the holes. "I call myself She Who Makes Well," Anna played, making the same grammatical mistake Big Red had made.

Khan, overwhelmed by pain and novelty, just stared at the pipe. Anna lowered it, disappointed. "Does he understand? Ask him if I may look at the wound."

"Freeze," Hashti told Khan. "She Who Makes Well will touch your shoulder. Move not."

Anna probed the torn flesh. Once, as her fingers brushed a nerve, Khan growled. "Freeze," Hashti repeated. Khan obeyed. His meekness worried Hashti more than the blood did.

But Anna seemed cheered by the inspection. "It's not as bad as it looks. If we keep it clean it'll heal beautifully—big carnivores have astounding recuperative powers. I'd like to sew the wound, but I don't dare use an anesthetic. His physiology is too different. Can you explain to him?"

"I'll try," Hashti assured the doctor. "But not in the middle of the street. Let's go the clinic, and then I'll talk to him."

Gay, a few feet away, cleared his throat. "He'd be safer and folks'd feel happier if you got him out of the center of camp. Can you do it in the barn?"

Anna nodded. "Easily, if you keep sightseers away."

Gay turned and clapped his hands at the crowd. "OK, everybody. The tiger's going to the barn. Clear out and give the doctor a chance to work. We'll tell you the details when we know them." Lumberjacks backed away.

Gay's easy cooperation with Anna startled Hashti. Had there been a rapprochement? If so, why hadn't relations with the tigers been mended? The barely-successful blockade run, and the wall itself, confirmed Killer's claim that Swamp City was hard pressed. But questions could be asked after Khan was tended to. Hashti guided him to the barn.

It had been more than two weeks since the trainer had entered a building. Warm humid air made her nose run. Sniffling, she tried to reassure the horses who pulled away, panicky, from Khan. The animals were well-groomed and stood in clean bedding, but too many stalls gaped empty. "Where's Herc?" Hashti asked. "And Blaze?"

Lance looked miserably away. Big Red answered. "We've been under siege. It was too dangerous to hunt."

Hashti stared. "That bad?"

Red nodded glumly. "That bad."

Hashti turned her back on the empty stalls. Once again, grief had to wait its turn.

They bedded Khan on sawdust and clean blankets in the tackroom. Anna stitched for two tension-fraught hours. The tiger tried to lie still, but pain avoidance is a reflex beyond conscious control. Finally Hashti strapped Khan's paws and sat on his neck. Anna worked with quiet concentration. Lance and Big Red supplied hot water and clean cloths. Just before noon they finished. Hashti freed Khan's paws while Big Red filled her washbasin with cool water and set it in front of the tiger. Khan lapped thirstily, then let his head drop. "I must sleep. Then I will hear the Names of Big Beaver and She Who Makes Well."

"Sleep well," Hashti told him.

The doctor stowed her gear in its bag and the humans stepped into the corridor. Big Red, wringing out the last of the towels, smiled proudly at Hashti. "You made it after all! Ready to tell us about it?"

She shook her head. "I'm not talking to anyone until I've had a bath."

The First-Inner knew how it felt to return from the wilderness. He grinned. "Fair enough. Lance, tell Lael to fire the sauna. When you're done, Hashti, come to the office for a council of war."

"No," Hashti told him.

The erstwhile boss's jaw dropped ever so slightly. "What? Why not?"

Hashti pointed with her thumb at the tackroom door.

"It's time to quit talking about tigers behind their backs. We'll meet here, so Khan can be in on it."

Anna's eyes crinkled in amusement. A flush rose behind Red's freckles. "Touché. We'll meet here."

Hashti sat in the steam for over an hour, trying to convince herself that she'd really returned. Two weeks of sweat and smoke sloughed from her skin in little gray rolls. Finally she sluiced the debris away with a pail of cold water, and dressed. Her clothes hung loosely— she'd lost more weight than she could comfortably spare. She'd done well to return when she did.

She found Anna waiting in the stable corridor, chatting with Lael and Georgia. Red had gone into the tackroom to practice tiger talk with Khan. Gay arrived last. "I'm having the men finish the palisade," he explained. "I figured it wouldn't hurt."

Anna nodded her approval. "They need to keep busy."

"They need more than makework," Lael grumbled. "Let's go talk."

Since harnesses were kept on pegs by the stalls, the so-called tackroom served mostly for repairs and long-term storage. Five people and a tiger filled the ten-by-twelve foot space to its seams. Red, who'd been squatting on the floor beside Khan, rose to take a seat against the far wall, on Hashti's waist-high workbench. His feet swung a few inches above the floor. Khan assessed the size fourteen boots. "Big Beaver has enormous paws! Do they come off, as yours do?"

"They do," Hashti assured him, glad to see his curiosity return. "But even lacking feathers, Big Beaver's paws are large."

Lael settled herself on a stack of spare horse blankets in the corner by the door. Georgia claimed a chest of leather straps. Anna sat on an upended bucket next to the workbench. She looked serene as ever.

Khan growled when Gay walked in. "That one killed lodgeless ones," he complained. "And he made you smell bad."

Gay flattened himself against the wall. "I don't think he likes me, Hashti."

"You're right. He says you made me smell bad. Behave or I'll sic him on you."

Gay sat on a barrel near the door, a nervous eye on Khan. If the tiger felt claustrophobic, he chose not to mention it. Hashti sat on the floor next to him and looked around at the humans. "What happened while I was gone?"

No one wanted to tell her. Gay twisted a harness strap in his hands as he finally started talking. "After I saw you were past helping, it took most of the day to get back. When I got here, two more men were dead—one jumped by a tiger, the other spilling contact poison on himself." Gay winced as he spoke.

Hashti knew how badly he'd wanted to be a savior for the camp. He was crushed by the deaths he'd been responsible for. She felt sorry for him.

He continued. "On top of that we had the blizzard—everyone cooped up in camp, with not enough to do and too much to think about. It was a pressure cooker. Pretty soon Sweat claimed lice were falling from Sam's bunk onto his, and a big fight broke out in the bunkhouse. I broke it up, but I had to use my fists to do it. I knew I was in trouble." He stopped, head hanging.

Big Red picked up the story, as nonchalant as if he were giving an academic lecture. "A wise manager knows when to seek advice. Gay and I reached an agreement about the tigers, but things had escalated beyond easy stopping. To keep the tigers out of camp, and give the men something to do, we started the palisade."

"But by then you were sure of the tigers' intelligence," Hashti exclaimed. "Didn't anyone try to talk to them?"

Anna spread her hands in frustration. "We tried. But friendly exchange is hard after the fighting starts. I was going to go out when my ankle mended. In the meantime, we needed to protect ourselves."

Things had been worse than Hashti ever suspected. Everyone stared at her. "Let's hear it from your side," Big Red said.

Gay lifted his head. "Yeah. What happened? When you pitched the beacon at me, I thought you'd lost your head. There was no way I could leave you there. So I crossed the stream and followed you on foot. All I found was your sweater and an empty hotbottle, hanging on a stick. I couldn't make any sense of that, but the tracks told their own story. There were signs of a scuffle, and Khan's prints, partly covered by something he'd been dragging. Something your size." His gaze drilled into Hashti.

She looked away, but the truth must out. "I was sort of chilled, and upset. I thought the scarecrow might act as a decoy for unfriendly tigers. Then Khan showed up . . ." She tried to gloss over the incident.

Anna, gray-faced, stopped her. "You're saying you were a hairsbreadth from freezing to death?"

Biting her lip, Hashti nodded.

"Khan dragged you away in spite of yourself, and warmed you out of the coma?"

Hashti nodded again. Anna took a deep breath. "It's a good thing that tiger likes you."

"Why?" Lael asked. "I mean, why Hashti?"

"He heard her sing," Gay replied. "She was always singing to the horses."

"He thought she was a cub," Big Red said. "Children learn faster."

"Wasn't it her soap?" Georgia asked.

"I think it was the horses," Hashti countered. "The tigers couldn't believe my pouncing ability."

"Khan's right here," Anna reminded them. "Shouldn't we ask him?"

This time Khan responded to the doctor's skillful piping. Hashti broke out laughing at his answer. "It was all of the above," she explained for those who didn't know the language, "but another thing most of all. Spunk. Remember I punched him in the nose the first time I met him? He decided there must be more to me than met the eye."

Georgia looked at the trainer, awed. "Is that how you backed down the big spotted tiger?"

Hashti sobered. "No. That tiger doesn't bluff and he has no sense of humor."

"All in good time," Big Red said. "Get back to your story."

Hashti saw her audience warm as she told of her adventures with the cubs. Anna grinned over Bunny Pouncer's bravado and Big Eyes' curiosity. Big Red's sandy eyebrows shot up when Hashti related the trigonometry lesson. Georgia, the bookkeeper, frowned. "I thought you said their number system was base four. Where did twelfths of a circle come from?"

"Most systems use twelfths for angular measure, whatever their other preferences," Anna said. "The thirty-sixty-ninety triangle is too neat to ignore."

Georgia nodded. Gay, grim and thoughtful, just stared at the wall. He'd been wrong all around, and was having his nose rubbed in it. Lael didn't look happy either. Her confident endorsement of the Code guidelines had been instrumental in winning support for Gay. "Why do the tigers care about angles, anyway? They don't build anything!"

"Travel," Anna said. "They have to be able to give and understand directions. They must have incredible spatial imaging and crystalline intelligence. And there's your answer to the hand-brain engima. Look what the tigers call themselves: 'speakers,' which really means 'those-who-name-themselves,' and 'lodgeless ones.' Other species developed speech in response to manipulative needs and the invention of tools. Tigers developed it as a consequence of nonterritoriality. Information exchange prepares them to cope with unfamiliar territory, and Name competitions replace territorial defense as a selective mechanism, creating a positive feedback loop."

"Oh," Lael said glumly, probably contemplating the penalties for assault on a rational species.

Tension rose as Hashti related the custom of the ordeal and the events surrounding Big Eyes' first kill. "She was going to let her own son die?" Lael exclaimed. "That's awful!"

Hashti answered slowly. "I guess a tiger that couldn't kill would eventually die anyway. It would have been even harder for Tree Walker if he'd been older, I suppose. And hard for Big Eyes, knowing he'd starve when he left his mother."

"Dreadful custom," Georgia muttered. She glared at Khan, tucking her skirt in as if to avoid contamination.

Hashti, too, found the subject uncomfortable. She hurried on. All too soon, she found herself relating what had happened at Cub-Of-The-Great-River Speaking Place. Once again faces twisted in distaste. "She ate him? That's barbaric!"

"What did you expect her to do?" Hashti countered,

tired of hearing people pass judgment on the tigers. "She doesn't use fire and can't hold a shovel. Should she have left him to rot? Or let wolves chew on her son's liver?" Anna, who seemed less interested in the tigers' actions than in Hashti's reactions, glanced at Big Red and smiled.

Gay still scowled. "And meanwhile, Khan and Sabra were rutting over the body."

Hashti winced. Khan, who'd been listening intently all along, recognized his human name. He heard the disapproval in their voices. "The hill beavers are angry with me," he said. "Why?"

"I sang of Big Eyes' death." Hashti had brooded on the subject herself. She took this opportunity to ask, "Why did you mate with Moon Chaser then?"

Khan looked puzzled. "She was in heat."

"But Big Eyes was dead and I was alone!" Hashti protested.

Khan's tail twitched in irritation. "Big Eyes did not (care?)! You were with Tree Walker and Bunny Pouncer." He curled his lips and shook his head a little, as frustrated with Hashti as she was with him. "Don't beavers come in heat? If I had left, Moon Chaser would have mated with Killer." He bit regretfully at his claw. "I did leave her, to help you. Now my shoulder is torn and I cannot return. She will finish her mating with someone else."

Anna shot Hashti a helpless glance. "I got about a tenth of that. Translate, please."

"I asked him how he could do such a thing. He thought it was a stupid question. Big Eyes didn't care, and I was with Tree Walker. He said if he hadn't mated Sabra, Killer would have. Khan's mad because she's still out there, while he's here with a wounded shoulder."

Big Red suppressed a smile. "Ethics are different

when mating comes once a year. I'd rather have Khan, than Killer, fathering cubs."

"Maybe," Lael said. "But no civilized race eats children's bodies!"

"On the contrary," Big Red said. "The Khatha find our Litany of Dust impersonal and uncaring."

"Lizards!" Gay spat.

"It's no worse than burning!" Hashti told him.

He regarded her as if she were a lizard, too. Or a tiger.

"I've heard all I want to know about cubs dying," Georgia said. "Tell us how you got back."

Hashti described her trip southward and the desperate run into camp. Then she outlined her ideas for making peace with the tigers and paying the company staff's way off the planet. Anna's eyes shone. "I think you're right, the tigers will never be a mainstream merchant power. But what they couldn't do on the frontier!" She glanced up at Big Red. "Can you imagine a more perfect Circlemate? Can you? Not territorial, so never homesick. Always ready for the next adventure. Natural navigators, superb descriptive ability. No need for fancy camping gear—"

"The perfect gypsy," Lael muttered.

Big Red smiled indulgently at Anna as she spoke, but he had difficulty restraining his own enthusiasm. "No, I can't imagine a better Circlemate. If no one else wants the tigers, First-In does."

"That's fine for you," Gay snapped. "What about the other hundred thirty-five people here? Will they have to sign their souls away to board ship, or will you buy the camp from them?"

Big Red rubbed his nose. "Will Oldearth let us get away with it?"

"No choice," Lael said, narrowing her eyes. "Hashti

was right about the export clause. Our work is our own, as long as it doesn't leave the planet." She lifted her chin as she faced the First-Inners. "First-In custom gives any Circle member authority to confirm a contract. What do you say?" All eyes followed hers. "Will First-In pay?" Lael repeated.

Big Red and Anna looked at each other. Five difficult months had forged a bond between them and the company employees. Hashti was sure the First-Inners wanted to help. But their first loyalty went to their own organization. "A Circle has to show a profit," Anna said. "Just like anyone else."

"Come up to the store," Georgia offered. "I can show you how many people and how much time it took to build this camp. I also know what First-Inners on exploration contract or diplomatic assignment could earn in that time. You'd come out ahead buying the camp."

"If that's true," Anna said, "we'll deal."

"On one condition," Big Red added, watching Gay. "I'm sick of wet-nursing this crew. Someone else has to take charge of the project."

Gay smiled slowly. "I can handle it, if you keep the tigers off our necks. And if I'm not hauled away on charges of treaty violation."

"Just keep your hands off your gun. And Sweat out of my hair."

"Yes, sir."

The meeting ended jubilantly. Tomorrow, on the solstice, the group would present the plan to the camp so all could join in the celebration. In the meantime, Anna hurried off to review Georgia's books. Big Red and Lael followed more leisurely, discussing fine points of the Oldearth contract. Gay lingered in the barn. "Did you want something?" Hashti asked.

He moved closer. "We haven't talked alone, since

you came back. Hashti, I felt like hell when I found that damn scarecrow. I thought I'd lost you."

She kept walking down the corridor. "You nearly did."

He scuffed at a wisp of hay on the floor. "Look. I was wrong about the tigers. And wrong about you. You're an impressive lady. I love you. Will you forgive me?"

In the sawdust Hashti saw Khan's footprints, uneven because he couldn't bear weight on his injured leg. She snarled at Gay. "You've got to be kidding!"

His jaw dropped a little. "You don't want me?"

"No!"

He ran to catch up with her. "Why not?"

She whirled to face him. "The first time I met Khan, you thought I'd hallucinated it. The second time, you intervened with a skunk gun. You tried to bully me out of going to the Rock with Ross. You made fun of me in the mess hall when I opposed your plan. Then you threatened to lock me up. You left me no option but the most desperate one, going after the tigers by myself. When I did, you tried to drag me home. Do you really think I'll kiss and make up?"

He was angry now, but not ready to give up. "I admitted I was wrong! Don't I get another chance?"

"You've had it! And another, and another. What about all the men and tigers who've died through your blind pigheadedness? Do they get second chances, too?"

His eyes narrowed. "Look, Hashti. You're upset. Your tiger's hurt, and you've been in the wilderness for weeks. I know it's hard to come back. This is no time to make decisions. Give yourself a while."

Hashti spoke very slowly, to penetrate his shield of stubborn confidence. "There you go again, telling me I can't make my own decisions for this reason or that! I've decided, Gaylord. We're through."

He flushed. "All right. So be it. Go flirt with Sweat. Maybe he'll take orders from you."

Hashti hurt all over as he stamped away. Was she being headstrong? He'd treated her well enough when tigers weren't involved. Should she run after him, hug him, apologize?

What kind of Name have you, Rose Cub?

That afternoon, while others enacted her plan to save the camp, Hashti pondered her own future. She'd come here to earn her Master's cap. With an active breeding and training program, she'd have had dozens of teams in her care. Now she'd have neither time nor need to expand the herd. They could build a First-In Core camp just fine with the horses they had. New Lebanon didn't need a horse trainer any more.

Where would she go when she left, Hashti wondered? She'd harbored hopes of going to Vandalia with Gaylord. No more. Home to Carolina? What future had she there? Wherever she went, she'd be separated from Khan. There was so much more she wanted to know about him!

He, in his enthusiasm for traveling beyond the stars, had not even asked if she'd be coming along. That hurt most of all.

Her horses could not console her. Deep in her closet on Carolina, as she packed for New Lebanon, Hashti had found her stuffed donkey, cherished companion of her childhood. He was not the plump and glossy creature she remembered. She'd cradled him tenderly, but her adult eyes saw that he was tattered, dingy, and faded.

Likewise her horses, though dear to her yet, had turned slow, clumsy, and inarticulate. Animals. *Leaf eaters*. Hashti expected more.

She tossed restlessly through the night. The next morning, with a hopeful glance at the starred-circle constellation hanging low above the trees, Hashti knocked on Anna's door. Anna answered in a robe and logging boots, as she had the morning before the trip to the Rock. Much had happened since then, but the same smell of pancakes wafted through the air. Anna saw Hashti sniff. "Come in," the First-Inner said, "and pour yourself some tea. Big Red will be here in a minute. We thought you might like breakfast without the whole camp quizzing you."

Big Red walked in. Kicking his boots against the threshold to shake off the snow, he grinned at Hashti. "Guess I won't need to fetch you after all. How's it going, Tiger Wrestler?"

The term roused bittersweet memories. "I'm fine."

"And Khan?"

"Stiff, but he insists it's temporary. He's afraid he'll miss the spaceship."

Anna set a plate of hotcakes on the table and pulled up a chair, leaning her crutches against the wall. "Tell him it won't be here for months. He's got plenty of time to mend."

Quiet settled as they picked up their forks. But the generous supply of pancakes with syrup and butter finally filled even seemingly bottomless stomachs. Too soon, Big Red cleared the table and poured another round of tea. Hashti summoned up her nerve. "Some of your Circlemates will get here before the rest of us leave, won't they?"

Big Red looked briefly at Anna, then back at Hashti. "They will."

Her throat was tight, but Hashti forced the question out. "Would you introduce me to them? I wondered if any of them would be willing to recommend me—"

Under the table, Big Red's boot nudged Anna's. The doctor smiled. "You want to join First-In, Hashti?" she asked.

"I do. If I can get the recommendations, that is."

"You have them," Anna told her.

The guildswoman frowned in confusion. "I thought I needed three."

"You have three. Sort of." Anna's eyes were misty. "There's me and Red. That's two. And we can witness to Ross's opinion. He picked you out the first week you were here. That's three First-In votes. Khan, who has tested your sympathy and found it ample, can cast the nonhuman part of the ballot."

Hashti stared at them. "That's it? It's that easy?"

"No, it's not easy," Big Red cautioned. "It's hard, dangerous work, and the decision is irrevocable. You'll find, when you're initiated, that you can't go back to the old life."

Anna's expression turned equally serious. "I think you'd thrive in a Circle, Hashti. And I'd love to have you as Circlemate. But First-In is a lot more than a Guild. Decide with your eyes open."

"I have," Hashti answered.

That afternoon, after coaching Khan for his appearance at the solstice party, she retreated to her room to wash and dress. She turned Master Will's picture to the wall as she prepared her present for the Phoenix. Her hand felt itchy and naked in her wool mitten when she walked up the hill with Khan.

It was half an hour before sunset. The whole camp had gathered in the Town Square. Men stepped hastily aside to make room for the tiger, and they glanced apprehensively at him as they stamped to keep their feet warm. People would move indoors for later merrymaking, but this part of the festival always took place outside.

Gaylord, as leader of the camp, stood by the Phoenix Nest and invited everyone to bring their gifts. Solemnly folk filed forward with offerings. Sweat, head bowed, tossed in a mangled piece of metal. "The bullet that killed Ross," someone whispered. Lance's eyes sought Hashti's as he laid down the nameplates of the geldings that had been slaughtered for food. "I never want to see a dead horse again," he muttered. Hashti knew the feeling. She wondered if Lance had found Hero's nameplate, hidden behind the molasses barrel.

Sweat's gift, and Lance's, were bitter memories to be consumed in the bonfire. But not everything would burn with the Nest. Hashti laid her own small packet in the insulated Egg, for although this gift was leaving her life forever, as gone as the old year, it would be resurrected to new life with a new person. Anna, too, laid her offering in the elaborately decorated Egg. Hashti guessed, from the tears on Anna's face, that the First-Inner had brought some memento of Ross.

The sun touched the horizon. Gaylord stepped forward carrying a lovely, polished sweetsap table. "We are done with slaving for Oldearth," he announced, heaving the table onto the Nest. "So much for doing other people's business!" The camp cheered.

Lael, wearing a fur coat over her holiday dress, put a sheaf of papers into the Egg. "May the debt contracts pass from Oldearth's possession into our own!"

An even louder cheer rose. Lael found herself hoisted onto Master Tam's broad shoulders.

Gay motioned for silence. "A week ago," he said solemnly, "we had no hope for the new year. But tonight we know that the Phoenix will indeed rise from the flames." He picked up a torch and looked toward Hashti. If anger or grief flickered in his eyes, none but the young woman saw. Gay would not let his own disappointments ruin a show like this. "Miz Hashti, light the Nest!"

The sun was nearly gone. Awash in conflicting emotions, Hashti hurried forward and took the burning brand. To the sound of cheering, she plunged it into the pyre.

Flames soared twenty feet into the air. Khan, mindful of his name, did not cower or whine, but he trembled against Hashti's leg as the scaffolding collapsed in a shower of sparks and the Egg tumbled into an inferno. "These hill beavers play dangerous games," she could almost hear him thinking.

Master Tam shoved a glass into Hashti's hand. "Does he get one?" Tam asked, with a gingerly eye on Khan.

Hashti shook her head. "He's dangerous enough sober." The carpenter beat a hasty retreat.

By the time the toasts were done, the fire had subsided into a glowing, searingly hot bed of coals. Most people were a bit light-headed. Clapping started up, an insistent rhythm. "We want the Egg! We want the Egg!"

Somebody handed Gay a fifteen-foot pole. Shielding his face with his arm, he approached the fire pit, poking and prodding until he had uncovered the Egg. "I would not go so near the fire," Khan said, *pianissimo*.

Gay retreated to mop his face, then stepped forward once more and maneuvered the Egg, hissing and steaming, onto the snow. The shell cracked loudly as it cooled.

Good luck went to the first person who could lay a hand on the Egg and keep it there. The hardier, or more desperate, souls of the camp crowded round. The first few contenders withdrew, cursing and sucking their fingers. Then another cheer went up. "Georgia did it!" A wide grin spread across the little bookkeeper's face.

Gay shooed everyone back. "Hashti lit the fire for us. Her companion will break the Egg."

"It is time, Beaver Teacher," Hashti sang. An awed murmur swept the square as the tiger limped forward. Hashti followed, ready to give assistance or explanations. Anna and Red, standing a bit apart from the rest of the crowd, smiled encouragement.

"I should break this many-colored rock?" Khan asked.

"Break it!" Hashti told him.

He sat back on his haunches, hampered by the stiff shoulder, and gave the Egg an experimental tap with his good paw. Nothing happened. Somebody laughed.

Khan's ears went back. The paw connected again. This time, the Egg shattered. Candy and presents skittered across the snow.

Khan understood that the cheering was for him. He roared impressively before he hobbled back to his spot on the edge of the square.

The cook had managed to provide sweets for everyone. Grown men scrambled through the snow for them. Lance, as youngest, read the tags on special gifts and distributed them. Hashti saw his eyes widen over his own package. He pushed through the crowd to her, scarcely deterred even by the tiger at her side. "Miz Hashti! Where did this come from? Are you a Master now? Can I be your 'prentice?"

Touched and saddened, she pulled off her mitten and showed him her bare hand. "No, I won't be your Master, Lance. I'm leaving the Guild. I hope my ring serves you well."

He pulled back, abashed. "Where are you going?"

Before Hashti could answer, Big Red tapped her shoulder. "What happened to our gift-bearer? Hashti, I think this is yours."

It was a tiny packet, even tinier than the one she'd given Lance, and it was wrapped in white silk. Hashti's breath caught as she loosened the ribbon and unfolded the cloth.

A gold earring, three-quarters of an inch in diameter, flecked with jewels. Emblem of the First-In.

Anna materialized at Hashti's elbow. The doctor nodded, unable to suppress the catch in her voice. "It was Ross's. He'd have wanted you to have it. Wear it with joy."

Khan nosed curiously at the glittering object, almost knocking it out of Hashti's hand. "What is that?" he inquired. "It (flashes?) like fire. I dislike fire, but I suppose I must (get used to?) it if I travel on the Burning Rock. You seem to like fire. Will you come with me? I tell much better stories than your horses."

Hashti's fingers tightened around the tiny gold hoop. "I will go with you, Beaver Teacher."

## About the Author

Marti Steussy hails from northern Minnesota, where she learned first-hand about cross-country bushwacking, camping at forty below, and skidding logs with a Percheron. ("Never did it with a tiger watching, though.") Her interest in the outdoors and natural science continues, but she also ranges in other directions as an ordained minister and scholar of ancient Near Eastern languages and literature.

She and her husband Nic, a small-town family physician, now reside in the South, where Marti preaches occasionally, writes, and works full-time toward a Ph.D. in Hebrew Bible. Her children, ages two and four when this book was completed, know how to cope with Mama's ambitions: "They found the power switch on the computer's surge protector. Ignore them too long, and the screen goes blank."

Marti's current hobbies include bicycling, bread-baking, volunteer ministry, and of course, the next book. "How do I find time? I married a saint and I don't dust baseboards."